Running Home

Katie Macmillan

Beneath the Cottonwood LLC

Contents

To all my cheerleaders. To those who breathed fire into my beaten soul. Who encouraged me, cheered me on, and pushed me along when I wanted to give up and quit. For believing in me when I didn't believe in myself. These words are alive because of you.

And to my Thomas. You are my home.

Grief is like the ocean; it comes on waves, ebbing and flowing.
Sometimes the water is calm, and sometimes it is overwhelming.
All we can do is learn to swim.

~Vicki Harrison

Chapter One

Sunday, June 10, 2018

It's a universal truth that airports possess a sort of hypnotic buzz about them. Eager travelers await to board their flights to take them to distant lands and foreign places. Families returning home can be seen laughing over freshly made memories. Children bounce with glee at the magic of flight. It's a bubbling, bustling atmosphere that Margaret looks forward to almost as much as the trip itself. As soon as she is through security and holds a steaming cup of caffeine, she settles into her plastic seat and lets her eyes wander through the crowds, watching the hustle and bustle, soaking in the contagious, almost tangible, buzz.

Usually.

Today Margaret's nose is buried in a book, her mind having drifted to another time and place, leaving her blissfully oblivious to the flurry of the happenings around her. Her eyes bore into the words scrawled across the pages between her fingers, eating up the world of colonial Massachusetts with a greed and hunger that she can never seem to satisfy.

When the microphone crackles announcing that her flight is beginning to board, Margaret groans and stuffs her book back in her bag with an audible huff. Forced to face the reality of the hard plastic seats of the airport terminal, she pushes her palms against her knees and rises from her chair. Her muscles tingle with warmth as she stretches her arms above her head and rocks on the balls of her feet.

Margaret's fingers fiddle through the belongings in her bag, intentionally drawing out the moment they grasp onto the boarding pass she needs to enter the jet bridge. When she can no longer put off the inevitable, she lifts her eyes with reluctance to peer around the terminal.

There's a little boy, sticky hands and face pressed against the window, eyes as wide as saucers, watching the airplanes on the tarmac take off into the heavens. Margaret guesses he's about three years old. The little koala backpack he wears is almost as big as he is, and there's a long, green dinosaur tail poking out of the zipper. He's squealing and bouncing up and down as he watches the massive aircrafts on the other side of the glass. She quickly looks away as her heart catches in her throat.

She catches sight of a young man handing a bottle of water to a woman who Margaret assumes is his new wife. The woman has a barely swollen belly. The type of belly where those who have never been mothers wonder if this young woman is pregnant, or if she just had one too many burritos at lunch. But Margaret is a mother. And she can tell by the way this young woman's hands keep fluttering to her belly, instinctively and intimately already connected in a thousand ways to the tiny human growing inside of her, that this woman did not eat too many burritos.

Margaret feels her pulse begin to race, her breathing turns short and shallow. She flexes her fingers, clenching and unclenching her fists. Heat rushes up her skin and her palms grow damp and clammy. She turns her now tear-filled eyes to the floor, cursing herself for looking around, and fighting the battle with her body to keep those tears from falling. She zeroes in on the scuffed-up Nike's of the person in line in front of her: when they take a step, she takes a step. She focuses on her breathing.

In.

Out.

In.

Out.

Step.

The once-white shoes have withered to a dull gray, and the laces are starting to fray on the ends.

In.

Out.

In.

Out.

Step.

She notices a crack in the rubber sole of the left shoe, snaking its way from the tip of the toes to the center arch before it disappears.

In.

Out.

In.

Out.

Step.

She's finally to the front of the line and with shaky hands passes her slightly damp and crinkled boarding pass to the attendant, only briefly glancing up to say a quiet, "Thank you," before moving through the tunnel to the plane.

Thank goodness I opted for first class, she comforts herself. *There won't be any kids in first class.* And she's right. There are no kids in sight as she takes her seat beside the window at the front of the plane.

The man in the seat beside her introduces himself as Keith with an out-stretched hand. Margaret notices the leathery tan of his arms, the thick veins snaking up their length. He's older, she guesses in his seventies. His long arms are sinewy and sculpted, and the heavy lines on his face make him look regal, rather than old. Looking him over, she assesses this is a man who has spent most of his life outside doing hard labor.

His deep, amber eyes steal her breath as she shakes his calloused hand, and she immediately feels as if she's looking into the eyes of an old friend. She introduces herself as Margaret.

"You travelin' for business or pleasure?" Keith's drawl is like honey, thick and sweet.

Neither, Margaret thinks, unsure how to respond to the kind man. Her hand reflexively starts spinning the sapphire ring on her finger, trying to decide how to answer his innocent question.

"That's okay, I've run away before too," he whispers as he pats her hand. Margaret looks up into his soothing eyes, his gentle touch sending a torrent of buried emotions flooding to the surface, and resists the urge to break down to a complete stranger.

"I'm...I'm not running away, I'm taking a vacation." It comes out almost as a whisper, and Margaret wonders if she'll ever be able to believe her own lie.

"Fresh air, white beaches, palm trees...they're all good for soul. It will do you good. You don't have to defend your choice, not to me. I don't judge. That's the Lord's job," he winks.

"How...why do you think..."

"Like I said, I've run away before too. I know what a runner looks like. I know what pain, and grief, and fear look like. I know how they feel. I've seen what they do to a person." He pauses, gives her an assessing look. "Can I give you some advice?" Margaret tilts her head in a barely noticeable nod, her eyes transfixed on his golden pools. "It's okay to run. Run until you get tired, until you can't run anymore. But when you stop to catch your breath? Stop to think too. Because that's when you'll realize it's time to turn around and run back towards wherever you came from."

Margaret paints what she hopes is a warm smile on her face for the old man, rolling his words around in her mind. Keith's skin is warm and electric as he gives her hands a small squeeze, and kindly says, "Now, I know you didn't want to spend the next handful of hours talking to an old man like me. I can tell by your bag full'a books that you had other plans in mind for this flight. So I'll let you escape into those books, Miss Maggie."

Her head whips up so fast, she hears a soft pop as it cracks in protest. The old man just winks at her again, puts some ear buds in, leans back and closes his eyes.

Margaret once again finds her heart caught in her throat, her hands trembling ever so slightly on the arm rests hugging her sides, Keith's warm touch still lingering on her skin. She closes her eyes and takes a deep, steadying breath, before pulling a book out of her bag. And as she opens the pages, she wonders how she could ever be able to stop running.

The thud of the rubber tires skidding along the runway jolts her awake. Margaret rubs at her face and feels warm tears on her cheek. Keith's eyes are soft, his brow furrowed in focus on her face as he places a warm hand on her knee, only to confirm her fear: her nightmare was probably a vocal one.

"Are you okay, dear?" he questions, his voice soft.

"Yes, yes I'm fine. Thanks." She mumbles back.

Margaret shifts her gaze to the tiny square window beside her and begins to discreetly clean her face. The perky flight attendant's voice flows through the loudspeaker, "Ladies and gentlemen, we've made a safe landing on the tarmac."

Obviously, Margaret muses to herself. The iron smell of the blood is so strong, she swears she can taste it. *How can dreams feel so real?*

"The weather is a lovely 87 degrees Fahrenheit, and there's not a cloud in the sky. Aloha, and welcome to Honolulu, Hawaii."

Margaret sighs. *I'm doing the right thing. Contrary to what my mother thinks, this is a good idea. It is. It is. It is.*

Right?

Aloha, Hawaii. Help me run away. Help me escape my nightmares.

As she's wheeling her carry-on through the airport toward the baggage claim carousels, Margaret looks at her phone for the first time since landing. She grins as she sees a simple text from AJ, her heart giving a little flutter in her chest: **Relax. And try to have fun. You deserve it. See you in a week.** She shoots him a quick text back, letting him know she landed safely in Honolulu and her vacation is officially beginning. She also finds three missed calls and a handful of texts from her mother, apparently eager to continue their conversation - if you can call it that. It was more like a lecture, in Margaret's eyes. Her stomach squirms with guilt but her head still pounds with pride, so she shoves her phone back into her purse and picks up her pace with brisk determination to power forward.

The carousel light comes on, and suitcases of varying sizes and colors begin to roll down the ramp. Thankfully, her suitcase is one of the first to make its appearance. She walks over to grab it but struggles to lift the massive luggage. *Oh for Pete's sake, I forgot how heavy this was,* she curses internally. She does an awkward dance of half walking, half skipping while clinging to the gliding suitcase as it continues to slide along the conveyor belt while simultaneously trying to heave the beast off the carousel. *I don't care, I stand firm that exercise is overrated.* As she's huffing and puffing, a large arm reaches around her and lifts the suitcase off the carriage with the ease of plucking a dandelion out of the soil.

"Holy hell, what do you have in this thing? Bricks?" a lopsided grin hangs on the face of a dimpled stranger in a carefree way that leaves Margaret wondering about the last time she was able to smile like that. It looks so...effortless.

She manages to slip out a few words without stumbling too much. "Thanks for your help. I appreciate it."

The helpful man just stares at her, the same lopsided grin hanging on his face, his hands buried in his pockets, his eyes scanning Margaret's face. An awkward pause passes, hanging heavy in the air. At least to Margaret it feels heavy. Everything feels heavy these days. Margaret's not sure what this man is expecting, or why he is just staring at her with that annoyingly easy smile on his face, so she just returns a sheepish grin, mumbles, "Thanks," again, turns around, and wheels her heavy suitcase down the hall toward the shuttles. She cringes as the sound of the stranger's light-hearted chuckle follows her away from the carousel, and she is left wishing airport baggage claims had holes to crawl into.

Margaret's suitcase *is* exceptionally heavy. She plans to do lots of reading while basking on the sandy beaches of Hawaii. And as a person who refuses to read electronic books because the smell of a fresh book is an aroma one should never leave home without, she has packed a suitcase that is about two-thirds books and one-third clothing and toiletries. The extra charge to check such a heavy bag was worth every penny, in Margaret's mind. One could travel the world, encounter countless loves, mingle with royalty, all without leaving the comfort of their squishiest chair - or in the case of the next seven days, the warmest beach. And now more than ever did Margaret love the escape and freedom that literature fed her soul.

Margaret finds the shuttle that will take her to her resort for the week, and after a thank you to the driver for helping her with her suitcase on the bus, she takes a seat, feeling her muscles instantly melt into the comfort of the chair as she sits. It amazes Margaret how traveling can be so exhausting when you spend the majority of your time sitting. *The irony*, she chuckles to herself. Between the exhaustion of traveling for twelve hours and the sudden heavy humidity of the island, her eyelids grow heavy and begin to droop. She lets the soft rolling and bumping of the shuttle bus lull her into a shallow, relaxing nap.

The brakes of the bus squeak in an ear-splitting protest as the driver pulls to a stop in front of a tropical oasis, snapping Margaret's eyes open. There are more palm trees than she can count, and the sun is screaming for her attention. A large stone sign near the bus stop reads *Hibiscus Cove*. The luxury all-inclusive, adults-only resort rests on the white sands of Waikiki beach on the Hawaiian island of Oahu. As she steps off her shuttle, her breath catches in her chest. Her eyes roam the shoreline of the whitest sand she has ever seen. If it wasn't 87 degrees and sunny, she would have sworn she was staring at a snowy canvas from her winters back home in Minnesota. Tall, swaying palm trees appear to wave hello to her. The thick, salty sea air hugs her bare arms. As tired as she was a moment ago from traveling, a new energy begins to buzz within her, the sights and smells around her intoxicating her senses.

"Aloha, and welcome to *Hibiscus Cove*." The woman's voice is soft, but it snaps Margaret out of her reverie. She gently places a lei around Margaret's neck with a smile warmer than the tropical sun hanging above the crashing waves. It reassures her she *has* made the right decision to come here, that she has yet to call her mother. A small pang of guilt pulses through her veins.

"Thank you," Margaret replies, as she rolls her suitcase into the lobby, returning the smile to the lovely woman. "Hi, checking in. Margaret Heller."

"Ah yes, here you are. Welcome to *Hibiscus Cove*. Here is the key for your home away from home." The concierge continues to explain all the amenities Margaret has at her disposal in the resort. But Margaret stops listening at some point, as she knows all she cares about or really needs to know to about is the food. The only other thing she plans to be doing this week is eating. Reading and food, her two favorite things. Okay, and tanning. You can't come to Hawaii without planning to let the sun color your skin. Pictures of upcoming sunny days stretched out on a chair, book in her hand, and a drink by her side swirl before her eyes.

When the concierge is finished, Margaret takes her key and heads to her private bungalow. After twelve hours of traveling, she eagerly awaits the comfort of a giant bed and a refreshing shower. But as she opens the doors and steps over the threshold, another surge of energy and excitement pumps through her veins. Her eyes roam across the room. A giant bed resembling a fluff of cloud stakes its claim near the center of the room, the wooden headboard ornately carved with delicate flowers, buds, and vines. Thick, plush carpet feels like pillows beneath her feet as she moves about, her hands gently tracing over the marble counter tops of the kitchenette.

She had splurged for the most expensive bungalow they offered. She wanted to be sure that if she got trapped indoors due to rain, she would still be living in luxury and have an amazing view. And what a view it was. The roar of the waves crashing on the beach thumps in her chest as she swings open the veranda door. Blues stretch as far as the eye can see, from the expansive ocean to the stretching skies, the blues both calm and energize Margaret's restless soul. She steps forward and sticks her toes through the bars of her patio gate, dipping them into the warm, silky sand before her. She is staying quite literally on the beach. And Margaret decides then and there that the veranda drapes will never be shut the entire time of her stay.

With the new vigor and excitement of being in a tropical oasis, Margaret abandons the idea of a shower and instead begins unpacking her things. She starts with her books, delicately pulling each one from her bags, treating them as if each were a fragile, expensive piece of art. After placing the last of her novels into the row before her, she slowly runs her fingers across their spines, as if to say 'hello' again. Her eyes browse over the different places she will travel this week: 1800s New York City, Modern Day New Orleans, 1970s Paris, and many others. She steps back, admiring the view, her heart swelling. There was something comforting in having a stack of books with her. It was like always having a best friend in your pocket.

After getting settled and soaking up the warm, ocean air from her veranda for a bit, Margaret heads back into her room in search of her phone. She finds the device buried in her purse, and looks at the time: 6:21pm. *Oh darn*, Margaret thinks sarcastically to herself. "Looks like it's almost 11:30 back in Minnesota," she announces to the empty room. "I wouldn't want to wake mom, so I guess I'll call her tomorrow." She smirks, tucking the phone back in her purse. The shower is softly calling her name, tempting her with its promise of satisfying warmth after a day of travel, but her stomach has a louder voice. She quickly ties her thick, chocolate hair back, slips on a pair of leather sandals, slides a book into a giant, colorful tote bag she purchased back home specifically for this vacation, grabs her room key, and heads out the door.

As Margaret strolls around the resort grounds, a smile crawls across her face as light and breezy as the tropical air whispering against her cheeks. The sun seems to make everything glow in a way only seen in movies. *Have trees always been this green? Is the sky really that blue? That can't be the same sky as in Minnesota. And since when does air have flavor?* The air is warm, thick, and salty as she walks along, until she gets closer to the dining area, when the flavor of the air begins to shift. With several different culinary venues to choose from, tantalizing new aromas begin to fill her senses. From fragrant meats to indulgent sweets, she scopes out her options. The smell billowing out from the open doors of a restaurant called Pacifica makes her mouth begin to water, but she stops in her tracks. Just outside the entrance to the restaurant is the man from baggage claim, enveloped within a large group of other adults. She stares for a moment too long, and as he looks up, their eyes lock. The same lopsided grin from baggage claim creeps up his face as he recognizes Margaret.

Seriously? Margaret huffs to herself. Feeling the blood begin to creep up her neck toward her cheeks, she spins on her heel and walks instead toward a small shack called The Huli Huli Hut. It smells just as delicious and poses no risk of an encounter with Baggage Claim Man.

The small hut has one big window at the front and is covered with a thatched roof. Large, vibrant flowers of pinks and purples hang around the roof and the single window, and lush, green ivy is growing up along the wall of the hut that faces the ocean. Looking through the window, Margaret can see a small kitchen with a man and a woman, their backs to the window, cooking on a huge, open-faced griddle. A large, beefy man running the ticket window smiles broadly at Margaret. "Aloha! Howzit, pretty lady?" Between the man's warm smile, the bright Hawaiian sun, and the invigorating sea air, Margaret can feel her body becoming lighter, as if a weight is slowly lifting off her chest, and her body is suddenly inflating with the infectious euphoria of the island. She smiles back, inhaling the delicious smell wafting past her. Her stomach rumbles at the aroma, and she realizes it's been hours since she last ate. She glances down the minimalist menu, eying her options.

"Aloha. Can I try the Huli Huli Chicken?" Margaret orders.

"You got it, pretty lady. Comin' right up. Feel free to take a seat on our lanai, and I'll bring it out when it's ready." His grin is beaming. "Mahalo!" The man waves and turns around to give her order to his coworkers manning the grill.

Margaret steps lightly, almost skipping, down a gravel path around the hut to find a spacious patio facing the ocean. She takes a seat at a table tucked away in the corner under the shade of a palm tree. As her eyes scan the horizon, she inhales deeply and takes it all in yet again: the warm breeze fluttering against her skin, the ocean waves crashing on the shore, the palm trees swaying, and cerulean waters as far as the eye can see. *Yes,* she confirms to her still-doubting heart. *I made the right decision. This is nothing like the view from my house.*

She reaches into her purse and pulls out her book just as the Huli Huli Man drops off her dinner. As she takes her first bite, savoring the sweet, pineapple taste of the chicken, she turns the pages and starts to lose herself into the world empirical Japan.

Reality couldn't possibly touch her here.

Chapter Two

Saturday, June 10, 2017

"**S**top! I want to watch Science Explorers!"

"Nooo! I want Elmo!"

Margaret groans and tries to ignore the sound of her children's bickering floating through their bedroom door. It is the worst kind of alarm clock, especially at six o'clock on a Saturday morning. But her little Irish twins, Jackson at five years old and Izzy at four, are already up and at it. Weekends mean nothing to children.

"Mooom! Izzy won't give me the marote! It's my turn to pick a show!"

She can't help but smile warmly to herself. She is not looking forward to the days when her children will be old enough to say words correctly. It is one of the most amusing things about being a mother, and her mind starts to wander to all the words her children misspeak: *marote* is remote, *friterfrater* is refrigerator, *lemalade* is lemonade, *purpalose* is purpose...but her warm and fuzzy thoughts are interrupted by more angry shrieks rippling up the stairs.

"MOOOM!!"

Margaret rolls over, wraps an arm around her personal furnace, and presses her cold toes onto his always burning skin. Having grown accustomed to the gesture, he doesn't even flinch. "Honey, the kids are calling for you," she nibbles playfully in his ear.

"Nice try. I'm tired, not deaf," he mumbles into his pillow. "I distinctly hear 'mom' out there. And besides, it's Saturday."

"Pretty please?" she whines, as her satin lips move from his ear down the scruff beginning to form on his chin and neck. "With cherries, and whipped cream, and..."

Their bedroom door slams open. "MOM! Why aren't you waking up? Izzy won't let me watch Science Explorers even though it's my turn to pick!"

Her husband further buries himself into his cloud of pillows as Margaret pushes herself off him in a huff. Today is his day to sleep in. Margaret will get her extra sleep tomorrow. She takes her son's warm, tiny hand within her own, and together they make the descent downstairs to find Izzy, sitting cross-legged on the floor, her face close enough to the screen that it makes Margaret's own head throb.

"Izzy, sweetie, back up. You're way too close to the TV. You're going to turn your brain to mush."

Izzy doesn't move.

"Mom. Just make her give me the marote!"

"Iz, it's Jackson's turn to pick the morning show. Give him the remote." Izzy doesn't move, frozen by the magic of the screen in front of her. Out of nowhere, a blur of green whips in front of Margaret's eyes, as Jackson, in his Ninja Turtle pajamas, tackles his sister. Screams and shouts fill the still-waking world as the siblings do what siblings at that age seem to do best.

"Enough!" howls Margaret over the ruckus, adding her own body to the wrestling match, eventually grabbing an arm of each child in each of her hands. *Thank goodness there's only two of them.* She lifts each child and places them on opposite ends of the couch. It always amazes Margaret how much strength she can muster up when playing referee to her children. *Exercise is overrated,* she tells herself as she proudly stares down at her accomplishment, trying to ignore her heavy breathing. The two children alternate between glaring at each other and glaring at their mother, arms crossed across their tiny, heaving chests.

"Now," Margaret begins in her best mom-means-business voice. "It's not even seven o'clock yet, and you two are already being mean to each other."

"I wasn't mean to her, I was just getting the marote! She wasn't listening to you!"

"No excuses. You both made bad choices. Izzy, you didn't give Jackson the remote when it's his turn to the pick the show. Jackson, you tackled Izzy instead of using your words. So now we are skipping morning cartoons, and instead you both go upstairs and get dressed while I get breakfast ready." More shouting and protesting erupt, but eventually the two children trudge upstairs, and a moment later Margaret can hear them opening their closets and dressers to retrieve fresh clothes for the day.

She plops on the couch and lets out a large sigh. How could she already be worn out when she has only been awake for less than fifteen minutes? So goes motherhood. She closes her eyes and lets herself drift away. Away to a place with palm trees, and white sand, and mornings that don't start until ten o'clock. Away to a place without arguments over the remote, or tears over the wrong-colored sippy cup, or tantrums from being told one can't have candy as a bedtime snack. *Inhale. Exhale. Ahhh, serenity.*

Boxed pancake batter is the greatest invention of all time, Margaret thinks to herself, standing at her kitchen counter. As she flips another pancake, two hands slide around her waist and pull her close. "Good morning, my love." Austin's lips peck her cheek, and she gags, fanning the air in front of her with theatrical flair. She whips around and starts pushing him away.

"Wish I could say the same about you. Your breath smells disgusting." Austin just pulls her closer, blowing more hot air into her scrunched up face. She shrieks and starts swatting at his arms with her spatula, as he laughs and pecks her nose before turning to go brush his teeth.

Margaret watches him walk away with a crooked grin hanging on her face. She's been in love with that man for thirteen years, and he still manages to make her heart skip a beat, though it's in different ways now. She used to look at him and it was his sculpted pecs and abs, his toned arms and back that made her skin prickle with fire. She would get lost in his deep ebony eyes and melt whenever he swallowed her in his arms. And while Austin still has the body that makes women everywhere do a double take, there are more intimate ways in which he now sparks a fire in her chest.

Nowadays, it is watching him play with the children that makes her heart melt. It's the way he prioritizes time with his kids before anything else. The way he always kisses her goodnight and goodbye. How he goes out of his way to keep up with the things around the house, like fixing squeaky doors and leaky faucets. It's how he comes home with a caramel macchiato from Caribou when she's had a rough day at work. It's the intimate, mundane pieces of their life together that fuels Margaret's love for her husband the most these days.

Margaret sets the pancakes on the table and calls the kids over to eat just as Austin walks back downstairs. The clinking of forks and knives begins to fill the house.

"What's on the agenda for today?" Austin asks between mouthfuls.

"Jackson has baseball at ten, and Izzy has dance at one," Margaret reminds him.

"Yeah!" shouts Jackson, fist-bumping the air. "I love baseball!"

"Can we really call what he does 'baseball'? The kids spend more time playing in the dirt than actually playing baseball. Do we *all* really need to go to that thing?"

"Jackson wants us all there, don't you, Jackson?" asks Margaret.

"Yeah! 'Cause I keep getting better! Last time I only knocked the tee over two times!" Jackson proudly explains.

"Point proven," mumbles Austin.

Margaret's eyes shoot daggers Austin's way before she resumes planning out the day. "We'll all go to Jackson's baseball practice, then after that we can go out to eat for lunch. Maybe to McDonald's and you two can play on the playground there before it's time for Izzy's dance lesson."

"Yay!" squeals Izzy. "Can I get an ice cream cone?"

Margaret answers with the code phrase every parent uses to say 'no' without actually saying 'no': "We'll see, honey."

The family of four finish their breakfast a little too slowly, soaking in as much of a lazy Saturday morning as they can, and then the usual "before activities" scramble ensues. There are hunts for missing socks and cleats, tears over ballerina buns made too tight, and squeals and giggles as little bellies get tickled along the way. The garage door slams shut behind them, and the minivan pulls out of the driveway only two minutes later than Margaret had originally planned to be on the road.

Margaret spends the drive scrolling through her Instagram feed and listening to Jackson excitedly tell everyone all the accomplishments he's going to make at practice today. As Jackson boasts about how he *knows* he's going to hit a home run *for sure* this week, Austin chuckles, reaches across the center armrest and laces his fingers between Margaret's. She glances up to see him smirking at Jackson's comments, and she feels a smile creep across her face as well. It's hard to tell if the smile is from Jackson's unrealistic but charming enthusiasm, or from Austin's simple but sweet gesture. It's probably a little bit of both.

Jackson's practice is like any other practice. There is a lot of down time, as one by one, half of the kids take their turn batting from the tee, while the other half attempt to field the ball. Some kids seem to really know what they're doing and pick up the skills quickly. Other kids spend most of their time drawing in the sand. Jackson is somewhere in the middle. Izzy is busy scribbling in her coloring book, and Austin is scrolling through his phone when Jackson comes up to bat for the first time that practice.

"Austin, pay attention – it's Jackson's turn!" Margaret announces, nudging her husband with her elbow. Austin looks up just in time to see Jackson successfully hit the ball without knocking the tee over; his first success all season. Margaret jumps from her seat cheering with the enthusiasm only a mother can muster at t-ball practice. Austin chuckles at his wife's over-excitement, and then joins in with a "Whoop!" of his own. When Jackson gets to first base and locks eyes with Margaret, his face is engulfed in the world's biggest, proudest smile. Margaret's pounding heart threatens to burst from her chest, her face beaming with pride right alongside him.

After Jackson's practice comes to an end, the family travels to McDonald's, where Margaret makes the announcement the kids had been hoping for: "It's a special day because Jackson didn't knock over the tee! So we will celebrate with ice cream!"

With half eaten chicken nuggets and crumbs of French fries littering the table, Jackson and Izzy run off to the giant play palace, leaving Austin and Margaret in the booth watching them from a distance. Austin drapes his arm around Margaret's shoulder and pulls her into his barreled chest. She instinctively leans in, her relaxed body melding perfectly into his own. Notes of mint and leather hit her senses when she breathes in a content sigh. He's worn the same cologne since the day they met, and every time she gets a whiff, she's reminded of their college days.

She's transported to the day she first laid eyes on Austin. Her college days had been long and grueling at the time, filled with late-night study sessions and exams that left one's mind trying to remember what was up and what was down. One of the local frat houses was hosting a party to celebrate the end of finals before everyone ventured home for the holidays with their families. Reserved and studious, Margaret wasn't one to be particularly interested in frat parties. But after her roommate begging her for hours on end, Margaret found herself primping in front of the mirror moments before locking elbows with her roommate as their heels clicked across the pavement on their way to the house.

The house was just as Margaret expected it to be, crowded wall-to-wall with bodies. Beer, weed, and body odor all mingled together to create a stench that made her stomach knot with nausea ever so slightly. Margaret grabbed a bottle of beer out of one of the many coolers, and pushed her way out to the patio, inhaling the clean night air deeply. After taking a swig, she scanned the scene outside: even outdoors there were still dozens of bodies rubbing against each other to the rhythm of the bass thumping (or perhaps the rhythm of their hormones, Margaret couldn't tell). One man caught her eye. He stood leaning against the wall of the garage, a red solo cup in one hand, the other casually buried in his pocket. He wore a basic white tee that contrasted beautifully with his dark skin and was just tight enough to highlight the sculpted body beneath. Margaret wondered if he was an athlete. A grin hung playfully on his face as he stared straight at her. His chocolate eyes poured over her as he sauntered her way, an easy confidence radiating in his swagger. As he approached, the intoxicating smell of mint and leather from his cologne left her skin and senses buzzing more than the alcohol in her hand. He clinked his plastic cup with her glass bottle, introduced himself as Austin, and the two fell into an easy conversation that lasted into the early hours of the next morning. Sitting in the McDonald's booth now next to Austin, she smiles as she recalls the feeling of finding "the one" after just one night together.

All too soon, the children are getting buckled into their car seats and the minivan is idling down the road toward the dance studio. "I'm going to be the best ballerina today, and I'm going to have the prettiest bow," Izzy chirps in one rapid breath.

"Oh I know you will, sweetie. The best and the prettiest," Margaret confirms, as again, Austin reaches over to hold her hand while he drives. They don't kiss at red lights like they did when they first started dating, full of blissful, naive love, but the hand holding? The hand holding has never died and Margaret always says a little prayer that it never will. She finds comfort and assurance in the feel of Austin's strong, rough hands in her own.

Austin has a desk job at an insurance company in the city, but in his spare time he enjoys building things and carpentry work. The third stall of their garage had been commandeered with sawdust, drill bits, a plethora of batteries of various sizes, and myriad of tools. She's lost count of how many bookshelves, benches, tables, chairs, and knick-knacks Austin has made over the years. Some of it is in their house, some of it he has given away to friends, others he sold to customers. All of his creations are unique and beautiful in their own way. And while Margaret loves and admires the work that is spit out from their garage, she particularly loves the way the hard work makes his hands feel – strong in a way that make her feel as if she never has to worry about him ever letting go.

They pull into the parking lot of the dance studio, and Izzy has escaped her car seat buckles, her tiny hands sliding the door open to release her from her prison. Dance lessons are the only time Izzy ever attempts unbuckling herself. Any other destination, and she sits like a lump, waiting for someone to do it for her.

"Yay! Dance time!" Izzy voices seems to linger behind as her body races toward the entrance of the studio. Austin comes around from the other side of the van and interlocks his fingers with Margaret's as Jackson trudges moodily along just in front of them. He hates having to sit for Izzy's dance class. It never mattered how many activities Margaret brought with her, Jackson would always pout and complain of being bored.

And while the hour-long class may drag on for Jackson, it always flies by for Margaret. She loves sitting behind the window of the classroom, watching Izzy twirl and sashay among her peers. She adores the way Izzy's brow scrunches in concentration, her lips pursed in focus, and how she periodically looks up at Margaret every time she completes a routine, her face suddenly beaming. And just as with Jackson's baseball, Margaret once again feels her heart swell in her chest as Izzy's face shines with pride and joy for all she is doing and learning. Izzy's joy is Margaret's joy.

On the drive home after dance class, Margaret stares at the trees rolling past her window while country music idles through the radio speakers. The rhythmic breathing from her children in the backseat floats to her ears, barely audible over the music emanating from the speakers, telling her that they have fallen asleep for a cat nap on the short drive home. And as Margaret turns her attention to the thick clouds high in the sky, she reflects on the day's events, her heart cracking ever so slightly.

It's such a bittersweet occupation, the job of a parent. Watching one's children grow and learn and explore fills your soul with immeasurable pride and joy, but that joy is a double-edged sword. For as much as a mother dreams of the people her children will grow to be, she simultaneously begs the world to keep her babies as babies forever.

Austin is chopping garlic, a kitchen towel draped over one shoulder, when Margaret idles down the stairs after spending some time playing with the kids. She grabs her own knife and cutting board, pulls a pack of chicken breasts out of the fridge, and starts dicing right alongside her husband. She playfully bumps her hip into Austin as she starts working, and he returns the gesture with a sly smile. "Alexa, play some Darius Rucker," he announces to their home smart system, and as the soulful, soothing voice of the country legend washes over the house, Austin begins to sway back and forth in time to the music, every so often bumping his hip into his wife. Margaret's rich laugh rides on the tune of the song, filling the kitchen with its warmth. Austin removes the knife from her hand, interlocks his fingers in her own, and pulls her in for a dance. Together they sway across the tile, Austin twirling Margaret into his arms. He dips her delicately just as the song comes to an end, and their lips meet in a soft, suggestive kiss.

"Gross!" Jackson's voice cuts across the sound waves. The lovebirds peel away from each other laughing, and Austin goes back to his garlic as Margaret instructs Jackson to go tidy up his room while dinner cooks.

Over their chicken dinner, Jackson is eager to entertain the family with repeated stories of his accomplishments at today's baseball practice. Ever the competitor, Izzy is right behind him, making sure everyone remembers how perfectly she accomplished her butterfly dance today. Margaret chuckles at the high-pitched, excited voices floating around the room, she and Austin sharing the look parents share when they know their children are the cutest, most adorable children to ever enter this world - *obviously*.

After the children announce they are full from dinner, Austin clears the table as Margaret begins the bedtime routine with the kids. First is bath time (with extra bubbles, of course). Squeals of laughter ring out as Margaret helps Jackson and Izzy make bubble beards and shapes their hair into silly styles. The tub is draining just as Austin makes his way upstairs, and he chases the dripping, towel-draped children into their bedrooms, roaring like a dinosaur all the way. He helps them get dressed into their pajamas – Jackson chooses his favorite Pokémon pair, and Izzy settles for her unicorn pajamas. As the kids run off to pick their bedtime books, Austin enters into the bathroom where Margaret is hanging up wet towels and getting toothbrushes ready.

"Tyler just sent me a text," he begins. "He says he and Carrie got a sitter tonight and went out to dinner. They were going to go see a movie after dinner but decided to see if we were up for hanging out instead. Want them to come over after the kids are in bed? I could get a fire going." Margaret loves the idea of an early summer fire with friends.

"Yeah," she answers. "I'll get some snacks together while you get the fire started." Austin starts texting Tyler their response as the kids come running back with their books. He takes their books from them, bringing the small stack into his room with him, while Margaret ushers the kids back into the bathroom and helps them brush their teeth with their favorite bubble gum toothpaste. As the kids dry their mouths and bound out of the room leaving giggles fading behind them, Margaret marvels at the amount of toothpaste that managed to find a home on the counter. In a rush to get the kids to bed and their night with friends started, she decides to leave the mess and makes a mental note to come back later and clean it up. After teeth are brushed, the trio join Austin in the king-sized bed, Izzy nestling herself next to her daddy, Jackson climbing into Margaret's lap. Three stories and two breaks for bed time snacks later, and Margaret and Austin are flicking off the bedroom lights, the kids already half asleep from the events of the day.

As Austin is getting the fire roaring out back, Margaret rummages through the kitchen cupboard and fridge, putting together a mishmash of snacks for her friends.

Margaret and Carrie first met each other ten years ago at their first job out of college. Margaret was going to be the new science teacher at Thomas C. Moore Middle School, and Carrie was the school's newest English teacher. Matching first-day jitters over their first job out of college built a foundation for their relationship, and the friendship never died. The women were maids of honor at each other's weddings and the first to be at each other's side for the birth of all their children. Carrie and her husband Tyler had three children of their own, and the two families seemed to have woven more memories together than apart over the past decade.

Rectangular butter crackers and cubes of various cheeses have been gathered on a tray, along with a bottle of her favorite wine for the ladies and a cooler of beers for the guys. Just as she walks out the front door, Tyler and Carrie pull into her driveway. Carrie jumps out of the car, her long, blond curls bouncing on her shoulders, and runs up to Margaret.

"Hey, girl! So good to see you!" Margaret smiles at how her best friend is as excited as if they hadn't seen each other for ages, rather than having just seen each other yesterday at work. Carrie gives Margaret a quick squeeze and takes the loaded platter out of her hands. "What can I help you with?"

Margaret gestures with the wine left in her other hand, "Let's bring all this out back, and then you can help me grab some chairs out of the garage."

Together they walk around back, where Austin is stoking the roaring flames inside a metal pit. He looks up and locks eyes with Margaret, giving her a mischievous grin thatmakes her heart flutter. He turns his attention to Carrie. "Hey Care Bear. Where's Tyler?"

"He's wrapping up a call in the car. Work called on our way here. Can't even have a date night without work interrupting. He's been putting in so many more hours with this new promotion," Carrie's voice is heavy as she sets the platter of snacks on a little table near the glowing fire pit, the flames already thick and dancing toward the sky.

Austin reaches for a beer from the cooler Margaret wheeled around, "Well that's what ya get when you're making the big bucks, eh? Gotta be a trade off somewhere."

"At this rate, I'd rather have his old salary with his time back." Margaret's heart cracks with the sadness in her friend's voice. She locks her arm in Carrie's and tries to change the subject. "Come on, let's go get the chairs so we can get this night started." As the two friends approach the garage, Tyler steps out of his truck. "Hey ladies. Austin out back?" The car door slams a little too rough, and Margaret is left wondering how Tyler is handling his new promotion. Are his feelings the same as her dear friend's?

"He is. We're grabbing chairs and we'll be back there."

"Oh, I can grab those," Tyler offers.

Margaret shoos him away with a wave of her hand. "Don't worry about it. They're not heavy and Austin's waiting for you. Plus it gives me and Carrie a chance to gab without you two overhearing." Tyler chuckles and meanders around the house to the back, gnats and mosquitoes stirring up from the grass with each of his steps. A moment later and the women hear the fizz of another beer popping open followed by the sound of tin cans clanging together. They gather together some folding chairs and head back to the fire without a word, Margaret unable to find anything to say.

As the flames lick the darkening sky and the stars begin to peek and flicker through the velvet curtain, the group settles into an easy, familiar rhythm. Tyler fills Margaret and Austin in on his new promotion at the marketing agency. He's recently become the new VP of his department and has had to work longer hours with the new transition, much to Carrie's disdain. Margaret and Austin share their plans and ideas for their unfinished basement they're going to start working on this summer.

Eventually the men split off into their own conversation about last night's Twins game (they lost to the Brewers, 3-1, and as a devout baseball fan, Austin took the loss to their rival team a little too hard), and the women discuss their own topics. Carrie begins the conversation, relenting her exasperation with Tyler's new job. "I mean, part of me feels bad for him, because he's working so hard, so much, and it's obviously causing him a lot of stress - I swear he's gained ten pounds just this past month, he's a stress-eater - but this other part of me resents him for taking the promotion. I mean, sure, the pay increase is nice, but we were doing *fine*. It's not like we needed the money. And now, with his long hours, I'm doing so much more of everything around the house. I carry so much more weight. And, I don't know, it just frustrates me, ya know?"

Margaret nods and takes a sip of wine, her foot flicking the air as it sits draped across her leg, and takes a moment to collect her thoughts. "I know it's hard," she soothes. "But hopefully it's only temporary. Maybe once he gets his feet under him, and more situated in the role, he'll be able to be more present at home. But in the meantime, call me! Let me know what I can help with. I'd be happy to bring dinner over any time or take the kids off your hands for a while. Izzy and Jackson always love a play date with your little ones." Carrie smiles in relief.

"Thanks. I know you're there in a heartbeat if I need it. I just might take you up on those offers here soon. I'm at my wits' end."

"Of course. Besides, I'm going to be needing to lean on you here soon: Austin and I have decided to start trying for a third." A high-pitched squeal cuts through the night air, but the husbands don't even flinch, too immersed in their own conversation, or maybe too used to their wives' theatrics.

"Shut up! Oh my goodness, that's so exciting! Three is the best. Seriously. It's so much easier than two. And Jackson and Izzy are old enough now where they'll be great helpers."

"Yeah, we haven't told them anything yet, obviously. Waiting until, ya know, I'm actually pregnant. But, yeah! Exciting, eh?" Even in the darkness of the cool, early summer evening, Margaret can feel her cheeks flush with warmth over the excitement and anticipation at what the future holds for her family. Carrie begins to rattle off all the reasons why having her third baby has been the easiest and their best decision.

Eventually the separate conversations meld together again, and all four friends are talking together about life, and TV shows, and kids. The banter and chatter comes easy, and the laughter and drinks flow freely. A soft breeze rattles the trees sending a shower of sparks cascading toward the heavens.

Early summer in Minnesota is one of Margaret's favorite times of the year. When you live in a state where six months of the year is cold, wet, and snowy, you come to truly appreciate and savor each day of gorgeous weather for the precious gift that it is. It's the sudden vibrant green trees, the return of the smell of freshly mowed lawns, and the aroma of logs burning on an evening fire with great company that fill her cup. Of course, she could do without the mosquitoes. There's nothing good about the mosquitoes.

As Margaret is soaking in the scene around her and sipping her wine, her eyes lock with Austin's across the fire, and it appears the fire isn't just contained in the pit. Her skin begins to prickle, and she can't tell if it's the flames making the blood coursing through her veins feel hot, or if it's her husband's smoldering stare. She's grateful the fire is dying down so her face isn't brightly lit; the man still has the power to make her blush without even saying a word.

Margaret pulls her gaze away from Austin's chocolate eyes as Carrie and Tyler stand up. "Well," Tyler huffs out. "I think it's time for us to get home. Babysitters are expensive these days." Margaret stands to bid her friends goodbye, and Austin follows suit.

Customary of the Midwestern goodbye, the group spends a handful of more time lingering in the driveway under the stars, unable to wrap up their conversations. Eventually Tyler and Carrie climb into their truck, and Austin comes up behind Margaret, wrapping his arms around her waist. The two stand at the top of the driveway watching their friends leave. As the ruby taillights fade down the road, Austin's lips begin tracing a trail down Margaret's neck. His warm breath mingles with the now-chilled night air, sending shivers down her spine as goosebumps pucker at her skin. She lets out a soft moan and presses into him.

"Miss Maggie," Austin drawls, nibbling her ear. "I think it's time we call it a night as well." He spins her around and wraps his fingers in her long, thick hair. His lips find hers, soft and sensuous. Margaret can feel his desire in the way his tongue explores her mouth, one hand on her hip, pulling her close. Suddenly, he sweeps her off her feet and is carrying her into the house. Margaret's heart beats faster as Austin carries her up the stairs to their bedroom, ready to fan a whole new set of flames.

Chapter Three

Monday, June 11, 2018

The intrusive rays of the Hawaiian sun stream through the veranda windows in Margaret's bungalow. Margaret can just make out the barely audible drum of the waves on the shore, just beyond her patio doors. She instinctively buries herself in the comfort of the downy pillows and luxurious blankets, trying to steady her breathing and calm her racing heart. Her clothes cling to her body, damp from the cold sweat coating her skin.

Inhale. Hold. Exhale.

Inhale. Hold. Exhale.

As her body calms, she lowers the thick blanket from her face, and slowly opens her eyes, allowing them to adjust to the tropical sun.

Inhale. Hold. Exhale. When was the last time I had a peaceful sleep?

She turns to the clock: 9:30. She brings the comforter back to her face, closing her eyes and inhaling the freshly laundered sheet's flowery scent. It calms her and reminds her of the giant flowers that decorated the Huli Huli Hut from her dinner the night before. Her heart feels a little lighter just thinking about that large man's bright, warm smile, and her nightmares start to melt to the back of her mind, tucked away until ready to pounce the next time her head hits the pillow.

Margaret pushes up on her elbow and gazes out the glass of the patio door. "Where does the earth end and the sky begin?" she muses. She throws her legs over the edge of the bed, slips on her sandals, and walks over to the door. When she steps across the veranda threshold, the crashing of the waves is magnified, and her senses shift from a dull, sleepy stupor to completely alert and awake: the view, the smells, the sounds. No need for coffee to wake you up here. There's a pair of wicker rocking chairs on her patio, and she scuffles over and sits down, staring out at waves dancing on the endless ocean. The air is warm and balmy, even at nine in the morning.

Margaret allows her mind to wander, just for a moment - she thinks of him. She closes her eyes, letting herself imagine he's here, wrapping his arms around her waist. As she feels his breath on her neck, the sound of the kids laughing and squealing from inside the bungalow drifts out, drowning out the sound of the waves on the shore. And for a moment, she lets herself feel it all, succumbing to the fantasy that was never meant to be. It feels so real, it hurts. "No!" her voice rings out, as her eyes snap open. She draws in ragged breaths, her chest heaving from the heartache of what is no more.

She stands up briskly, giving her arms a shake to rid herself of the sudden jitters flowing in her veins, and walks up to the mirror above her dresser. She runs her fingers through her hair, ruffling up some volume, and pinches her cheeks for some color. "Screw a shower," she announces to her reflection. "I need to get into a book." So she throws a t-shirt over her tank top, grabs her book off the bed, and heads out the door to find some breakfast.

Margaret's steps are brisk and precise, her sandals flapping on the pavement with each step as she searches for a place to grab some breakfast. Her eyes catch a little cafe nestled in a palm tree cove on the resort. A wooden carving of a mother and baby dolphin stands beside the open door of the bright yellow building, and the words "Waikiki Eats" written in bright green on a wooden sign hang above the entrance. The cafe is humming with the sound of conversations among the scattered tables as servers walk among the guests, carrying trays of steaming plates and full cups. Margaret grins at a sign by the door that says, "Pick your seat and your company!" She chooses a booth by a window with a view overlooking a garden decorated with the brightest, biggest flowers Margaret has ever seen.

A woman with sun-kissed skin and thick, onyx hair with waves like the ocean walks up to Margaret's table with a smile. "Aloha! Welcome. Here's our menu.

Can I get you anything to drink right away?" Margaret smiles back - smiling comes so easy here - and asks for a glass of water. She begins to scan the menu as the woman walks away to grab her water. While there are some comfort foods that sound familiar to her, there are several new foods she's never heard of before. There's *linguiça, malasadas, loco moco,* and *poke* - all foreign dishes to this Midwestern native. Margaret decides to be adventurous, and when the beautiful woman returns with her water, she orders the breakfast platter with *linguiça*, eager to try something new. The waitress flashes her captivating smile as she departs with the order, and Margaret starts fishing through her bag for her book.

She looks up just as she pulls the novel onto the table and notices Baggage Claim Man enter the cafe accompanied by a small group of other guests. Margaret quickly dips behind her book, peering over the cover to get her first real look at the man. His shaggy hair is ruffled and unkempt, as if he just rolled out of bed. He's wearing a plain white t-shirt, and he's already got his swimming trunks on for the day. Margaret guesses the man must be planning to hit the waves after some breakfast. He takes his eyes off the hostess and starts to scan the room. Margaret quickly averts her eyes and focuses on her book, hoping the man doesn't recognize her. Bonus points if he doesn't even see her at all.

She is so focused on actively *not* looking up to check on the man, that she's reread the same sentence three times by the time the waitress returns to top off her water and let her know her breakfast will be ready any moment. Margaret thanks her and takes the opportunity to do a quick scan. She finds Baggage Claim Man sitting at a table on the other side of the cafe, his back now to her.

A sigh of relief escapes Margaret, and she returns her attention to her book. Not long after, her breakfast platter with *linguiça* is delivered, and Margaret is pleased to discover the Portuguese sausage is a delicious, salty treat with just a hint of sweetness. It is the perfect accompaniment to her eggs and rice. As she devours her breakfast, she falls deep into medieval times, becoming a knight in the king's army, and very quickly forgets about Baggage Claim Man. And that's exactly why she loves her books - they let her forget.

Margaret strolls leisurely through the resort as she makes her way back to her bungalow after a very satisfying and delicious Hawaiian breakfast. "It's a beautiful day to tan with a book!" she declares to herself, pulling out all the bathing suits she packed for her trip. She eyes the modest one-piece suits next to a few more tantalizing bikinis. She had packed the one-piece suits; they were all she owned. She can't remember the last time she wore a bikini, wanting to always hide the baby-weight she's never been able to lose and the stretch marks that claimed her as a mother. Odette was the one who sent a couple bikinis along. "It's a vacation! A time to try new things and find a new you! Wear the bikinis," she had urged as she drove Margaret to the airport.

But as Margaret stares at the bikinis in the drawer before her, her stomach flips at the thought of looking down and seeing her pale stretch marks clawing violently across her soft belly. She snatches a one-piece and slams the drawer closed.

Margaret stands before her reflection after changing into her bathing suit. Looking at herself, she feels as if she's aged ten years in the last one. Purple circles hug the skin around her eyes, and she swears she's developed frown lines. Her unkempt hair drapes well past her chest, as she hasn't ventured into a salon in over a year. "What's the point?" she mumbles. The usual wave of feelings she can never seem to shake off begin to creep up her into her chest. Regret. Despair. Fear. Anger. The high-pitched ring of her cell phone makes her jump. She runs to her phone, grateful for even a temporary escape from her anguish. The screen tells her it's her mother, and Margaret curses to herself for forgetting to call her earlier.

"Hey, Mom. Sorry I haven't responded to you," Margaret apologizes.

"Good Lord, Margaret, are you trying to give your mother a heart attack? Here I am thinking you've been attacked by a strange man, or run over by a crazy taxi, or something terrible. You shouldn't be there by yourself."

"I'm fine mom, everything's fine. I made it to the resort, no problems. How are things back home?"

"Oh everything is fine here. Same old, same old." Margaret can almost see her mother through the phone, her apron on for the day already covered in flour, hand waving dismissively. "So you made it to Hawaii, great. Was that so hard? That's all I wanted to know. I still think this trip was a bad idea. I don't like you halfway across the world by yourself."

"It's hardly halfway across the world, mom, and I know. I know what you think. You made that clear before I left. But this trip is good. It's gorgeous here. It's good for me," Margaret defends, feeling the heat in her body begin to rise.

"Home is what's good for you. Your mother is good for you." Her mother lets out a heavy sigh, and Margaret lets the air between them hang heavy, not adding a word. "Just do your mother a favor and check in once and a while, okay? I worry about you on your own. I don't like you there by yourself, especially in your state."

"I will. I'll touch base, promise." Margaret smiles. It's still comforting to know her mother is worried about her, even as a full-grown woman.

"Alright, well I just wanted to check in, see that you're okay. I'll let you get back to pineapples or coconuts or whatever they have in Hawaii that they apparently don't have in Minnesota." Margaret rolls her eyes.

"Bye mom." The phone call went better than Margaret had anticipated it would go with her overbearing, critical mother. She lets out a sigh and looks around the room. Having a momentary connection back to Minnesota suddenly makes Margaret feel very lonely. The room seems bigger somehow, and the air quieter, heavier. Before she can dwell too much on the change in the atmosphere, Margaret throws a bright yellow sundress over her bathing suit, gathers her thick hair into a messy bun, fills her beach bag with three books, sunscreen, complimentary snacks and water from her mini kitchen, and a towel, and heads out the door to the beach.

As soon as Margaret's walk to the beckoning shore changes from concrete path to luscious Hawaiian sand, she slips off her sandals, relishing in the way the silky soft sand ebbs and flows between her toes with each step. She still cannot get over how white the sand is. "It seriously looks like snow," she chuckles to herself as she walks toward the shore. This portion of the beach is only accessible to vacationers of The Hibiscus Cove Resort, so it is wonderfully quiet. A few other beach goers speckle the sandy shore, but for the most part, Margaret can have her pick of anywhere on the sand to relax. Before she lays out her towel, she takes the opportunity to walk along the edge of the ocean, her feet getting kissed with the froth of the waves as they flow in and out of the shore. The water is blissfully warm on her toes, and the sand beneath her feet dances and moves with the waves, tickling her soles as she walks. She keeps her head down as she strolls along, eying the shells scattered along the sand as she wanders.

A long line of luxurious lounge chairs spread across the high end of the beach, up and away from high tide and close to a little tiki hut serving beverages at the top of the sand. But Margaret has her heart set on stretching out on the silken beach, where she can be close to the ocean waves. She settles on a patch of sand to spread out her towel. She takes her time slathering her sunscreen across her body (only SPF 15 - got to get that tan!), looking around at the scene before her. There are a few surfers straddling their boards out a distance in the water as they wait for some surf-worthy waves to make an appearance. A stray wisp of a cloud drifts lazily overhead, barely a blip on the unnaturally blue sky. A group of albatross appears to be roaming the shores for a snack, their impressive wingspan catching Margaret's eye. Peaceful contentedness washes over her, the Hawaiian sun blanketing her in a warmth that seems to reach to her spirit even more than it warms her skin. It startles Margaret, the feeling so foreign to her, yet coming so easily. She closes her eyes and inhales deeply, letting the feeling flood her veins. When she opens them again, she decides it's time to dive into her book before the feeling goes away.

She has barely begun reading when an employee from the resort walks up to her, wearing the same contagious Hawaiian smile as all the other employees she has encountered so far. "Aloha, my lady. Can I bring you any beverage while you enjoy the Hawaiian sun today?"

"Ooh, I would love a strawberry daiquiri, if you have them." Margaret eagerly replies.

"We do, miss. I will get that right out for you." *Sunshine, the beach, and complimentary drinks delivered right to me. I could get use to this.* The young man returns from the beach-side bar with her beverage. She sips on the cool, tropical drink as she loses herself in the comforting pages of her latest book.

The sound of a woman squealing in delight as a young man pulls her into water wakes Margaret with a jolt. It takes her a moment for her fuzzy mind to recall where she is. She glances around the beach, trying to scope out anyone who could deliver her another beverage. As she's scanning her surroundings, her eyes lock on Baggage Claim Man. He's standing with his hands on his hips, the salty sea water dripping from his shaggy hair. He is wearing a wet suit, but has it unzipped and pulled down off his torso, resting casually on his hips. Margaret guesses by his attire, dripping hair, and the small pile of surfboards stacked haphazardly by the group, that he's just finished surfing. Baggage Claim Man starts to look around the beach, so Margaret quickly averts her eyes in an attempt to, once again, not be noticed.

As she buries her eyes in her book, she can't stop thinking about how she could really use another drink. Some ice-cold water sounds exquisite after dozing off and baking in the sun. Margaret gives it another minute of staring into the book praying for someone to come ask if she needs anything, then gives up. Her parched throat and hot skin are too uncomfortable to ignore. She slips her book into her bag, hauls it over her shoulder, and starts walking to the beverage hut situated at the top of the beach, where the sand meets the grass. The silky sand has been baked by the sun to be a deliciously hot massage on her feet. Margaret has always been a freeze baby (perhaps it's from living in the tundra of the north), so there is no such thing as too hot in her mind. She savors the heated beads flowing through her always cold toes.

The beach bar is one long hut of straw, grass, and flowers, with stools nestled around the bar. A bartender stands in the middle, whipping up some sort of yellow and pink swirled concoction. Two other workers walk around and behind him, cleaning cups, running tickets, and wiping down the counter. "Aloha! Howzit this beautiful day?" the bartender asks Margaret.

"Aloha," Margaret smiles back. "Can I just get a glass of ice water?"

"You got it pretty lady."

"Ice water? That hardly sounds like the type of beverage one should be enjoying on a sunny Hawaiian beach. You need to spice it up a little bit. This is the tropics. Have some rum!" Margaret cringes at the voice coming from behind her. The man steps to the side and pulls out the stool right next to her, taking a seat. She reluctantly looks up into the eyes of Baggage Claim Man. Margaret smiles at him as she tries to find her voice.

"I fell asleep in the sun. My body desperately needs some water. I'm more parched than a lone camel in the desert." Margaret's words spill out in a speedy, nervous cadence. Baggage Claim Man lets out a robust laugh and smiles. He has brilliantly white teeth. And only one dimple, on his left cheek. *How weird*, Margaret thinks.

"Don't camels store water or something in their humps? And that's why they can live in the desert?"

Margaret's mind falters for a moment. "Uh, yeah, actually I think your right. Or maybe it's fat. One or the other, anyway." She feels her face beginning to burn with embarrassment.

"I'm Will." Will offers his hand to Margaret. She takes it reluctantly, her mind churning through excuses to flee the scene and recover to the isolation of her lounge chair.

"Margaret."

"Margaret, I like it. You're my friend from baggage claim, right? The woman with the insanely heavy suitcase." Margaret averts her eyes, suppressing the urge to groan audibly. Will just laughs a warm, honey-like laugh that sings as it floats around her, and she looks back up at the man before her.

"I'm guessing by the book in your hand that your suitcase may have been stuffed with a few things to read?"

"I never like to leave home without a book."

"Or a mini library?" He lets out his kind, soft laugh, relaxing Margaret just a bit. "So Margaret, are you here on business?"

"No."

"Oh. Do you live in Hawaii?"

Margaret can't help but laugh. "Did my pasty white skin give it away? No, I don't live here. What would make you think that?"

"Well, I don't know. I've seen you around in a couple places, but every time you're alone. And you have a book. Every time. I would figure someone who keeps their nose in a book, choosing to miss out on this beautiful island, must either be a frequent traveler to the area, maybe here on business, or a resident. I mean look, you even have a bag of books with you right now." Margaret looks down at the bag by her feet. It's half open, revealing the three books she stuffed in there on her way out this morning. "So what's your story then?" he asks.

Margaret takes her eyes off her books and looks up at Will. His eyes are the same soft blue of the Hawaiian sky with flecks of dark ocean blue and seaweed green speckled throughout. A small, tropical oasis right in those kind eyes. "I don't have a story. I'm just a Midwestern girl visiting Hawaii. And I like to read." She tries to sound nonchalant. "What's your story?" she pries.

"Ah, me? Well I'm just here for my little sister's wedding. One of those 'destination' things. The wedding isn't until Friday, but you know, gotta get the whole family out for a big family vacation. Make the most of it while we all come down here, ya know?" He grins at her with his one-dimpled smile, and Margaret smiles a genuine, soft smile in return. Her mind wanders to family memories of all her loved ones together over fire pits or picnic tables or living rooms, just enjoying each other's company. Suddenly there's a lump in her throat, and she can feel her heart erratically increasing its speed. She quickly stands up from her stool, pulls her bag of books over her shoulder, and grabs her glass of ice water from the bar.

"Well, Will, it was nice to meet you. I'm going to take my water and get—"

Will cuts her off, "Back to your books?" He chuckles warmly. "It was nice to meet you too, Margaret. Enjoy your books." He winks at her, and Margaret smiles back. As she turns to head back to her lounge chair near the waves, she thinks about Baggage Claim Man. Will. That wasn't *so* bad, having to talk to him. *Could have been worse,* she reminds herself.

Back in her bungalow, Margaret cozies herself deep into the pillowy comforts of her bed. It's been a long relaxing day of reading and sunshine today, and Margaret feels content as she reminisces on her first full day on the island and the stories she explored beneath the tropical sun. After changing for bed, she plugs in her phone, her eyes catching the date at the top of the screen. Dread washes over her, as her mind drifts to tomorrow. But before she can fall into the dangers of reliving the past, she grabs her book, opens the pages, and says a little prayer that her book will work extra hard tonight to drift her to a sleep far from reality and her nightmares.

Chapter Four

Sunday, June 11, 2017

Margaret avoids opening her eyes, and instead reaches lazily across the bed, looking for her personal furnace. Between her fingers failing to find skin and the roar of a dinosaur chasing squealing kids drifting in through the cracks of the bedroom door, she realizes morning has arrived. Austin must be downstairs with the kids.

It's one of the things she adores the most about Austin, his love for his children. It doesn't matter how early in the morning it is, or how tired he truly feels: if the kids want to play, he plays. And not just a "sit on the couch while they bring him pretend food" type of play. He plays in a hands-and-knees-on-the-floor, all-in sort of way. For Margaret, mornings are the worst part about being an adult. She does not like to function before getting her daily cup of coffee to kick start the day. She smiles to herself as Austin's stomping T-Rex footsteps thunder from the floor below and stretches her arms and legs, waking up her body. She grabs her bathrobe as she walks out the bedroom door and heads downstairs.

The scene she enters in the living room makes Margaret chuckle to herself. Jackson has his Nerf gun aimed at Austin's back as Austin roars and stomps toward Izzy, who is bravely brandishing a plastic sword at the approaching dinosaur. Margaret watches for a moment, savoring the joyfulness ringing in her children's laughter, then makes her way to the kitchen to get her coffee. As the noise of the banging cupboards reaches her children's ears, they come running into the kitchen, squealing with glee at the sight of their mother. Their tiny but strong arms wrap around Margaret's legs, and she kisses each of their heads. She turns her attention to Austin and smirks at the sight of his heaving chest, trying to catch his breath.

"Nothing like a morning workout to get my day going!" He jokes cheerfully, grinning at his wife across the counter and puffing his chest with bravado.

"I'll stick to my cup of coffee, thanks," Margaret smirks in return.

The kids run off upstairs to continue playing, and Margaret is left staring into her husband's brown eyes over the rim of her coffee cup. With his smirk still hanging playfully on his chiseled face, he idles over to his wife and pulls her into his chest. His arms consume her and she instinctively starts to melt into him, her face finding the crook of his neck, her empty hand gripping his hip. He removes the coffee cup from her other hand, as his soft lips climb from her collar bone up her slender neck, sending shivers down her spine. "Round two, Miss Maggie?" Austin playfully whispers in her ear. Margaret's rich, melodic laugh bounces around the kitchen.

"In your dreams," Margaret responds. She playfully pushes Austin away, grabs her cup of coffee, and smacks his butt on the way out of the kitchen. She turns to look back at him as she leaves the room and is pleased to see he's grinning, eying her backside as she exits. She absolutely loves that after nearly a decade of the monotony that marriage can be, they still flirt with each other daily.

Margaret is standing under the bright lights of her vanity, curling her thick hair, when Austin walks into the room. He stops and leans against the doorway, arms across his chest, watching her. Margaret loves when he watches her get ready. It makes her feel desired, and her mind flashes back to last night. Their eyes connect, and Austin drops his stance at the door and sidles over to her. He kisses her cheek as she continues to curl her hair and starts to dig out his toothpaste from the vanity drawer.

"What are the kids doing? Did they get dressed?" Margaret asks.

"Yeah. Both are dressed, teeth brushed, and hair combed," he replies, wetting his toothbrush. "Do we really have to go to this thing?" She doesn't answer, and instead gives him a glare that tells Austin it's not up for debate.

Margaret has one brother, AJ (short for Aaron James). AJ was the older one, but only by fifteen months. Being so close in age, they grew up as best friends. As kids, wherever one was, the other was not far behind. Their father left the family in the middle of a random winter night when Margaret was just six years old. AJ stepped right up to being the most important man in her life, even at his young age of eight. He slid into the protective big brother role effortlessly, and Margaret was just as devoted to her big brother. She has fond memories of sneaking into her brother's room well after bedtime and perusing comic books together by the glow of a flashlight within a cave of sheets. When Margaret experienced heartbreak for the first time as a high school sophomore, AJ's shoulder was there for her head to rest on as tears poured out of her trembling body. She remembers feeling the clench of his jaw as he laid his head on top of her own, awakening Margaret to just how fiercely her brother loved her. She was also fiercely devoted to her brother, covering for him when he took their mom's car after she had gone to bed to go to a party and ended up putting a rather large dent in bumper. Their unbreakable bond continued well into college and adulthood, each of them thinking they loved the other more.

AJ was now married to Odette, and the two were expecting their first child, and today they were having a gender reveal party. And while attending the event was not up for debate with Austin, Margaret felt his pain. She didn't want to go any more than he did. She never understood all the hullabaloo over finding out the sex of one's baby. Sure, it's exciting, but party worthy? It didn't help that Margaret wasn't a fan of Odette either. Odette and AJ had been married for two years, and she still didn't understand how the couple worked together. Her brother was the most humble, down to earth, modest man she had ever met. He was the Midwestern stereotype: a grizzly, buff, lumberjack of a man. And Odette was the most glamorous, high maintenance, and image-driven woman Margaret had ever met. She came from a wealthy Southern family and had grown up in a lavish life of housekeepers and perfection - a far cry from the cabin in the middle of the woods she and AJ had called home. Margaret once tried to talk her brother out of being with Odette, but AJ had become extremely defensive and upset during their conversation. He told Margaret that Odette was the love of his life, and he was the luckiest man on Earth to be the one she chose to be with. Margaret never again mentioned her feelings about Odette and has since tried her best to find a common ground to build a friendship on with her sister-in-law. She has yet to find that ground.

Margaret lets the last strand of hair to be curled slip out of the iron, then unplugs the device. She runs her slender fingers through the fresh curls, loosening them up a bit and creating some more volume to her already voluptuous auburn locks. She turns to plant a quick kiss on Austin's cheek, and informs him "We're leaving in five," as she walks out of the bathroom. She rounds up Jackson and Izzy and helps them slip their feet into their shoes. Almost five minutes to the dot after her announcement to Austin, and he's backing the mini-van out of the garage, everyone loaded up inside ready to go.

About three minutes later the family is rolling back into the driveway. Margaret hops out of the passenger door before Austin has even put the car in park and runs inside the house. Thirty seconds later, and she's climbing back into her seat, clutching the baby's gift she had forgotten on the dining room table, and ignoring Austin's playful banter on her forgetfulness.

They pull up to the party and it is just as elegant as Margaret would have expected. Instead of the usual blue or pink one would expect at a gender reveal party, Odette has opted to decorate with gold and silver - gold for a girl, silver for a boy. A lavish buffet table decorated with parfaits, mimosas, fruit kabobs, and other various brunch items sits at the back of the yard, with an elaborate three-tiered silver and gold cake at the center. There's a bubble machine sending iridescent orbs floating around the guests, and Jackson and Izzy run straight towards it, captivated by its works.

Margaret scans the yard, and finds Odette, the guest of honor. She takes her sister-in-law in from afar; her silky blond hair is perched in an elaborate bun atop her head, and she's wearing a glamorous floor-length dress that is the brightest white Margaret has ever laid eyes on. It both hugs her body in all the right places, yet seems to drape effortlessly over her curves at the same time. *How does she make pregnancy look sexy?* Margaret thinks to herself, both impressed and slightly jealous. *I don't care if it's exercise. I still think exercise is overrated.* Margaret finds Austin's hand, and together they walk to the corner of the yard where Odette and AJ are chatting with some friends of theirs.

"Margaret!" Odette squeals, as if they've been lifelong friends. She kisses each of Margaret's cheeks in a flashy greeting. "Oh I'm so happy to see you here. Hi, Austin. You're looking as dapper as ever." Odette pecks a pair of kisses on Austin's cheeks as well. AJ walks over and buries Margaret in a bear hug, kissing the top of her head. He reaches across and shakes Austin's hands without releasing his little sister. She doesn't mind. AJ's arms are her second favorite place to be after her husband's arms.

"Where are the rascals?" AJ asks, looking around the yard.

"They ran towards the bubble machine," she answers. AJ spots the children, releases his sister and heads towards his niece and nephew with an excited bounce in his step. Margaret's heart pumps warmth through her veins as she watches him make his way toward her children. AJ is an amazing uncle, always doting on and playing with her kids. A smile grows on her face as she thinks of the wonderful dad he's going to become.

Odette's musical voice snaps Margaret out of her daydream. "Thank you so much for coming. I can't wait to hear the big news and share it with y'all," For all the little things that grate Margaret, she does love the woman's southern drawl.

"We're happy to be here," Margaret smiles.

"Well don't let me keep y'all just standing here! Help yourselves to what's on the table. We'll do cake and the big reveal in a little while - eek!" Odette claps her hands excitedly then shoos the couple toward the food.

Margaret and Austin walk together to the elaborate spread and fill up their plates. Margaret piles extra food on her plate, knowing the kids will be back soon and asking for food for themselves. As she and Austin take their spread to a table, Margaret scopes the yard for her two children, but instead notices her mother walking towards her. She instantly feels her muscles stiffen, bracing herself for whatever nagging is about to come her way.

"Hi, my baby," her mother says, as she pulls Margaret in for a brisk hug.

"Hi, Mom."

"Hey, Nancy! Lookin' beautiful as ever!" Austin exclaims as he takes Margaret's place in her mother's arms. Margaret rolls her eyes. Austin is such a schmooze with her mother, though she can't totally blame him. Her mother, Nancy, adores Austin. From the day she first brought him home, Margaret was sure Nancy Kranz loved Austin more than her own daughter. As soon as Nancy is done squeezing her son-in-law, she turns her attention back to Margaret, giving her an assessing look.

"Margaret, have you been getting enough sleep? You look tired. You would think now that school's out for the summer, you wouldn't have an excuse to be tired anymore." *An excuse,* Margaret thinks to herself. Margaret is a teacher, and her mother frequently tells her she is "wasting her brain" as a teacher. Margaret tries to see it as a compliment, to see how her mother thinks she is able to achieve great heights, but she just wishes her mother saw that being a teacher *was* a great height.

"Even though school ended last week, we still have to be at the school to wrap up grades, clean the classrooms, and close the school up," Margaret explains.

"Ah, well. I saw a commercial for some eye cream that appeared to do wonders. I'll get that for those circles under your eyes. They're dreadful."

Margaret sighs and glares at Austin, who is standing behind her mother trying to suppress a chuckle. Just then, squeals of "Grandma!" fill the air, as Jackson and Izzy come running toward the group. Nancy bends down to squeeze her grandkids, kissing each of them multiple times on the head.

"Oh my babies!" she coos over the pair. She stands up and announces in a sing-song voice, "Who wants a dollar?" Both kids start jumping up and down with excitement. Nancy fishes out two dollar bills and hands one each to Jackson and Izzy, who grab them from her and run off to play with the bubbles again.

"Mom! You can't just give them money every time you see them!"

"Ah, who cares. It's just a dollar. And how else am I going to make sure they keep liking me more than their other grandma?"

Margaret huffs and throws her hands in the air, looking to her husband for support. Austin just laughs, enjoying her annoyance. "You know there's no competition there anyway, mom." Austin's parents moved to Canada during Austin's freshman year of college, and they have never made any real attempt to get to know their grandchildren.

Austin grew up an only child, and when he and Margaret were dating, he often talked about how he was sure his parents never wanted children, and that he was not part of their plan. Margaret always assumed he was exaggerating until she met them for the first time. It was Margaret and Austin's first Christmas together, and they were flying to Canada to spend it with his parents. Margaret had never met more self-centered people. Not a single photograph of Austin was found anywhere in the house. In fact, if you didn't know any better, you would have thought Mr. & Mrs. Heller were a childless couple and always had been. Austin didn't even receive a Christmas gift from them (though she did notice gifts under their Christmas tree addressed to each other). And when she asked Austin about it on the flight home, he just shrugged his shoulders, and said, "They stopped giving me gifts when I turned eighteen."

Margaret thought things would change when babies entered the picture. After Jackson was born, she tried video calls, emailing pictures, sending cards and letters with updates, but all of her interactions went unanswered. They were always too busy to take a phone call, and she never once received a response to any email or letter she sent them. They did fly down to Minnesota for two Christmases since the kids had been born. And while they only stayed for one day and didn't bring any gifts for Margaret or Austin, they did at least bring a toy for each of the kids on both occasions.

Margaret notices AJ climbing up on a chair, and suddenly his charismatic voice is booming over the guests in the yard. "Thank you so much to everyone for coming out here today." Odette strides over and plants herself to his side, beaming with excitement. Margaret feels a flood of warmth and joy for her brother and his wife. "It's time for us to cut the cake and see what baby Kranz is going to be!" Everyone claps, including Odette, and AJ climbs down from the chair. He pecks Odette's cheek and the two of them walk hand-in-hand to the buffet table. The guests make their way over as well, and soon everyone is crowded around, anticipation hanging in the air. For as much as Margaret thinks these parties are a dumb idea, she can't help but feel giddy too. Odette picks up the knife, and AJ wraps his hand around Odette's slender fingers. Together they cut the cake and pull out a slice. "It's a...GIRL!" AJ shouts, holding up a slice of pink cake beneath a pile of frosting for all to see. The whole party erupts in cheers. Joyful tears are streaming down Odette's porcelain cheeks, and AJ dips her for a deep, celebratory kiss.

Margaret is teary-eyed as well, as her heart floods with emotions. She immediately starts daydreaming of future holidays, birthdays, and random days in between of all of their kids: cousins growing up and making memories together. Memories they will all cherish forever.

The Sunday Kranz tradition is to have a big family dinner at Nancy's lake house, and even though the family was all together for celebrations in the morning, the tradition still stands. So it's only a matter of hours before Margaret's family is pulling into Nancy's driveway, her childhood home.

Margaret loves her mother's house. It was more of a cabin than a home, filled with old, rustic charm, and sitting on ten private acres of lakefront property. Nancy's father had built the cabin himself, and she inherited the home when her parents retired and wanted to downsize. Margaret had so many fond memories of this house. She used to spend hours of her childhood combing the beach for crayfish and snails. She and AJ loved to spend their days exploring the woods that overtook half of the property. She recalls the two of them encountering all sorts of creatures, from cute, furry ones like rabbits, squirrels, deer, and even opossums, to the not so cute ones. There were plenty of snakes, spiders, and bugs in the woods as well. Margaret remembers one summer fondly, when AJ got sprayed by a skunk that had crossed their path. Their mother made him take tomato baths for a week after that. Her childhood was also filled with fishing off the dock. So much fishing. The dock jutting out into the lake faced west, and Margaret always loved ending her summer days catching some crappies while watching the sun set over the water. The winters were just as fun as the summers. There was ice skating, ice fishing, snow shoeing, and more snowball fights than Margaret could count.

Austin puts the car into park, and everyone starts to unload. Jackson unbuckles himself and runs up the driveway, and Margaret helps Izzy undo her latches. Nancy is standing on the front porch, her apron covered in flour, holding out her arms for her grandchildren. Margaret instantly feels comfort wash over her, as she makes her way up the driveway towards home. If she looks hard enough, she can see her mother twenty years younger, standing on this same porch, in that same apron, calling her and AJ in for Sunday dinner. In all her years of life, Margaret can think of only two times she has missed a Sunday at her mother's house: the Sunday she and Austin were in the Florida Keys for their honeymoon, and the Sunday Margaret gave birth to Izzy.

Everyone says their hellos on the porch and then makes their way inside. Odette is in the kitchen chopping vegetables, and again Margaret finds herself analyzing the woman. *Who wears stilettos while chopping vegetables?* She tries to shake it off and smiles warmly at Odette. "Hey, Odette. Where's AJ?"

"He went out to the dock. Hey Austin - if you go out there, bring a couple beers for you both. AJ asked me to come in and grab one for him, but your mama sucked me into choppin' these veggies for her." Austin eagerly grabs two beers out of the fridge and heads out to the dock, the kids running ahead of him to go dig in the beach.

"Come on now, Margaret. Make yourself useful. You can prep the salad," Nancy orders, as her head is in the oven, checking on her casserole. Margaret heads over to the fridge, digs out a head of lettuce, and begins chopping. She attempts to make small talk with Odette as she chops.

"Hey, congrats again on the baby girl, Odette. That's so exciting. You guys are going to love having a little girl."

"Aw, thanks hon. We're so excited. 'Course, I woulda been excited no matter what. I am just a big bundle of joy - and gettin' bigger every day!" Odette giggles. Margaret offers a chuckle along, but can't help scanning Odette's body. A small ripple of jealousy flows through Margaret's veins; she definitely wouldn't call Odette 'big.'

"You look great, Odette. You're positively glowing," Nancy offers, giving Odette's hand a squeeze. Margaret tries to push away the memories of her mother lecturing her on weight gain when *she* was pregnant and her comments about the importance of losing the baby weight "and then some" after both of her pregnancies. Odette blushes at Nancy's comment and keeps working away on her cutting board. The sound of the kids squealing in the sand along the shore drifts in through the windows, washing away some of the bitterness flowing in her veins at the moment.

After a while longer of small talk, dinner is ready, and everyone gathers around the picnic table out on the lawn. Nancy sets a steaming casserole dish of tater tot hotdish in the center of the table, Margaret places the bowl of salad next to the hotdish, and Odette brings over the plate of fresh veggies. The air is filled with the savory aroma of the tater tots, ground beef, veggies, and gravy as talks of baseball, fishing, babies, and jobs fill the air. Soon everyone is leaning back, rubbing their bellies in satisfaction.

"Grandma," Jackson pipes up. "Is there any dessert?"

"Dessert? What's dessert?" Nancy teases.

"Grandma!" whines Izzy. "You know what dessert is! Don't tease!"

"Okay, okay," Nancy concedes. "I did make dessert. I made salad!" Nancy winks at Odette as she rises from the table to get the dessert. The children cheer in delight. Because in Minnesota, salad is the best kind of dessert - Snickers Salad. Nancy returns with bowl full of diced green apples, cool whip, and crushed snickers bars, all mixed together. A deliciously crisp, sweet end to dinner a perfect summer night, and Margaret's favorite kind of "salad."

The family ends the night with a roaring bonfire. After a couple of toasted marshmallows, Jackson climbs into Austin's lap, and Izzy curls up in Margaret's - a sign that they're ready for bed and it's time for the night to come to a close.

Everyone says their goodbyes, Nancy reminds Margaret she'll be bringing over some of that magic eye cream, and the family loads into the car. As Austin drives home, Margaret reaches across the armrest, taking his hand in her own. She absentmindedly strokes his hand with her thumb as she stares at the stars out her window. The sound of the children's rhythmic breathing fills the car, and a sigh of perfect contentment escapes Margaret's lips. She listens to her babies breathing, feels the strong comfort of her husband's hand, and reminisces on how wonderful the weekend was.

Chapter Five

Tuesday, June 12, 2018

Margaret jolts awake drenched in a cold sweat. The beautiful Hawaiian morning sun is a stark contrast to the dark abyss of her nightmares she just left. Her heart threatens to tear through her rib cage, its erratic hammering cracking her ribs with each beat. Nausea teases her stomach. Even as she sleeps, she can't escape the demons that haunt her from that summer day one year ago. Margaret peels the slick sheets from her body and makes her way to the bathroom on shaky feet. A torrential storm rages through her mind of all the memories that once were and all the heartache of what will never be. Gripping the sink with one hand for balance, she uses her other hand to splash cold water on her face. She takes a moment to try to focus on her breathing.

In.

Hold.

Out.

In.

Hold.

Out.

After a moment of calculated breathing, Margaret slowly slides herself down to the bathroom floor. Curled in the fetal position, she rests her damp head on the cool tile, closes her eyes, and tries to will away the nausea. *It's been a whole year. 365 days,* she reports to herself. Tears swimming beneath her lids begging for release.

Eventually, Margaret is able to drift back off to a restless sleep.

It's Margaret's stiff, sore muscles that wake her up the second time. At thirty-three years old, her body is starting to resent when Margaret does things like sleep on cold, hard bathroom floors. She's able to sit up without a wave of nausea overcoming her. With her back against the wall, she stares absentmindedly into nothing.

"Guess my nightmares can find me anywhere," she mumbles to the void.

And then it comes. Like a wave crashing into her soul. Her heart shatters into a thousand pieces of shrapnel, slicing through her body, damaging her, killing her from the inside out. Something inside of her breaks. The dam that she worked so hard to build the past year, the dam that was supposed to keep her grief and pain trapped inside, is torn down. And with it, a waterfall of tears and grief consumer her. And for the first time in almost a year, Margaret doesn't try to fight the grief. She lets the tears fall. She lets the pain, anguish, and despair rake over her body. She trembles as her anguished wails fill the empty bungalow, bouncing off the walls, magnifying her pain and loneliness.

And while she tries to focus on the fact that she's survived for a whole year, all she can think is, *Do I even* want *to survive?*

Margaret eventually manages to get herself out of the bathroom, and searches for her phone. As she's walking around the room, she passes the giant mirror hanging above the dresser, pausing to assess herself. Her eyes are deeply bloodshot, the dark circles beneath more pronounced than ever. Tear stains decorate her cheeks, and her hair is begging for a wash and a comb. Margaret sniffles, turns, and keeps trudging around the room. She finds her phone on the floor, next to her bed.

She has a few different messages on her phone. The first she opens is from Carrie, and her heart jumps to her throat. She hasn't spoken to Carrie in months. How could she after what happened? The message reads: ***I know it's been a while, but I just want you to know I'm thinking of you today. I'm still here if you ever need anything.*** Margaret's stomach squirms as guilt fills the pit of her belly. She reflects on the last year, trying to pinpoint how it happened - how she became so alienated - but she can't find an exact moment. Margaret decides to bypass Carrie's message, unsure how to respond. *That's how* *it happened - I never know what to say. There is nothing to say and everything to say all at once.*

She flips to her message from AJ: ***Thinking of you today.***

She also has a message from her mother: ***Don't do anything foolish today.***

Even in her current state, she chuckles at the stark contrast of two of the most important people in her life. And she is pleased to see she also has a message from Odette - a simple heart icon. And for just a small moment, peace is able to enter her still trembling body. She wants desperately to call AJ. She looks at the clock: It's almost one o'clock here, which means it's five o'clock back home, and AJ is just getting off work. Margaret decides to call him.

Her stomach churns as she waits for him to pick up.

"Mags, are you okay?"

"No," and that's all she can get out before she loses control. The tears begin to fall again, and she convulses in uncontrollable sobs.

"Margaret. Margaret, it's okay. You're okay. Talk to me, Margaret." But she can't stop. She just wants her brother to wrap her in one of his bear hugs, so she can feel safe. "Margaret, breathe. Shhh. You're okay, breathe." AJ continues to be a steady, comforting voice on the phone, and Margaret's meltdown begins to ease. "There, that's good. Breathe. Keep breathing, I'm here. Talk when you're ready."

It takes a moment to find her voice, her throat is raw and hoarse. "A whole year," is all she gets out. AJ's deep sigh fills the air hanging between them and she realizes she's not the only one in pain today. The line is achingly empty, as the two siblings share their mutual grief thousands of miles apart. Finally, AJ speaks.

"I know," his voice cracks. "I know."

"I want to come home. This was a dumb idea. I can't be here."

"No." AJ's voice is firm. "No, Mags. You have to stay out there. You need to do this, if only to just say you did it. To say you were strong enough. Because you *are* strong, Mags. You are one of the strongest people I know. Definitely the strongest sister I have." Margaret smirks through the silent tears as she hears his smile across the phone.

"I hurt everywhere. Everything hurts. How does it still hurt so much after so much time?" She's not expecting an answer, she knows AJ can't provide her the answer she needs.

"Margaret," AJ begins, drawing out his words as he assembles his thoughts. "I don't think it's ever going to stop hurting. I don't think that's the point." Margaret doesn't respond, waiting for AJ to give her more. "Your world isn't meant to go back to what it was before. I know, ugh, I know this hurts to hear - because it's killing me to say it - but, Mags? You've got a new life now. You have to find it, and then accept it. And I really, truly think Hawaii can help you do that. If you let it. But you gotta let it. Don't come home."

The air hangs thick between them, as Margaret digests his words. Her eyes fill, then the tears tumble silently out and roll down her cheeks. *A new life? What if I don't want this new life?* Her sniffle breaks the silence between them.

"Margaret? Can you promise me you'll stay? Promise me you'll try to let Hawaii help you?"

No, she thinks. *I don't want this life.* "Yes."

"I love you, Mags."

"I love you too, AJ. Thanks for talking with me."

"What are big brothers for?" he smiles through the phone. Margaret feels new tears welling in her eyes, as she reflects on fierce protection and immense love her brother has showered over her throughout her life.

"I don't think most big brothers do as much as you do, AJ." She hears AJ clear his throat, and the ice in her chest is momentarily warmed. "Okay, I'll let you go now. Talk to you later."

"Bye, Mags."

The silence in the room is deafening when she hangs up on her brother. She focuses on the sound of her pulse throbbing in her head, the stress and anxiety of the last several hours make her feel exhausted. She suddenly realizes she hasn't eaten all day. She glances over at the mirror, then says out loud to the empty room, "Well I'm not going anywhere looking like this today." Margaret notices a room service menu next to the TV, and she walks over to pick it up. Scanning down the menu she opts to skip the Hawaiian cuisine today and go with some much needed comfort food. She picks up the room phone, and orders herself a cheeseburger, fries, and a chocolate malt.

After eating some comforting, greasy carbs, Margaret spends the rest of her day drifting between losing herself in her books and floating in and out of fitful sleep.

At some point, Margaret wakes to discover the once vibrant sky has shifted to a canvas as black as the darkness clawing at her heart. Beyond the patio door, the night sky is splattered with stars, as if God became bored and decided to decorate with glitter. The milky reflection of the moon shivers on the rippling surface of the ocean. She glances at the clock on her bedside table and sees it's almost ten o'clock. She stares at the ceiling, contemplating her latest dream. In the dream, she and Austin had been cuddled up together in bed, talking about everything under the sun, just skin and sheets and giggles all tangled together. It's one of the things Margaret loved the most - random, late night pillow talk. They would talk about it all - the big things, the little things, and all the things in between.

The dreams are worse than the night terrors that leave her drenched in a cold sweat. The nightmares are always the same. Margaret knows what to expect, knows exactly how the visions will tear her heart apart. The nightmares are blunt, direct, bold, and predictable. But the dreams? The dreams are never the same. They each weave a delicate, beautiful story. A lie. The nightmares break her heart retelling the painful story of what happened. But the dreams carve a hole, painting a gut-wrenching picture of what will never again be.

Margaret forces Austin out of her mind and herself out of bed before another emotional breakdown consumes her. She grabs a sweatshirt, throws it over her head, and walks out to the patio. The cool, night air is a welcoming touch on her hot, sticky skin. She closes her eyes, letting the sound of the waves on the shore soothe her with their comforting rhythm. Her eyes snap open as she decides she's going to go for a walk on the beach.

As she passes the mirror, she catches a glimpse of her reflection. "Yikes," she assesses. Her puffy, red eyes seem to consume her face. "At least it's dark out," she concludes. She slips her phone into the pocket of her shorts, her room key into the other, and leaves her books behind.

The sand is cool to the touch, now that the moon has replaced the sun in the sky. The air is still heavy with humidity, but the soft breeze coming off the ocean makes Margaret grateful she pulled on a sweatshirt before leaving her room. As she descends closer to where the sand meets the sea, she notices a small fire on the beach, a few yards to her right. A small group of people are gathered around it, their laughter rising into the air with the fire's ashes. Margaret feels a ping of sadness as she thinks about the fires back home with her family and friends.

The sand becomes firmer and cooler as Margaret advances closer to the beckoning waves. Reaching the water's edge, she wraps her arms around herself and digs her toes into the sand, letting the ocean kiss her feet. Her gaze floats out to the vast ocean before her, and she tries to focus on the way the moon dances across the water with each passing wave. But no matter how hard she tries, her mind continues to wander back to Minnesota, where her heart is. It's not here in the palm trees and white sand. It's trapped thousands of miles away, with all the things she loves and misses most. In the safety of darkness, she gives in to the yearning of her heart and lets her mind focus on her family. She imagines Austin wrapping his arms around her from behind, vacation stubble scratching her cheek as he buries his face in the crook of her neck. She pictures the kids running along the water's edge, kicking up the salty sea as they go, and stopping every few feet to pick up a shell to add to their collection. Her chest constricts tightly around her heart, the grief becoming a physical ache she can feel deep in her bones.

Margaret drops down in the damp sand, letting the waves gently roll over her legs. A feeling of complete and utter emptiness washes over her with each caressing wave. She feels nothing. Even her tears have stopped. Today has been exhausting. Margaret contemplates what would happen if she laid down to sleep right here and let herself be carried away with the high tide when it came.

She's jolted from her thoughts when she suddenly hears footsteps kicking up sand coming her way. Her body tenses, her muscles constricting in fear as she suddenly realizes how alone and vulnerable she is. *Oh, God. Please just keep walking. Please keep walking,* Margaret prays, as the heavy footsteps creep closer. A man plops beside her, kicking damp sand across her legs.

"I thought it was you, Margaret," Margaret senses his eyes on her, but refuses to look his way, afraid of what he might see in her face. She stays focused on the moon's simmering reflection. After a moment's pause, Will turns to watch the ocean as well, and together they spend the next few minutes in silent company.

The silence becomes too much for Margaret, and she speaks up, still keeping her eyes focused on the black expanse before her. "Were you with that group of people at the fire?"

"Yeah. We were trying to roast pineapple chunks over the fire. You know, more of a Hawaiian campfire instead of the usual s'mores?" He chuckles to himself and continues. "Turns out they are *not* too tasty over a fire. Pineapple that tastes like ash and smoke is not delicious. Not nearly the same as a pineapple grilled with some brown sugar and cinnamon." Margaret realizes she's carrying a small smile, and she silently thanks Will for bringing some light to her day, even if it is minimal. She notices him move to face her again and feels his assessing stare. "I didn't see you at all today. Were you out finally exploring this beautiful island on what was a beautiful day?" Will inquires.

Margaret chews her lip, debating how much to share with Will. "No," is all she says for now, as her fingers find the familiar sapphire ring and begin spinning it. Will doesn't push and instead turns his attention to the stars. Margaret steals a sideways glance at the man. His stubbled face is tilted toward the heavens as he gazes at the celestial view above. From the side, she notices the long lashes that blanket his eyes. As she assesses him, she gets the sudden urge to tell him everything, to just release the monstrous weight from the depths of her chest. The idea of spilling everything to a perfect stranger that she doesn't ever have to see again is sounding more and more appealing as she mulls it over in her mind.

Her heart begins to race, and her palms grow clammy and damp. Her breathing comes in ragged breaths. Will pulls his gaze from the blanket of stars and locks eyes with Margaret. Those sky-blue eyes rake over her face, assessing the pain she's sure he sees in her eyes. Margaret is overcome with vulnerability, and she desperately wants to fall apart to someone, anyone. There's something comforting about Will's presence that makes her decide to just let everything out.

"I wasn't out exploring the island or doing anything today because I locked myself in my bungalow all day. Because I couldn't stop falling apart today." Margaret's confession rolls out in one quick breath. Will's eyes radiate comfort and safety.

"Do you want to talk about it?" he asks.

"No."

"Would you like to just keep sitting here?"

"I don't know."

"Would you like me to leave?"

"No." It comes out faster than Margaret would expect, but she realizes it's true. She doesn't want Will to leave. His presence is comforting, and she realizes it's been a long time since she had someone besides her brother to comfort her. It's her own fault for pushing everyone away, and she thought she was doing fine with just her brother. But her days on the island and Will's presence tonight make her realize that maybe she isn't strong enough to be on her own. She looks back at Will, who has turned his attention to tracing lines in the sand with a broken shell. "Will?" He turns to her and drops the shell, giving her his undivided attention. Margaret hesitates, trying to find her courage, "Will you take a walk with me? I lied when I told you I didn't have a story. And I want to tell you my story." Will's soft, genuine smile affirms to Margaret she's making the right choice.

"I'd love to listen to your story," he responds. He stands up, reaches down to help Margaret to her feet, and together the two take a moment to brush the sand off their bodies. Will turns to Margaret with outstretched arms and offers, "Lead the way."

They walk side-by-side in silence, only the rhythmic crashing waves filling the air, the stars and the moon lighting their path along the sand. Margaret fidgets with her wedding ring, her heart palpitating aggressively in her chest. She can't seem to find her voice, and a million fragments of thoughts are swirling in her brain, making it impossible for her to figure out where to begin or what to say. Thankfully, Will doesn't seem to mind. He idles along, hands in the pockets of his shorts, eyes turned once more to the sky. He doesn't pressure her to talk, doesn't ask questions. He just waits patiently; and for that, Margaret is grateful. After a few minutes of strolling in the froth of the waves, she finds the words she's been searching for.

"I'm not married anymore," she begins. She notices Will glance at the sapphire ring on her finger, but he doesn't say anything. "I met my husband in college. We were married for nine years." She feels her voice start to crack, but she's determined to keep going, now that she's started. "I was a mom too. A mom to two beautiful kids, Jackson and Izzy. Jackson was five, Izzy was four." Margaret's heart starts to crack, and she stops walking. She feels the tidal wave inside of her gaining momentum. "I'm a widow," she whispers, the tears starting to fall. Will moves from her side to stand before her, holding her in his gaze. She forces her eyes to meet his. His brow is furrowed in concern, his stare piercing. "They call you a widow when your husband dies. But they don't have a name for a mother who loses her children," she whispers, and the torrential storm that's been swirling inside of Margaret all day is unleashed yet again. Her knees hit the cool, damp sand, her chest heaving in heavy sobs. Will slowly lowers himself beside her, as she trembles and shakes, her anguished cries piercing the empty night. Cautiously he places one arm around her trembling shoulders, and when she doesn't protest, he uses both arms to wrap her in a strong embrace. Margaret melts into him, taking comfort in the strong embrace. She sobs uncontrollably into his chest, letting all the pain, grief, and heartache from the last year flow through her tears. Eventually she is able to steady herself with deep, slow breaths. Her heart reclaims its regular beat, proclaiming its strength and survival through another battering storm. She inhales deeply and slowly unwraps herself from within Will's arms. She meets his eyes, and she's touched to see he looks genuinely concerned over her, a complete stranger.

"I'm sorry," she sniffles. "I'm so sorry. You don't even know me. You can go, I'm sorry."

"I won't go unless you want me to. Do you want me to leave?"

Margaret assesses him. Now that she's opened the dam to someone she barely knows, she feels the pull to tell him more.

"No. Can we keep talking?"

"Of course."

The two strangers make themselves comfortable on the beach, side-by-side, legs outstretched into the rolling waves, each pulse of the ocean blanketing them in a warm, frothy blanket. Margaret begins again, this time with a steadier, stronger voice.

"It was a year ago today. Today is the one-year anniversary," she fiddles with her wedding ring once again. "There was a storm, a tornado. The rain was coming down in sheets, you could hardly see a foot in front of you on the road. And the wind. The wind was howling and whipping. It all came out of nowhere. Austin, my husband," she stops, realizing she hasn't said his name out loud in months. "He was picking up the kids from daycare. I was going to meet them all at home. But," she pauses, wiping her still running nose on the sleeve of her sweatshirt. "But they didn't make it home." Margaret stops and takes a moment to steady herself. She looks over at Will, that same furrowed, concerned look on his face. His eyes are dark, intense, piercing into her. He doesn't say anything or pry with any questions. He just watches her, letting her guide the pace and depth of the story. "It was a semi. Which I guess was kind of good, because I was told it was quick. So...so the only comfort I have is knowing that they didn't suffer." Without giving it any thought, Margaret leans her head on Will's shoulder. She suddenly feels heavy and empty at the same time. Hollow, with no light inside of her, yet full of heavy, suffocating sadness.

"That's why I read so much. When I read, it's the only time I don't think of them. Because they're everywhere. Even after a year, no matter where I go or what I do, I can't escape them. I see them in everything, hear them in everything, want them to be with me in everything. And that's why I came to Hawaii. I thought maybe they wouldn't be able to reach me in Hawaii. Because Hawaii is so different from Minnesota. I knew the anniversary was going to be hard, and I thought there wouldn't be anything in Hawaii to remind me of them." Margaret becomes aware of her heavy tears making an ever-growing damp circle on Will's shoulder, but he doesn't move or say anything. He keeps listening, letting Margaret empty her broken soul to him.

"And today, with it being the anniversary, I don't know. It just, it hit me harder than it has in a long, long time. And I've been a hot mess all day. I thought coming out in the cover of night would be perfect," she lifts her head and smiles softly at him, while wiping her nose and cheeks. "Nobody would see me and my horrifically puffy, red eyes. I could come out here and listen to the waves and just…be, or cry, or think, or I don't know. But you ruined that." She gives him a very small elbow to the side. Will looks at her, a sad smile hanging on his face. He runs his hands through his hair.

"Man, Margaret, I don't even know what to say."

"You don't have to say anything. Listening was enough. I haven't talked about it in months. I saw a therapist shortly after it happened, but, I just felt like, 'What's the point?' The therapist wasn't going to bring my family back. So I stopped. I haven't really talked about it much since." Margaret draws circles in the sand as she speaks. The air is heavy as Will gazes out at the ocean, seeming to contemplate what Margaret has shared with him.

"How long are you on the island for?" he asks.

"I go home Saturday."

Will seems to take this fact and digest it a moment. "Can we exchange numbers? I am here until Sunday, and I just, I don't know, I want to make sure you have someone while you're here. If you need anything. If that's not too weird?"

Margaret rolls this idea around in her mind a moment. She hasn't given her number out to a man in over a decade. *It's not for romantic purposes*, she tells herself. *And it would be nice to not be* totally *alone, in case I do decide on some company.* "Yeah, sure. We can do that." Will smiles at Margaret as they dig out their phones and add each other into their contacts.

After exchanging numbers, the two new friends continue to keep each other company in the sand, gazing at the decorative sky, the rumbling waves filling the air between them.

"You don't have to stay here with me." Margaret's voice breaks the silence.

"I don't mind. I could sit and listen to the ocean all day. It's nice to do it with company."

Margaret assesses him as he smiles at the stars sprinkled across the sky, and a flicker of contentment lights up Margaret's heart for just a moment, as she thinks about how he is right: it is nice to sit with some company.

Margaret's not sure how much time has passed when Will breaks the silence. "So, what are your plans while you're here?"

"Reading. I came to Hawaii to read and get a tan while doing it."

"Wait, that's literally all you plan to do while you're here?"

"Well, and eat Hawaiian food," she smiles at him.

"You're kidding right? No luaus? No volcano hiking? No whale watching, snorkeling, surfing?" Will is looking at her in astonishment.

"No, I wasn't planning on it," Margaret shrugs.

Will just shakes his head in disbelief. "Well, that needs to change." He slaps his knees and pushes himself off the sand, reaching out a hand to Margaret. "You ready to call it a night? Or do you want to sit out here longer?"

"No, I'm wiped. Calling it a night sounds like a good idea." She takes his hand, and the two spend a moment dusting the sand off themselves before they start walking away from the ocean and towards the resort. They come up to the abandoned fire pit Will's family had occupied prior to their walk. The fire has been reduced to smoldering ashes, the log benches around it lay empty.

"Oh, I'm so sorry. I made you miss your fire with your family."

"Margaret, it is perfectly okay. I am glad I was able to be with you tonight. Thank you for telling me your story. I know that can't have been easy."

Will's smile is hanging soft and genuine on his face, making something deep within Margaret's chest pinch tight. She turns her attention to her toes, and goes back to spinning her ring. "Thanks for listening to a total stranger. And thanks for letting me destroy your shirt," she smiles in what she hopes is a warm smile, and Will chuckles.

"Goodnight, Margaret. I hope tomorrow is a better day for you."

"Thanks, Will. Goodnight."

The two part, Margaret to the north side of the resort where the private bungalows reside, Will to the south side where the high-rise hotel sits. As Margaret enters her room and looks around, she once again feels the familiar weight of grief and sadness descend on her shoulders. But as she sinks into the comfort and safety of her giant bed and opens her nearest book, she thinks that perhaps the weight of sadness she carries around all the time feels slightly lighter tonight.

Chapter Six

Monday, June 12 2017

It's hard for Margaret to stop hitting the snooze button. With students gone for the summer, she wants to begin her summer vacation. too. But she still needs to go into the school to clean up her classroom, finish posting grades, and there's the end of the year lunch that the PTO puts together for all the staff at the school. Margaret does love any excuse to eat good food.

She moans and rolls over to wrap her arms around Austin, but she's met with nothing but air and cool bedsheets. Pushing herself up on her elbow, she peers towards their master bathroom, and notices light beaming through the cracks of the doorway. Austin must be going into the office early today. She groans and falls back into her pillow. After a few moments, her better half walks out of the bathroom, a towel around his waist, and heads toward the closet. Margaret drinks him in from her perch on the bed, reminiscing on their college life when they could lay wrapped beneath the sheets as late as they wanted.

As Austin begins buttoning a shirt, he notices Margaret staring at him and grins coyly at her not-so-subtle interest. "So looks like you're going in early today?" she asks him.

"Yeah, I want to dip out early today so Jackson and I can play catch before his practice tonight," Austin explains, planting a kiss on Margaret's cheek. She smiles at him a moment longer, then reluctantly rolls out of bed herself to start her own morning routine. As she's brushing her teeth, the tell-tale sound of the bedroom door creaking open and the pitter-patter of tiptoes running across the carpet alert her that Izzy has crossed the threshold. Margaret peeks out the bathroom door as Austin picks her up and moves to sit with her on the edge of the bed. He kisses her forehead and rubs her back, as she nuzzles into his chest, and Margaret quickly grabs her phone to snatch a candid picture.

"I'll grab her some breakfast before I leave. You can keep doing your thing," Austin explains, as he carries Izzy with him down to the kitchen. Margaret finishes doing her hair and makeup, then shimmies into jeans and a t-shirt. She walks into the kitchen just as Austin is kissing the top of each child's head. They hardly react to his touch, their eyes glued to their favorite morning cartoon as they scarf down some cereal.

"Jackson, when did you wake up?" Margaret asks.

"He came out just as I was pouring milk into Izzy's bowl," Austin responds on behalf of Jackson. "I made a pot of coffee, there's still some left in it for you," he explains, as he gives Margaret a quick peck on the lips. "Love you, babe. See you later." He grabs his thermos of coffee off the counter, his keys from the key holder on the wall, and heads toward the garage.

"Love you too," Margaret shouts his way, as she heads for her favorite spot in the kitchen - the coffee pot.

Margaret is not quite sure how it happens almost every time she's in charge of drop off, but per usual, she and the kids are scrambling to get out of the house on time. They make the ten-minute drive to the daycare center, and Margaret helps the children out of their seats. Once their little feet hit the floor, they take off running to the doors of their favorite place. It's always reassuring for Margaret that the kids love their daycare so much. It makes drop offs so much easier on her heart.

She meets the kids at the front door, takes out her parental key card, and swipes to unlock the doors. As the alarm system clicks to alert it has been unlocked, Margaret takes each child by the hand, and together they walk into the building. Because Izzy and Jackson are so close in age, they are in the same classroom at the daycare—the pre-K room. They all walk to the room together, and Margaret meets their teacher in the doorway.

"Good morning, Jackson. Good morning, Izzy. How are you guys all doing today?" Miss Sally, the lead teacher of the room, asks the kids.

"Good," they reply simultaneously.

"Okay kiddos, mommy's gotta go. Give me my kisses and hugs!" She squats down to reach their level, and Jackson and Izzy wrap their arms around Margaret's neck. She inhales their scent, the familiar aroma squeezing her heart, and kisses the tops of their heads. Sally ushers the kids into the room and smiles a warm goodbye to Margaret.

Margaret is eager to get back on her way and into work, so she doesn't linger, knowing her children are in good hands. She arrives at the middle school just as she's finished off her second cup of coffee for the day. She leaves her thermos in the car, making sure to grab her water bottle instead. As she walks through the door of her classroom, she pauses to assess the view. A warm feeling spreads through her body as she contemplates how wondrous it is that the learning her students do extends far beyond these four walls. But just as quickly as the joy of learning enters her veins, it's soon replaced with a cool longing for time to slow down; the end of the school year always leaves Margaret a little sad. While it's great her students are growing and moving forward, she has spent the last nine months spending day in and day out with them, and they each impact her in their own ways. After a moment's pause contemplating life's many trajectories, Margaret sighs and sits down at her desk, ready to finish submitting grades so she can start her summer too.

Margaret is deeply focused on her computer screen when Carrie walks into her room, and she jumps at the sound of her friend's voice.

"Hey girl!"

"Hey. What's up?"

"I just needed a break. My eyes are spinning from looking at my screen all morning. Lunch is soon, so figured I'd start my lunch break a little early and check in on my favorite person," Carrie smiles, as she takes a seat at the desk closest to Margaret's computer. "Did you hear Rachel isn't coming back next year?"

"No, do you know why?"

"Apparently she's going to teach at The Prestige Academy. I don't know, I don't think you could pay me enough to work there. Those rich kids? And their parents? No thanks." Margaret smiles listening to Carrie. Her friend always has gossip to share. She zones out a bit as Carrie continues to talk about The Prestige Academy and the horror stories she's heard about the place. Margaret is focused on getting as much done as she can while she's here. She wants to get summer started as quickly as possible.

"Anyway, that's why Rachel will fit in perfectly over there. Are you almost done? I want to start walking down to lunch," Carrie concludes.

"Yeah, okay. We can head down." The two women walk together towards the main entrance. Every year the PTO puts on a wonderful end of the year picnic out on the main lawn for all the teachers and staff at the school. Lunch is usually catered in from a local restaurant, and Margaret is excited to see where their lunch is coming from this year. *It's the simple pleasures in life*, she thinks to herself, as she makes guesses at what she'll find on the tables.

As the women come up to the front doors of the school, their principal is standing in the doorway. "Hi, Margaret. Hi, Carrie. Thanks for taking a break to come grab some food. We're actually moving it into the cafeteria this year. The weather is looking ominous, and we didn't want to get caught in a storm." Margaret leans around the principal's shoulder to take a peek outside, and sees heavy, black clouds making their way towards the school. Carrie pulls on Margaret's arm, focusing her attention back to the lunch ahead.

"Sounds good, thanks," Carrie says on behalf of both of the women, as she leads Margaret away from the doors and into the cafeteria. They make their way towards a long table laid out with an array of food choices and take their place in line.

Margaret peers out the window on the wall across the room and notices the wind picking up. The trees are starting to strain their roots, and the sky is shifting from onyx to emerald. She feels her stomach start to squirm.

"Hey, are you okay?" Carrie asks, noticing Margaret's distraction.

"I didn't know it was supposed to storm today, and Jackson hates storms. He gets really scared and nervous. If I give him a heads up, he usually does better. But we were rushing this morning and I didn't watch the news and didn't know it was going to storm. I'm sure he's panicking right now, and I just hate that."

"Oh, man, I'm sorry, Margaret. He'll be okay. He does have Izzy in class with him, doesn't he? Hopefully that will help his nerves and give him some comfort."

"Yeah, hopefully," Margaret concedes, as she grabs a plate, and starts scoping out the choices before her. Looks like this year the PTO brought in one of Margaret's favorite cafes, The Buttered Crumpet. There's an array of sandwiches, salads, soups, and desserts. The two friends fill their plates, then take a seat among their peers. Margaret falls into the easy chatter about school and summer plans, and soon forgets to worry about Jackson and the impending storm.

After lunch, Margaret is back in her room, but her focus has changed. She has finished inputting the remaining grades for the year and is now cleaning around her room. Beakers need to be washed and boxed away. Bunsen burners need to be locked in the cupboards. Textbooks need to be stacked on the book carts and wheeled to the library storage room. As she's giving her chalkboards a wash, the sound of hard, heavy rain pellets hammering the window begins to fill her room. Margaret turns around to peer through the rain-streaked glass, assessing the weather.

The pine trees that line the road are threatening to snap from the howling wind that carries sheets of torrential rain on its back. The sky swirls in an eerily green glow, as sticks, leaves, and other debris fly past the window. Margaret looks at the clock and her heart aches for Jackson as she pictures her son trembling in fear of the storm. It's three-thirty. She could technically leave now, pick the kids up early, and get them home where they feel safe. But as she's contemplating putting those plans in action, the tornado sirens begin to sound their sinister wail. The only place Margaret is going now is the gymnasium.

She pulls her phone out of her pocket as she makes her way to the gym, and after glancing at the screen, she stops dead in her tracks. Carrie, also headed to the gym for safety, finds Margaret standing in the hallway, and stops at her side.

"What's up? Why'd you stop? Let's get going. Gym. Tornado. Come on, sister," Carrie urges, pulling Margaret's arm to get her to join the wave of staff all making their way to the gym.

But Margaret doesn't budge. She looks up at Carrie, panic in her eyes. "I missed a call from Austin while I was cleaning my room. He sent me a text when I didn't pick up." Margaret shows the phone to Carrie. Carrie's eyes shift to concern as she reads the screen: ***Leaving now to grab the kids. Glad I went in early so I could get Jackson before the storm, just no baseball tonight I guess. See you at home.***

"Okay," Carrie starts, continuing to pull Margaret's arm. "Let's get to the gym and digest this in there." Carrie successfully gets Margaret to the gym, where they huddle together over the phone. There's a dull hum of chatter from all the staff, and the lights flicker slightly. "Okay, what time did he send that?" Carrie asks.

Margaret reviews the screen. "Thirty minutes ago."

"Okay, so maybe he's home already?"

"Yeah, maybe," Margaret agrees, her stomach tying in vicious, sickening knots. "I'm going to call him," Margaret decides.

"No, don't call. If he *is* driving in this, you don't want him on his phone. Just wait. Wait until it dies down."

"Yeah. Yeah, you're right," Margaret agrees, and she puts her phone in her lap. Her fingers dance and tap across the back of her phone. She tries to ignore her heart pounding in her chest. Carrie reaches over and firmly grasps her friend's hand. With her other hand, she plugs an ear bud into Margaret's ear and one into her own ear. She starts playing one of Margaret's favorite songs, "Living" by Dierks Bentley, and Margaret's heart slows down a little bit. She rests her head on her friend's shoulder as she listens, and she sends up a little prayer of thanks for great friends.

The sirens dissipate and the wind fades. Eventually there is nothing left of the storm but the soft drizzle of lingering rain. Margaret hasn't moved her head from her friend's shoulder, and Carrie has kept the music rolling throughout the ordeal. Margaret's nerves haven't disappeared, but the comfort of her best friend and the music have at least helped her manage them. The rest of the staff in the gym begin to stand, and Margaret and Carrie follow suit.

"I'm calling it a day. I'm going home," Margaret announces.

"Good idea. Give the kids a hug for me."

Margaret smiles at Carrie, and the two friends part ways for the day. Once back in her classroom, she quickly rounds up her belongings and heads out to her car. The air is still humid and heavy from the afternoon storm, and Margaret can almost taste the rain lingering in the air. The parking lot is littered with branches and sticks. A young tree on the far side of the lot has been uprooted, and large pieces of hail are strewn haphazardly about that have yet to melt. As she's walking across the parking lot, she pulls out her phone to give Austin a call, but it goes straight to voicemail, making Margaret's stomach churn.

"Don't panic. Don't panic. Don't panic," she chants out loud to herself. She's a notorious worrywart, and Austin is always giving her grief for her mind jumping to the worst conclusions. If he's ever just a few minutes late coming home from work, Margaret always jumps to the conclusion that it must be because he's been in an accident. If she gets a headache, the first thing she assumes is it's caused from a tumor. If the kids get hurt playing, she is quick to do a swift exam for any broken bones. Margaret hates that about herself. She never used to be so quick to assume the worst, but then she got married. She was surprised at how deeply she could love someone, and that scared her. And once Margaret became a mother, she quickly discovered her heart now lived outside of her body, and she discovered what it means to love fiercely. The fierce, deep love she has for her family scares her more than anything else.

Margaret speeds home, ignoring the speed limits. Her heart is pounding in her chest, and she keeps glancing at her phone sitting in its holder on the dash, praying for a text to pop up from Austin, or even better, a phone call. But the screen stays ominously dark the entire drive home. As she comes down their street, she notices more branches and debris all over. There's a lawn chair stuck up in a tree, a garbage can tipped sideways in the middle of the road, and several smaller trees along the street are uprooted. Margaret hits the button on her garage door opener as she pulls the van into the driveway, and immediately feels a wave of nausea wash over her—the garage is empty.

She parks in her usual side of the garage and turns off the ignition. She sits in the car for a moment, just focusing on her breathing, trying to relax. There could be any number of reasons why they aren't home yet. Maybe Austin stayed at the daycare during the storm to wait it out and they didn't leave as soon as it was over. Or maybe when it started to get bad, they pulled off into a gas station, or a Target, and are still there, or on their way back home now. Or maybe he never ended up leaving. Maybe it hit his office as he was wrapping stuff up, so he ended up waiting it out at his office before going to get the kids.

Yeah, okay, there are lots of reasons why they wouldn't be home yet, she tells herself, as she heads into her home.

Margaret tries to make herself busy in an attempt to keep her mind from running through all the dark scenarios it conjures up. She tidies up the kitchen, which was left a mess after the hectic morning. Then she takes the chicken breasts out of the fridge and starts to prep them for dinner. Her mind is still racing, so she fills the house with music, blasting her smart system as loud as it goes, and tries to lose herself in Darius Rucker's voice. Margaret finishes dicing the chicken and has sliced some peppers and onions for the fajitas she plans on making. When she's finished, she looks at the clock: she's been home for over an hour, and the house is just as empty now as it was then. Austin and the kids still aren't home, and Austin has not called or sent any text since he last mentioned his plans for pickup. She turns off the music, the only sound now is that of her own heart, beating vigorously against her chest.

Margaret wipes her hands on her apron, unlocks her phone, and calls Austin again. Again, it goes straight to voicemail. She feels her panic rising, as her stomach twists and turns, and she fights to keep both nausea and tears at bay. She debates calling daycare, but with it being prime pickup time for all the kids, she knows the odds of anyone answering the phone right now is slim to none. With trembling hands she calls Carrie, who picks up on the first ring.

"They still aren't home, and I haven't heard from Austin since the text I got at school," Margaret's voice is shaking as she explains the current situation to her best friend.

"Okay, okay. It's okay. I'm sure there's a good explanation," Carrie begins.

"I'm going out. I'm going to drive to the daycare."

"Well did you call the daycare first? To see if they even got picked up?"

"No, there's no point. Nobody will answer the phone right now because pickup time is always so hectic."

"Okay, do you want me to come with you?"

"No, I'm okay. I'll call you later."

"Yes, you better! Okay, love you, Mags. Be safe."

Margaret's heart is stuck in her throat, so she hangs up without saying goodbye. And a moment later she is on the road, heading to her children's daycare.

The drive to the daycare is littered with broken tree limbs and debris. Margaret's heart is beating so forcefully against its cage, for a moment she wonders if hearts can get bruises. The sky still hasn't cleared up from the storm. Dark, heavy clouds refuse to release their grip on the city.

Margaret hasn't driven far when she sees the unmistakable red and blue flash of police cars up ahead, just where the road starts to curve. As she drives closer, she notices the southbound lane of the road is completely blocked off by cones and a squad car. Margaret's driving slows as she comes up to the curve, and notices large, black skid marks scarring the road from her side, the northbound lanes, across the median and up towards the southbound lanes around the corner.

As she takes her car around the curve, a horrific scene unfolds before her. A large freight truck is on its side, splintered wooden crates spewing out of its broken hull. Produce is smashed and splattered across the pavement. Pinned beneath the front-end of the freight truck, is another car. Except it looks nothing like a car. The vehicle is folded like an accordion on itself. Shards of glass and pieces of shredded metal pollute the road. The scene is swarming with police cars, ambulances, tow trucks, and a fire truck. Dozens of first responders are walking about the scene, talking into walkie-talkies, talking to each other. Margaret notices they are putting tools back into their trucks rather than taking them out.

Margaret's knuckles go white on the steering wheel. Her driving slows almost to a stop, and she's grateful the road she is driving is empty, so she can assess the scene. The vehicle under the freight truck is unidentifiable. It appears to have been ripped to pieces in order to rescue whoever was inside. She can't make out what kind of car it is, only that it is black - the same color as Austin's car. *But there are thousands of black cars on the road,* Margaret tries to assure herself as her heart tries to escape her chest.

But then she sees it. The bent license plate of the crushed car lies face up on the median: 861-XLR. Austin's license plate.

Margaret feels a wave of nausea rush over her. She immediately pulls over, throws her door open, and runs out across the median toward the wreckage. Two police officers spot her right away and come running to intercept her. One officer grabs her by the arm and pulls her into him to keep her from running through the hazardous debris that litters the pavement.

"Let go of me! I have to go in there! That's my husband's car! My husband, my kids! That's his car!" Margaret screams hysterically. She doesn't even recognize her own voice.

"Ma'am, you can't go in there," the officer's voice is as firm as his grip. "It's unsafe, and it's..." his voice trails off.

"Please," Margaret begs through heaving sobs. "Please. That's my husband's car. That's our car. That's the license plate over there. My family..." The rain has resumed its descent from above, and the drops mingle with the tears running down her face. "My kids. My husband." Her voice is a barely audible mumble, a whisper of dread escaping through her lips. She stops fighting against the officer's restraint. Margaret doesn't want to look at the wreckage before her, yet she can't tear her eyes away. The car doesn't even look like a car, it's a heap of tangled, ripped metal. She can't make out its doors, windows, anything. The tires are the only thing that help her understand it's a car she's looking at. There's a funny taste in her mouth, and she realizes it's iron. Blood. The smell of blood is in the air.

Margaret turns to look at the officer holding her. She sees it in his eyes: the answer to the question she's too afraid to ask.

"Where are my husband and kids?" she manages to whisper.

The officer holding Margaret looks straight into her eyes, concern written across his face. The second officer asks, "You sure this car belongs to your family?"

Without taking her eyes off the officer whose hands grip her arms in a vice, Margaret responds with a cracking voice, "Positive. The license plate on the median behind me reads 861-XLR. That's my husband's license plate." She pauses for a moment, gaining strength to ask the question a second time. "Where is my family?"

The cold rain picks up, chilling Margaret to the bone - a stark contrast to the burning fire pulsing through her veins with every anxious beat of her heart. She assesses the man holding her, her heart violently screaming to break out of her chest, her stomach churning. His weathered face softens, his golden eyes grow wet, and no words need to be spoken.

Margaret will look back on this moment later and recall how it felt as if her heart physically shattered at the realization before her. A sharp pain radiates from her chest, as she collapses in the stranger's arms with a gut-wrenching wail. Her agonizing cries send birds flying from the trees, and the rest of the first responders on the scene stop in their work to give pause to the woman in mourning.

The officer with Margaret pulls her close and tight, letting her fall into him. Her legs have become like jello, unable to hold her body upright, and the officer walks her over to the nearest squad car. He guides her onto the seat, and watches her carefully, as her sobs rake through her in trembling waves.

"My name is Officer Garrison. But you can call me Brian. I'm so very sorry." The officer is still holding her hand, his grip firm and strong, and he squats down to be at Margaret's eye level. She refuses to look at him, refuses to accept that which is standing right before her. She clutches at her chest, trying to catch her breath. Officer Garrison squeezes her hand.

"Is there somewhere I can take you?" he asks. *Home*, Margaret thinks to herself, her heart shattering in her chest, realizing home will never be the same again. Margaret looks up from the floor of the car and meets the somber eyes of Officer Garrison. She tries to find her voice, but words fail her. She can't think, she only feels.

Brian digs in the front pocket of uniform, and pulls out a small, damp notebook and a pen. He hands the items over to Margaret. "Can you write it down? Wherever you want me to take you? I don't want you driving right now." Margaret's shaking hands take the notebook from the officer, and in barely legible handwriting, she scribbles down the first address that comes into her mind.

They drive in near silence. The only words spoken during the twenty-minute commute come from the gruff voice of Officer Garrison at the wheel. "Don't worry about your vehicle. We'll bring it to this address when we've finished clearing the scene." Low rumbles of thunder in the distance mirror the growling rumble of pain rolling around in Margaret's chest. The squad car pulls into an asphalt driveway as black as her heart. Thick, fat raindrops roll down the window she is absentmindedly staring out. Brian puts the car in park and turns around to face Margaret. "I'm going to go up to the door on my own first. I'll be back to get you after talking to the homeowners."

Margaret doesn't respond, her glazed-over eyes focused on the blurred trees beyond the window. Everything is blurry, so blurry. She can't tell if that's from the rain on the window or from the silent tears welling in her eyes that refuse to stop their journey down her face. A blur of khaki makes its way from the squad car to the front door of the house. She leans her head against the cool glass of the window and allows her heavy eyelids to drop. A moment later, her eyes snap open with the jolt of the car door springing wide. AJ's face swims before her, his eyes reflecting the storm clouds still rolling lazily across the sky. The sight of her big, protective brother releases the tiny dam Margaret had built in her chest, and she falls into his arms, great heaving sobs racking her body once more as he leads her into the house.

Brian and AJ continue exchanging words, but Margaret can't make out any of what they are saying, it's just a mumble of sound her ears are too tired to try to decipher. Odette comes traipsing into the entryway to meet them at the door, a large, fluffy towel in her hands and tears swimming in her eyes. Her short, crisp sniffles echo off the walls, as she wraps Margaret in the towel, takes her out of AJ's arms, and leads her to the couch. She gently lowers Margaret down to sit, and immediately starts taking Margaret's soaking wet sneakers off her feet. Margaret is suddenly very aware of how wet and cold she is, the chill reaching down to her bones. As if reading her mind, Odette leaves her side momentarily, and returns with more towels. She starts by drying Margaret's feet, then moves to the stringy hair clinging to her face and neck. Margaret closes her eyes, absorbing the soft, caring touch of her sister-in-law. She tries to listen to AJ and Brian talking at the door but can only pick up bits and pieces.

"...seven fatalities during today's tornado..."

"...lost control in the flooded road..."

"...likely instantaneous..."

"...here's my number..."

The shrill whistle of a teapot beckons Odette into the kitchen. The thud of the front door tells Margaret the two men have finished their conversation. She sits in her bundle of warm towels, refusing to open her eyes and accept the reality before her. A cupboard bangs shut. A drawer rolls open, cutlery clinking inside as it slides. A small *thunk* as it closes. The ting of a spoon inside a ceramic mug. Deep, ragged breaths from AJ, seemingly still by the front door. Odette's bare feet moving swiftly and lightly across the hardwood floor of the kitchen. The couch sinks, as someone takes their place at her side. She inhales his familiar, comforting scent, and rests her damp head on AJ's shoulder, his body trembling beneath her. He finds her hand, squeezing it tightly. Together, brother and sister cry.

Odette's hands flutter about effortlessly as she removes Margaret's rain-soaked clothes clinging to her frigid skin. She inhales deeply, allowing the steam wafting about the room to relax her overworked lungs. Odette's slim fingers intertwine in Margaret's, and she firmly grasps Margaret's elbow with her other hand, guiding Margaret into the shower. "A nice, hot shower will do some good. How's that temperature?" Margaret moans her approval, unable to articulate any words. "Okay, I'm gonna go put these clothes in the wash and get you something fresh to wear. I keep my best wash over there - apricot mint. It's divine. Use that, get a nice, thick lather, alright sugar? The aroma will do wonders for you. I'll be back in a little bit."

Odette closes the shower curtain, and Margaret hears the bathroom close behind her. Margaret stares about the shower - there's a rack of AJ's shower supplies, and a rack of Odette's, similar to the setup in her own shower she shares with Austin.

Shared.

Reality slaps her in the face, rubbing salt in the gaping wound of her heart, and she slides to the floor of the shower, letting the hot water run over her empty shell of a body. She doesn't know how long she's been sitting on the shower floor, her tears mingling with the water running over her, when a pair of soft hands coaxes her off the floor. Odette's pink eyes are swimming with tears as she turns off the shower and helps Margaret into a towel. As she lets Odette lead her to the guest bedroom, she notices her tears have stopped. Maybe she wasn't actually crying in the shower; maybe it was only the shower wetting her face. *I have no tears left.*

Odette lowers Margaret's wrapped body onto the bed. A neatly folded pile of clothes waits for her at the end of the bed. *I can't move*, Margaret thinks, unable to decipher if her shaking body is just chills from the shower or the grief rolling in waves within her.

As if reading her mind, Odette begins to carefully dress Margaret. Odette's occasional sniffle is the only sound filling the room as the young woman gently cares for her grieving sister-in-law. When dressed, she wordlessly picks up the damp towel from the floor and leaves the room, without looking at Margaret.

Margaret releases a heavy, rattling sigh and closes her eyes, focusing again on the sounds around her.

A new voice is in the house. A woman's. Her mother's.

A sudden howl ricochets off the walls, and Margaret envisions AJ holding their mother's hand on the couch as she wails over the loss of her grandkids and son-in-law.

The guest room door opens and closes softly. Someone sits beside her, and suddenly Margaret feels the light touch of slender fingers on her scalp, and the gentle pressure of a brush running through her damp curls. She keeps her eyes closed, relishing in the calming, massaging sensation of Odette brushing her hair. Her heart suddenly swells with gratitude for her sister-in-law, and the care she has shown her since arriving on her doorstep however long ago. Heavy tears escape her closed lids, and roll down her cheeks as Odette works, her shoulders heaving in rolling sobs.

Odette finishes, and helps Margaret lie down in the bed, pulling the plush comforter around her. "You're gonna stay here, love, okay? Your mama's here, me and AJ too, if you need anything. You just let us know. Don't matter if it's the middle of the night. You let us know, ya hear?" Odette's pink and puffy eyes are swimming with compassion, locked fiercely and protective with Margaret's own.

"Odette..." Margaret stammers, locking eyes with her sister-in-law. Her own storm of emotions is mirrored in Odette's eyes, swimming with grief and tears. "Thank...I..."

"Sh-sh-sh. I know. Try to get some sleep now, okay? We're here when you need us. You're not alone." Odette squeezes her hand and rises from the bed, shutting the door behind her as she exits the room.

You're not alone, Margaret repeats to herself. *Then why do I feel so utterly alone?* She wraps the thick blankets tight around her and scans the room, catching sight of her phone sitting on the nightstand by the bed. Someone must have brought it in here while she was in the shower. Staring at Margaret from the screen are two text messages and a missed call from Carrie.

Everything okay?

You're killing me, Margaret. Let me know how everything is.

Margaret stares at the screen, her mind as empty as her hollowed out chest. "How is everything?" she whispers to the room. "Everything is...nothing. There is nothing anymore. My life is gone." Margaret's hands tremble on her phone, as she begins typing a response to her best friend.

They're gone. They were in an accident. The officer said it was instant. They're all - Margaret's fingers hover over her phone, as she realizes she hasn't said it out loud yet. She inhales deeply, tears sliding down her face, and finishes her text. - **dead.** She hits send, sending off her entire heart with it. She stares at the ceiling, her body shaking, but no tears make their escape. The floorboards of the hallway outside her room creak, as someone makes their way toward the door. Margaret quickly closes her eyes and tries her best to appear asleep. The door creaks open slowly, and Margaret's muscles stiffen as she prays to be left alone.

"Look, she's sleeping," AJ's soft voice explains. "Let her sleep. She's probably exhausted."

A loud sniffle and cough cut through the air.

"I can't do *nothing*, AJ. She's my daughter. Look at her..." Nancy's voice is coarse, rough, as it gets stuck in her throat. Margaret keeps her eyes closed, acutely aware of how little energy she has to keep this day and its memories alive any longer. She hears someone's feet cross the doorway, and a moment later her mother's hand softly caresses her cheek, wiping at invisible tears no longer rolling down her face. Nancy starts trembling, as sobs begin to roll through her body. AJ wordlessly guides Nancy out of the room, closing the door with a soft click behind them.

After waiting a moment to be sure the room is empty, Margaret lets her body relax. She can't remember ever seeing her mother cry, let alone have her completely fall apart. She wonders if she should have reached out to her mother, broken her facade and squeezed her hand. But it's too late and too complicated to dwell on it any further. Exhaustion overcomes her, everything in her body suddenly feels so heavy, especially her eyes. She lets her lids fall, drifting away from the horrors of reality.

Margaret wakes in a cold sweat, the sheets of the guest bed clinging to the now dampened pajamas Odette has lent her. She bolts upright in the bed, her chest heaving, hands shaking. She squeezes her eyes shut, trying to focus on calming her breathing. Splashes of her nightmare—her memories—flash before her: the offensive, stark flashing red and blue lights, the icy rain on her burning skin, the metal scraps scattered around the ground.

After gaining her composure, she pulls the sheets off her sticky body, and throws her legs over the edge of the bed. *I need some fresh air*, she thinks to herself. As her feet hit the lush carpet, she notices a pile of blankets or towels near her bed. She creeps closer and discovers her mother, sleeping at the foot of her grieving daughter's bed, and her heart jumps to her throat.

The window at the other end of the room beckons Margaret, and she raises the frame slowly, careful not to make too much noise at the risk of waking her mother. A waft of the cool, early summer midnight breeze washes over Margaret's face. She closes her eyes, relishing in the feel of the crisp air on her feverish skin. She looks back at her mother, and guilt creeps into her veins. Margaret and Nancy's relationship has always been strained. Nancy was never one for showing affection. At least to Margaret, anyway. She was always very open about her adoration and pride for AJ. Margaret always had to work hard to get her mother's approval, and even when she did, she always questioned if it was genuine.

But somehow, seeing her mother at the foot of her bed speaks volumes to Margaret.

Her mind flashes back to when Izzy had to get stitches. She had been jumping on her bed when she fell off, slicing her leg on the corner of her nightstand. Izzy's piercing wails sliced through Margaret's heart as she raced her to the ER. That was the day Margaret realized her heart was living outside of her own body; her child's pain was her own pain. Tears had streamed down Margaret's face as she sped down the highway, wishing she could do something, anything, to take her daughter's pain away.

And now, her own mother was here, lying at the foot of the bed, doing the same for Margaret.

She crawls back into the bed, pulls the blankets up to her chin, and silently cries herself back to sleep.

Chapter Seven

Wednesday, June 13, 2018

The day is cloudy when Margaret awakes. She stretches sleepily, hugs one of the many downy pillows within reach, and stares out onto the Hawaiian shore from beneath the comfort of her blankets. Soft gray clouds tumble across the sky, as if it is unsure if it wants to let the sun through or claim the day for rain instead. Her mind wanders to her walk last night with Will. A soft smile creeps on her face as she recalls how comforting his presence was. But the warmth and comfort fade as her memories of years ago battle for space with the memories of her new life. Her mind tries to replay her worst memories, and the suffocating feeling of aloneness threatens to take her over again today.

The aloneness is the worst. It's different than lonely. Margaret doesn't feel lonely, she knows she has people who love her dearly, who will answer any time their phone rings. But the aloneness? It's the feeling that nobody out there understands Margaret's pain. She's in it alone. Because how can anyone possibly understand the gut wrenching, heart breaking, soul crushing trauma she has endured? The aloneness is the most suffocating of any of her feelings, wrapping its gnarled claws around her chest, squeezing her heart in a vice she can never seem to truly escape. So she shut people out and replaced them with books. She reads morning, noon, and night. She always makes sure she has a book in her purse or a book downloaded on her phone. Because with a book, she is never alone. With a book, she can escape the world and all its unforgivable pain.

But last night had been different for Margaret. She wasn't sure what compelled her to spill her story and pain to Will. Maybe everything had been bottled up for so long, it was just ready to topple out to the next person who pried. Or maybe there was something about Will that made it easy for Margaret to talk to him. Or perhaps it was the scenery, the moon hanging above the ocean and its rhythmic waves. Whatever it was, Margaret was glad Will had reached out and glad that she had let him in on her story.

She wipes a single tear that has escaped her eye, throws the blanket off of her, then climbs out of the bed with determination. She walks her bare feet out onto the patio. The air is a little bit cooler today, the wind blowing strong off the ocean, carrying the salt with it. Margaret takes a moment to inhale the beachy smell deeply, letting it seep into her veins, relaxing her body.

She walks back into the bungalow and starts brewing a cup of coffee. As the coffee is brewing, she finds her phone and decides to text her brother.

I made a friend last night. Glad I stayed, thanks for pushing me. <3

Just as she hits send, a knock taps on the door of her bungalow. She sits on the bed for a moment, confused why anyone would be knocking on her door. She strides toward the door and peers out the peep hole. A resort employee is standing at the door, holding a basket of something Margaret can't quite make out. She steps back and opens the door.

"Aloha! Margaret Heller? You have a special delivery," the woman explains, holding out the basket for Margaret. Margaret is speechless, as she robotically takes the basket from the employee.

"Thank you," she manages to get out.

"You're welcome! Have a beautiful day!" The woman turns and leaves Margaret with her gift.

Margaret's eyes rake over the basket, which appears to be a collection of various Hawaiian goodies. A beautiful pineapple sits tall in the middle, surrounded by a variety of other treats. There are two cards within the basket. The first Margaret pulls out explains all of the foods in the bundle: the pineapple, ohia lehua honey, haw flakes, lychee jelly fruit bites, Sweet Li Hing Mui, coconut syrup, pineapple gummy bears, arare rice crackers, a can of Spam, and dried lemon rings. After reading the list of treats in her basket, Margaret reaches for the second card. She opens it to find a personalized messaged: "Hope you're finding the peace you need in Hawaii. Here are some treats to enjoy with your books! Loving and missing you from MN. XOXO Odette." Margaret's eyes mist over as she thinks fondly of her sister-in-law back home.

The past year has taught Margaret the ever important lesson of never judging a book by its cover. She had previously had so many reservations about Odette, simply because she never took the time to really get to know her. But this past year, Odette had been one of the biggest sources of strength for Margaret. She had come to treasure her sister-in-law and counted her as her dearest friend.

Margaret is pulled out of her reverie with the ping of the coffee pot - her morning cup of caffeine is ready. She walks with her steaming mug out to the patio, taking pleasure in the aroma of the rich, Hawaiian coffee mingling with the salt of the sea breeze. As she's sipping on the smooth beverage, its warmth coursing through her veins, she resolves that she's still going to read on the beach, even if it appears rain might be lingering at the seams of the day. She empties the mug, enjoying every last drop of the unique local flavor, and makes her way back inside to get ready for the day.

Margaret has opted for a light sweater over her tank top and her favorite pair of ripped jean shorts. After towel-drying her long, brown locks, she decides to let the beach breeze finish the process. She loads a couple of books into her bag along with some snacks and her sunglasses, grabs her phone and room key, and heads out to get comfy on the beach.

As she's strolling down the path towards the ocean, she smells breakfast wafting her way from the food lounge to her left. She decides breakfast on the beach sounds like a lovely idea and makes a detour to collect some food to bring with her down to the waves. There are several restaurants in this corner of the resort that are serving breakfast. She decides to go to a little hut that appears to have a to-go window for service.

The hut is similar to the Huli Huli Hut Margaret ordered from on her first night in the resort. But instead of being decorated with giant Hawaiian flowers and ivy, this hut has carvings all over its wooden walls. Dolphins, sea turtles, flowers, pineapples are all etched into the weathered siding. Margaret takes a moment to take in all the carvings, lightly running her fingers across the grooves. They appear to be carved by various people. Some of the art is extremely delicate and intricate, others almost childish and playful. The artwork reminds Margaret of her children, but instead of it saddening her, she smiles, allowing a particular memory of Jackson's first drawing of a fish flood her heart and mind with a brightness the skies are lacking this morning. She smiles softly, longing to be given a piece of art from him again. Her hand falls limp to her side. She inhales deeply, shakes the thought out of her mind, and walks up to the menu hanging by the hut's window.

"Aloha! Howzit this beautiful morning?" the man at the window asks Margaret.

"It would be beautiful if the sun was shining."

"Ah, every day is beautiful when you're in Hawaii." The man winks at her, his mouth offering a wide, bright smile.

"I suppose it's hard to not have a beautiful day in paradise." Margaret smiles. "What's in the acai bowl?"

"Ah, the acai howl is a Hawaiian favorite. We blend acai berries with pineapple, bananas, and strawberries. Think of it like a thick smoothie, ya know? Almost like yogurt, but a different texture. Then I put fresh fruit and granola on top. Very yummy. Wonderfully fresh and fruity!"

"Oh that does sound lovely. I will have one of those please. And a bottle of water," Margaret orders.

"Coming right up!"

Margaret leans her back against the hut and closes her eyes, focusing on the feel of the wind on her face. After only a moment, her order is ready.

"Here you are! Enjoy. Aloha!"

"Mahalo," Margaret smiles, as she turns and heads toward the ocean.

"*'A' ole palikir*!" the man shouts in return as Margaret descends back down the path. She's not sure what it means, but she decides she likes the way it sounds. Margaret takes a spoonful of her breakfast as she wanders down the path, and closes her eyes at the deliciously sweet, smooth experience. She pauses to slip her sandals off her feet, stuffing them inside her tote.

Walking barefoot in this silky sand is one of her favorite experiences so far. As she's walking, she scans the horizon, looking for an open lounge chair beneath an umbrella to claim as her own. Her eyes catch Will playing beach volleyball with a group of adults. She lets her gaze linger for a moment, watching him play. His body is lean and slightly muscular in a natural way. His back is to her, and she watches the muscles in his shoulders flex as he reacts to each movement of the ball. After a moment, the volleyball flies over Will's head, landing with a thud in the sand, and he quickly turns to retrieve it. His eyes connect with Margaret's, and immediately a huge, beaming grin grows on his face. She smiles broadly in return, surprising herself at how easily it comes.

After a quick wave, she continues walking, spotting a chair down closer towards the waves. Margaret gets settled on the lounger, takes out a book, and begins reading as she dives into her acai bowl. It's not long before her phone pings. She digs into her bag for the device, expecting to see a response from AJ regarding her text from earlier this morning. Instead, she sees Will's name lighting up the screen. She stares at the phone, trying to understand why her heart is suddenly racing.

Hey stranger. Put the book down and come play some volleyball with us. ;)

The thought of playing volleyball with a bunch of strangers gives Margaret minor anxiety. ***I'm going to pass and enjoy my book. Thanks though.*** Margaret hits send and goes back to her book. A moment later her phone pings again. She expects some reply from Will, but this time does see her brother's name when she looks at the screen. She smiles and opens the text.

That's awesome, Mags. Make the most of it. I hope you'll have some great stories for me when you get home.

Margaret chews on his words, second guessing her response to Will. Maybe she should join them; AJ would want her to. She looks over her shoulder to peer back at their game. They're all laughing together, seemingly on a break between games. *Nope. Not going over there.* She turns and gets ready to dive back into her book just as a resort employee walks over and asks her for a beverage order. She orders herself a Mai Tai. *Sun and books,* Margaret reminds herself. *That's what I came here for. Not volleyball with strangers.* And with that thought, she stretches out comfortably on her beach chair, the sun's honey rays kissing her skin, and opens her book once again, ready to lose herself in the pages.

Margaret reaches the end of her book and runs her fingers gently over the curling pages; the island humidity has affected more than just her hair. She closes the cover and lets out a satisfied sigh as she gazes across the ocean. She really enjoyed that particular book. While reading it, she traveled to Europe and built cathedrals through the eyes of a medieval cathedral architect. It was enlightening and a great escape from reality. As she absentmindedly watches the waves rolling on the shore and thinks about the finished book, she catches the flash of a dolphin breaching the waves. She perks up, scanning the horizon for more movement. After a moment, another dolphin breaks the water. Margaret feels giddy with excitement. Dolphins are one of her favorite animals. She pushes herself up from the chair and runs toward the water, stopping when the waves hit her knees. She continues staring out across the blue expanse, willing the dolphins to keep dancing for her. She's not disappointed. The dolphins start jumping with more frequency. There appears to be a pod of them racing parallel with the beach, cutting seamlessly across the waves. The sun breaks through the stubborn clouds, its rays flashing on the backs of the graceful sea creatures. The pod begins to fade into the distance, and as Margaret watches them disappear, she hears steps splashing into the water behind her. She tries her best to ignore the sudden visitor at her side, soaking up the last dance from a dolphin as it disappears from her view.

"Well that was something, wasn't it?" Will asks, breaking the reverie Margaret was basking in. The afternoon sun is quickly becoming blinding on the ocean as the clouds continue to dissipate from the Hawaiian sky. Margaret turns with her hand above her brow, shielding her eyes, and faces Will. His face and shoulders are tinged pink from sun, and patches of fine sand cling to his glistening skin.

"Forgot the sunscreen today?" Margaret asks.

"Ah, am I pink?" he asks, holding out his arms to look at them.

"Just your face and shoulders,"

"Must have sweat it off," Will grins in resignation, not seeming to give too much thought to the pain he'll be in later. "What are you up to?" Margaret gestures towards her lounge chair with her books and tote bag, an empty Mai Tai glass propped up in the sand next to the seat.

"Just finished my latest book."

"Perfect timing then! You can join me for a hike," Will states excitedly.

"Oh, thanks, but no. I'm about to order another drink and start another book."

"Margaret. This trip probably cost you a nice chunk of money. Don't waste it. We're about to go hike a volcano. When is the next chance you're going to get to hike a volcano if you don't do it now?" Margaret just stares, unable to come up with a good retort. "Come on, come with us."

"I don't know anyone in your family. And it feels weird intruding on your family hiking adventure. I'll stick to my books. You enjoy your vacation with your family."

"Okay, if my family makes you uncomfortable, then we'll do our own hike. There's plenty of trails and excursions to choose from," Will presses. Margaret chews on the inside of her cheek as she considers the offer.

I mean, he's right. When am I ever going to get to climb a volcano again? She thinks to herself, AJ's last text flashing briefly before her eyes. "I don't have any hiking gear. All I packed are flip flops."

"There are shops here on the resort that I know have tennis shoes for sale. Other than good footwear, you don't really need anything else."

Running out of excuses, Margaret concedes. "Fine. But I need some time to go back to my room and get ready."

"Sounds good. I need to shower off all this salt and sand anyway. There's a shuttle bus leaving in an hour we plan on hopping on. It will take us to the base of the volcano. There's a shop there where you can get your shoes. Then from the drop-off point there are about half a dozen different trails we can choose from to hike. Sound good?"

"Yeah, sounds good."

"Great. I'll meet you at the shuttle station in an hour - don't be late!" And with that, Will begins jogging back up towards the resort. Margaret gets a funny feeling in her stomach that she can't quite place. Nerves? Excitement? Perhaps a bit of both? Whatever it is, she tries to ignore it as she packs up her belongings from her chair, and heads back to her room, suddenly acutely conscious of the sparse choice of clothes she packed to choose from.

Since Margaret feels she has plenty of time before needing to meet Will, she decides to check out one of the several retail stores on the resort for footwear there. Her efforts are successful, and she purchases a pair of tennis shoes and some socks, as well as a bag of tropical trail mix. After checking out at the sales counter, she starts meandering towards her bungalow. As the unnamed emotions continue to squirm inside her, she decides to call her brother on her walk back to her room. He answers on the second ring.

"Mags! Hey sis. How's today going?"

Just hearing his voice calms Margaret, and a large smile blankets her face. "Hey AJ. It's going alright. I spent the first half of my day on the beach reading. And just as I finished a book and looked up, a pod of dolphins swam and jumped across the horizon. It was beautiful."

"That sounds awesome. I bet you were happy you were able to catch it. So what's the second half of your day looking like?"

Margaret pauses, the mysterious feelings swimming inside her. "I think I'm going hiking."

"You think?"

"I mean, I am. I am going hiking with a friend."

"A friend? The one you said you made last night?"

"Yeah."

"That's great, Mags. I'm glad to hear you're going to be doing something besides reading, you book nerd," AJ teases playfully.

"Yeah, me too." Margaret finds herself smiling again.

"Where are you hiking?"

"He didn't say exactly. Some volcano. We'll be taking a shuttle to wherever it is and going from there."

"Wait. Your friend is a 'he'?" AJ's tone has completely changed.

"Yeah."

"So you're going hiking on a volcano halfway across the world with a total stranger? I don't like that, Mags. I don't like that at all."

Margaret becomes defensive. "He's not a total stranger. We've talked a handful of times since I've been here. I first met him at the airport when we landed, but last night, I went to the beach to try to calm down and find some peace, and he found me. We took a walk and I just told him everything that's happened. He's nice. His name is Will. I actually think you'd really like him."

AJ seems to ignore all the positive things Margaret just explained to him. "So not only is he a total stranger, but he also knows how broken and vulnerable you are? And you're going to be alone in some volcanic jungle with the guy?"

"AJ stop it, you're making me angry. Will's not like that. You've never met him, and you have no idea what you're talking about. And it's just a hike. It's not a big deal. And *you're* the one who told me to make the most of my trip."

"Yeah, I didn't mean go meandering off into a volcanic tropical jungle with strange men," AJ huffs. Tension hangs in the air between them, as neither speaks. "I love you, Mags. I just worry about you."

"I know," Margaret whispers. "Look, it will be fine. Will's family is going too." Margaret leaves out the fact that they'll be on a different trail.

"Okay, well why didn't you say that in the beginning? Just, just be safe, okay? And shoot me a text when you're back at the resort, so I know you're back safe and sound?"

"Yes, I will. Promise."

"Okay. Well in that case, have fun, Mags."

"Thanks," Margaret smiles into the phone, excitement starting to flutter deep within her belly. "Love you, AJ. You're the best big brother a girl could ask for."

"Yeah, sure, whatever," Margaret can hear his smirk through the phone. "Love you, Margaret." And with that, AJ hangs up. Margaret puts the phone back in her bag and picks up her speed as she continues the trek back to her room, a slight bounce in every step.

Margaret arrives at the resort shuttle terminal about fifteen minutes early. She makes herself comfortable on one of the several wooden benches and pulls out a book from her backpack.

"Leave it to Margaret to pack a book for a volcanic hike," Will's voice flows over her shoulder. Margaret closes her book and turns to look at him. He's wearing a navy-blue athletic shirt that hugs his body just enough for her to make out his muscles hiding beneath it. His khaki shorts have about half a dozen pockets, and she wonders if they are filled with anything, or just for show.

"I don't go anywhere without a book," Margaret retorts. Will smiles at her, as a small group of fellow hikers descend upon them, gathering behind him.

"Margaret, this is my family. Well, some of them," everyone is beaming at Margaret. "This is my mom and dad, Jack and Mary," Will begins introductions, gesturing to his parents. "That's my brother Kyle, my future brother-in-law Chris," Will grabs a petite blond woman next to him and gives her a tight squeeze. "And this pipsqueak is my little sister, Kara. The one getting hitched in a couple of days." Kara laughs and pushes Will away.

"Hi," Kara holds her hand out to Margaret. "Nice to meet you." Margaret smiles as she shakes Kara's hand. The woman is positively glowing, and she fondly recalls the giddy feelings leading up to her own wedding day years ago. "Hopefully Will has been being nice to you. I hear he's been stalking you the last couple of days." She throws her big brother a playful smirk.

Margaret smiles between the two, reminded of her and AJ. "He's been stalking...but he's not so bad." She flashes back to their late-night beach walk last night, and a twinge of those un-namable emotions stir in her belly. Will just grins at Margaret, his arm loped around his dad's shoulders. Suddenly, looking at the small crowd around her, Margaret feels very self-conscious, as if she's intruding on a family affair. As if able to sense her discomfort, Will's mother speaks up, breaking the ice as they wait for the shuttle.

"So Margaret, Will was telling me you're a voracious reader. I'm a bit of a bookworm myself. What do you enjoy reading the most?"

"Well I just finished <u>Pillars of the Earth</u> by Ken Follett, and it was absolutely breathtaking. So well written and incredibly immersive. His research and attention to detail was amazing. I will read just about anything I can get my hands on, but I probably gravitate to historical fiction and fantasy the most." It doesn't go unnoticed on Margaret how easy and comforting it is to talk about books. She feels herself relaxing.

"Ah, I love historical fiction too. I recently read <u>Salt to the Sea</u> by Ruta Sepety, and it was incredibly well-written," Mary replies. The two smile at each other, and Margaret can feel her nerves slowly dissipating.

"Here comes the shuttle!" shouts Kyle. The bus pulls up to the transit station, and the group loads into the seats along with some additional tourists. Margaret walks to the back and takes a seat next to a window, Will plopping into the empty seat beside her.

The bus driver spends a few moments waiting for any straggling tourists to wander into the transit station, and as they wait, the two new friends sit in comfortable silence, listening to the small hum of conversation around them. Margaret is looking out the window, following a flock of birds in the sky, when the bus doors squeak shut and the wheels jerk the vehicle forward into motion. She continues watching the birds travel one direction as the bus takes them another, and she can feel Will's eyes on her.

"I'm glad the sun came out. It's going to be a beautiful day for a hike," Will states.

"Yes, it really is," Margaret responds, not taking her eyes off the window. She can't quite explain it, but now that they're on the bus and moving towards their destination, the giddy anticipation she was feeling earlier has been replaced with anxious trepidation. She's suddenly worried about being alone with Will, replaying her conversation with AJ in her head.

They continue the rest of the drive in silence, with Margaret worrying that Will can hear her heart pounding in her chest. The bus clambers to a stop and all the passengers file out. As Will and Margaret exit the bus, they join the small crowd gathered around a young man with outstretched arms.

"Aloha, everyone! Welcome to Diamond Head State Monument! It's a beautiful day for a hike, right?" The young man's face appears to be in contest with the sun for who can shine brighter. A few people clap, everyone is smiling. "There is only one trail to hike up to this volcanic crater, and it is steep and it is strenuous. Some of it is paved, some of it is not. This trail has a unique history, so enjoy the ghostly military remnants that are speckled throughout the trail and be sure to take lots of pictures - both along the way and once you reach the top! The sun has decided to grace us with her beautiful presence this afternoon, so that means it's hot. Make sure you have water with you! If you didn't bring any water, there is water available for purchase in the shop to my right," the man gestures toward a small building. "Be safe, drink lots of water, and enjoy the view from the summit - it's one you shall never forget!" And with that, the man waves his arms in a flourish toward the head of the trail, and the group travels as a flock towards the trail's mouth.

"I thought you said we'd be doing a different trail from your family?" Margaret whispers to Will, panic rising in her chest as she intrudes on a family affair.

"Huh. I was planning on it, but looks like there's only one. Ah, who cares? There's tons of other people here too, it's not like you're intruding on anything. Look, we'll just let everyone in my family get ahead of us, and take our time at the back of the pack, if that makes you feel more comfortable."

"Yeah, I like that idea," Margaret responds, thinking it's more than just feeling as if she's intruding on a family affair. *If we go slow and steady at the back, nobody can hear my heavy breathing as I struggle up this mountain.* Margaret looks questionably up the steep path ahead of her. *I still think exercise is overrated,* she affirms to herself.

Will and Margaret let the rest of the group put some distance between them, and then they begin their ascent. Their adventure begins in that familiar silence Margaret is growing ever comfortable with. She appreciates Will not pushing for more about her past, and enjoys his steady presence, even when no words are exchanged. After several minutes into their climb, Will does decide to break the silence.

"How ya doing?"

"Fine," Margaret lies. Her legs are already starting to burn. *Damn elevation.*

"You wanna talk about anything?"

No, she says to herself. *Talking while climbing a mountain is a terrible idea.* "You can tell me more about your family." Margaret figures if she gets Will talking, she won't have to use up her precious energy talking herself.

"Yeah, okay. Well, you met my immediate family - my mom and dad, Kyle, and Kara. It's always been the five of us. I'm the oldest, then Kyle, then Kara. We have some aunts and uncles and cousins here too, they're just all off doing things with their own families right now. Chris, Kara's fiance, has family here too, though I don't really know them at all. Let's see, what else..." As Will thinks about more to elaborate on, Margaret marvels at how easily he can hike and talk at the same time. "We're all from Colorado, born and raised. My dad started his own manufacturing business and was extremely successful. Was able to sell his business and retire at only 55. Kyle does construction, Kara just finished nursing school, and I am a business analyst. Nothing too exciting." Will glances at Margaret and must notice her struggling to keep up with his pace on their climb, because he suggests they take a break for some water.

Margaret gladly agrees, the sun scorching her from its perch above the trees. "Alright, looks like there's a good place to stop just a little way ahead." They walk a little while further, and come upon an overlook, where crowds of tourists are gathered taking selfies. A soft "oh" escapes Margaret's lips as she wiggles her way onto one of the overlook perches.

"Beautiful, right? And this isn't even the top yet." Will is smiling out towards the expanse in front of him.

"Breathtaking is right," Margaret whispers, as she takes a moment to collect her own breath. The pair take some pictures from the top, move aside to let other tourists take in the view, and take a moment to have a water break. Margaret takes some time to absorb the sounds of the nature that surrounds her as she rests. The music of chirping birds fill the air. "Do the trees look greener than normal here?" she asks Will.

Will laughs and looks around. "You know, I think they just might." They continue to sit and rest for a moment, and Margaret takes out her phone to snap a few more pictures. She sends a couple to AJ, along with a text letting him know they're halfway up their trek to the crater, which is a total guess. She's lost of sense of space and time while on her body has protested the laborious trek. She tucks her phone back in her pocket and turns to Will.

"I'm ready when you are," she informs him. Will slaps his knees, pushing himself off from the against the rail he had been leaning on.

"Alright then. Let's keep going." They resume their hiking in silence, until Will asks, "So do you want to tell me about your family?"

Margaret chews on his invitation, deciding what to say, as they come upon a set of stairs leading to a tunnel carved right through the mountain. Lights glow along the footpath of the tunnel, casting shadows of the tourists on the walls as they journey onward. "Well I have just one brother, AJ. My dad left when I was young, so AJ and I are really close. And then it's just my mom. Just the three of us. Well, now there's Odette too. She's married to my brother. I didn't care for her when they first met, but she's become my best friend this past year. And they have a little girl, Mary Kate." Margaret trails off, her heart catching in her throat, as she thinks about the part of her family that's been missing for the past year. She blinks rapidly to keep the tears that have suddenly flooded her eyes from falling. Will doesn't say anything and together they simply walk, exiting the tunnel, which leads the pair to another set of stairs. Margaret glares at the stares before her, tears stinging at her eyes, channeling her anger at the unfairness of the world to the physical exertion laying before her. She feels an inexplicable urge to tell Will more. She inhales deeply as she takes her first step onto the staircase before her, and the tears that had been begging for release slowly and silently carve a path down her face.

"Jackson had the biggest heart of any five-year-old I know. He was always focused on the emotions of those around him. If he thought someone was sad, he tried to cheer them up," Margaret's voice cracks, but she keeps going. "Izzy was my wild child," she chuckles. "She was so spirited and so full of energy. She always worked so hard at anything she did and she was fearless, adventurous, brave." Their trekking has slowed, and Margaret feels Will's eyes on her. She focuses on staring straight ahead, avoiding his gaze. "Austin," she wipes at her face. "Austin and I met in college. He was the yin to my yang. I was the grounded planner, he was the spontaneous adventurer. He was so good at making me laugh and reminding me to take life easy. He was my very best friend."

"They sound like a wonderful family," he offers.

"They were," Margaret whispers. "The best." The tears are flowing freely now, but she doesn't fight them. "I can't stop thinking about them. I see them everywhere. We're hiking in this beautiful tropical island, so far removed from anything I would normally attach to them, but they're still here. Like right now, I think about Austin holding my hand as we hike, the kids running ahead of us, completely unphased by all these stairs, their energy boundless. I don't know how to stop thinking about them. And it's been a whole year. How does it still hurt so much after a year? I just can't figure out a life without them."

They continue climbing the stairs in a slow silence, as Will appears to digest Margaret's words. They reach yet another staircase, and Margaret lets out an audible groan that bounces off the compressed walls around them. Will breaks the silence as he takes the first step onto the newest staircase.

"Maybe you're not supposed to figure out how to stop thinking about them about them all together, but maybe you're supposed to figure out how to make it hurt less when you do," he begins. "Maybe it's like Newton's law." Margaret gives Will a perplexed look. "You know, Newton's law? For every action, there's an equal and opposite reaction? So in this case, the action is: you had this wonderful life, right? A wonderful family who was your whole world, your greatest source of joy. Well what's the opposite of that? Now that they're gone, it's your greatest source of pain. And you can't avoid it, you can't escape it, because it's science. Newton's law."

Margaret gives a small chuckle at the strangeness of comparing her grief to a science algorithm, but as she mulls over his words, she realizes there might be some sense there. They reach the top of the staircase, exiting into an historic military bunker. Together the pair walk over and lean on one of the walls, taking another water break.

"So, what I'm saying is, you can't stop thinking about them all together because they were such a big, important part of your life. And besides, you don't *want* to stop thinking about them, they're your family. You want to keep them and their memory alive, just without it hurting so much. But the pain is so great because they were such a big, important part of your life. But, maybe, as you keep living, keep moving forward and filling your life with *new* joyful things, the pain will begin to subside. Your world will expand, therefore they won't take up so much of it, so the pain won't take up so much either." She thinks about what he is explaining and tries to imagine a world where her pain and hurt are no longer a part of her; a world where she doesn't have to run into books to escape her grief. Will doesn't add anything more to the conversation, and they continue on their trek, climbing the last set of stairs to the summit, and letting the chatter from the fellow tourists fill the air around them.

As they reach the peak of the crater, Margaret's heart flutters and her breath catches in her throat. Her soft tears have stopped their flow, and she wipes her face. The beauty in the view ahead is astounding. She slowly steps forward, Will right behind her, toward the rail that runs along the edge of the crater. She grips the metal bar with both hands and looks out at the scene before and below her, breathless. The sparkling blue ocean expands as far as the eye can see, its water lazily rolling in the distance. As she looks around, she can see the whole island. Lush, green tropical jungles cover the land, and again Margaret thinks about how the plants here look unnaturally vibrant, a special shade of green reserved just for the island. Birds of all sorts are seen flying through the air, the flashes of color dashing in and out of trees and soaring over the ocean. Margaret looks up at the sky, the bluest sky she's ever seen, and inhales deeply. The smell of the salty ocean, the earthy vegetation around, it all fills her senses. She closes her eyes, face tilted towards the heavens, relishing in the warm sun on her cheek, the thick air blowing her hair. She realizes she's crying again, slow, soft tears escaping through the corners of her sealed eyes. *The world is so beautiful*, she thinks to herself, heart pounding with adrenaline in her chest. *I've missed seeing it.*

Margaret and Will don't talk on the trek back down, and Margaret takes the opportunity to continue listening to the birds and world around her. When they get back on their bus, she decides to send some of her pictures from the top of the crater to AJ and let him know she's on her way back to the resort. She scrolls through the abundance of photos she has to choose from, picking her favorites to add to the text. After she hits send, she looks over at Will, who is also on his phone, his brow furrowed. There's an emotion written on his face that Margaret can't quite place. Anger? Confusion? Concern? Margaret studies him for a moment, but decides she doesn't want to pry, so she turns to look out her window, enjoying the tropical view flying past her.

After they arrive back at the resort, Margaret and Will are left standing at the shuttle station, as Will's family say goodbye to Margaret and walk back towards their rooms. Will sticks his hands in pockets and rolls back and forth on the heels of his feet.

"So what did you think?" he asks Margaret. "Better than spending your afternoon in a book?" He flashes her his playful grin.

Margaret grins in return. "It was breathtaking. The beauty of it all was so intense it moved me to tears." A smile crosses Margaret's face as she dreamily recalls the afternoon. She turns her attention back to Will, who is studying her intensely, a deep look in his eyes. She looks away, feeling heat rising up her neck.

"Do you want to go get some shave ice? Cool down a bit after the hike?" Will asks.

Margaret chuckles. "You mean shaved?" She emphasizes the *d* on the end.

It was Will's turn to laugh. "No, smarty pants. Shave ice. The locals call it shave, not shaved."

Margaret chews the bites her lip, her stomach swirling with emotions. The last two days have taken such an emotional toll on Margaret, and she really just wants to be alone. "Raincheck?" she asks.

Will's smile only crawls halfway up his face this time. "Sure. But I'm going to hold you to it." She smiles back and starts twirling her wedding ring. Will glances down at the movement, taking in Margaret's change in demeanor. "You going to call it a day then?"

"Yeah, I think so. I think I'm going to go back, take a cold shower, and order some room service," Margaret explains.

"Okay, cool. Sounds good. Well, have a good night, Margaret."

"Thanks, Will. You too."

Will smiles and turns on his heel. Margaret watches him walk away, his hands in his pockets.

"Hey Will!" She shouts in his direction. Will turns on the spot, locking eyes with Margaret. "Thanks for pushing me to come today. I'm glad I did." His signature one-dimpled smile leaps across his face.

"You're welcome. I'm glad you did too." He turns back around and continues walking away.

Margaret watches him leave, trying to assess the feelings inside her. She wants to be alone. She wants to read, and escape, and recharge after today. But at the same time, she doesn't want Will to leave her. His company has been so comforting. Will has become a speck down the path, but Margaret watches him turn and head into the Waikiki Eats cafe. For a split second she considers walking into the cafe as well and joining him at his table. But she decides against it and ends up walking back to her bungalow alone with just her thoughts.

After her shower, Margaret wraps herself in the complimentary bathrobe provided in her room and orders herself some room service. She takes her time scanning the menu, her mind set on trying another local dish. She finally settles on something called *manapua*, and after placing her order over the room phone, she goes searching in her tote bag for her own phone.

When she pulls it out of her bag, she sees a handful of texts waiting for her, as well as a missed phone call from her brother. She decides to call him back before opening the texts.

"Margaret! Hey sis. How was the hike? You dead?" Margaret can hear his smile through the phone, and her heart pinches with homesickness.

"Not dead yet," Margaret playfully responds. "The hike was beautiful. It was just astounding. I mean, the hike itself was disgusting and awful and brutal and I still think exercise is not worth my time, but once to the top? Just stunning. I've never seen anything like it," Margaret recalls dreamily.

"Yeah, the pics looked pretty wonderful. And how was your time with your new friend?"

"Will was great. He's just a really good listener. I find it easy to talk to him, which is nice to have."

"Well I'm glad you have someone to talk to out there. I mean, I wish it wasn't some strange guy, but whatever. As long as you don't stop texting and calling me, I won't fuss over it."

Margaret smiles, her chest warming with her big brother's protective love, even from halfway around the world.

"Anyway, it's late, I was just crawling into bed when you called. So I'm gonna go. Some of us actually have to work in the morning. Talk to you later, Mags."

Margaret chuckles at his playful banter. "Bye, AJ. Give Mary Kate a kiss for me."

"Will do. Bye." A click later and the room is filled with silence again. Margaret pulls out the texts she had missed. One was from AJ asking her to call him and check in. Another was from her mother complaining she hasn't heard from Margaret yet today, and then she had two texts from Will. She decides to respond to her mother before she forgets.

I'm doing fine, Mom. Went hiking up a volcano today, just grabbing some dinner now and calling it a day. She adds some pictures from her day to the text and sends it off. Finally, she opens her messages from Will, a giddy smile plastered to her face before she even reads the first word.

I'm really glad you came with me today. And I'm glad you enjoyed it.

We're going on a dolphin tour tomorrow - you in?

Margaret's heart starts to flutter and she's again left questioning why. So many emotions spin through her mind, it's hard for her heart to decide which to let in. She spins her phone in her hand as she debates how to respond to Will. A knock on the door makes her jump out of her thoughts. "Room service!" a perky voices announces from the other side. Margaret checks that her robe is secure, then opens the door.

"Aloha, ma'am! I have some *manapuas* for you!"

"Yes, thank you!" She takes the platter from the employee, the aroma tantalizing her taste buds before she's even opened the lid.

"*A hui hou,*" the woman says, as she waves and turns back the way she came. Margaret closes the door and carries her steaming dinner out through the patio doors to the wicker table that occupies her patio. She walks back into her room to grab her book to read while she enjoys the Hawaiian cuisine, and as she's walking back outside, she hears her phone ping. She stops in the doorway of the patio, debating whether to grab the phone or ignore it. She decides to go and see who the text is from.

She picks up the phone: it's Will. *Are you deep in the midst of your next book? Trying to come up with an excuse? Or flat out ignoring me? ;)*

Margaret taps the phone, trying to decide what to say. *What if I told you it was a little bit of all of the above?* She pauses just a moment before hitting send. A playful smirk wisps across her face for just a moment before she remembers her dinner is waiting for her outside. She makes herself comfortable at the table and opens her platter - steam flows out of its cage, swirling its way into Margaret's senses, and her mouth instantaneously begins to water with anticipation.

The platter is filled with a few white, doughy buns. Margaret takes one in her hands, giving it a soft squeeze. It's supple yet full. She slowly pulls the bread apart, more steam releasing from the confines of the bun. A sweet and tangy shredded pork fills the cavern inside the dough. She takes a moment to inhale the aroma, and then takes a bite. An audible "yum" escapes from her lips.

Her phone pings as she digs into the second bun. Margaret takes it in her hand as she chews and sees Will's name on the screen. She taps the text to open it: *I would tell you that your fate is sealed: you're coming dolphin watching with us tomorrow.* Another text pops up in the conversation as she's reading. *Meet me at the Huli Huli Hut at 7 tomorrow morning.* Margaret almost chokes on her meal.

You didn't say it was an early tour. I'll be sleeping. She chews slowly, savoring her dinner, as her heart dances inside her chest, waiting for Will's response.

You know you'd rather be watching dolphins dancing in the sunrise surf. Hope to see you at the Huli Huli Hut.

Margaret finishes the last of her delicious buns and stares at her phone, debating if she should go or skip. As she's staring at the black screen, it lights up with another text from Will. She opens the message but is surprised to see there's no text. Only a picture.

It's Margaret, at the top of the crater from their hike today. She's facing the ocean, her arms outstretched, head tilted to face the heavens. The expanse of an impossibly blue sky fans out behind her, and several strands of her unruly hair have escaped the bun atop her head, blowing wild and free in the wind. But Margaret isn't focused on those details. She's zoned in on her own face. Her eyes are closed, and there's a stream of wetness and dirt on her cheek from where her tears had fallen. The corners of her mouth are tilted upwards in a subtle, yet profound smile. Margaret can't stop staring at this woman, this woman she can't believe is actually her.

She decides she won't cancel. Tomorrow she's going on another adventure.

Chapter Eight

Tuesday, June 13, 2017

Margaret's not sure what time it is when she wakes up, but there's a tall glass of orange juice and a bagel slathered in cream cheese on the nightstand. A neatly folded pile of blankets lies where her mother had been keeping watch the night before. She stares at the popcorn pebbles on the ceiling, trying to think of anything but yesterday's events. She focuses her attention again on the sounds around her. The soft buzz of chatter filters in through the bedroom door, but Margaret can't make out the conversation or decipher the owners of the different voices.

She stares at the small plate of breakfast on the white nightstand beside her, trying to decide if the hollowness she feels is from a lack of food or lack of a will to live. Yesterday hits her like a bag of bricks, flashes of the scene hammering her already shattered soul. The bent license plate on the muddy grass of the median. The abrasive red and blue flashing lights of the emergency vehicles clogging the scene. The never-ending rain, tinting everything in its bleary, gray overcast. Officer Garrison and his khaki-colored uniform. And the mangled lump of metal that had previously been a vehicle. That's the image most vivid in her mind. The one she wishes she could unsee, yet the one that refuses to release its hard, vivid grip from her memory.

Margaret buries herself under the thick blankets, and howls, her heart ripping as her new reality slams a menacing blow to her thoughts. Footsteps thunder down the hallway, and the bedroom door bursts open. Big, burly arms wrap around her shaking body, and she turns to bury her face in the comfort of her big brother's trembling, heaving chest.

Eventually the tears ease their flow, her breathing slows, and the swelling pain in her chest begins to subside. In its place she is left with a thundering headache pounding mercilessly behind her eyes. She pulls away from AJ and looks up at her big brother. His usually sparkling, playful eyes are a tired, bleary pink, but otherwise he looks as handsome as ever. Margaret always teased him that he got the looks of the family genes, she the brains.

"They're gone. They're really gone," Margaret whispers.

AJ pulls her close again, squeezing her tightly. "I know," his voice cracking. Margaret closes her eyes, letting AJ's comforting arms squeeze her into a sense of safety. The door squeaks slightly as someone slowly peers in. Margaret's mother clears her throat.

"Margaret?" Margaret can't find her voice, so she says nothing. "Margaret, what do you need?"

The world to stop spinning, my husband back, my kids alive. A new life, Margaret thinks. "I need some ibuprofen. I have a raging headache."

"Okay." Margaret hears the door close behind her mother.

"You know," AJ begins. "Having not eaten in who knows how long probably doesn't help this headache you have." He pulls away from her, turning towards the bagel and juice. "You need to eat something. Here."

Margaret takes the glass reluctantly and sips, glaring at AJ while doing so. The cool liquid slides refreshingly down her throat, and she suddenly feels ravenous. She hands the glass back to AJ, and he swaps it for the bagel, grinning his 'I told you so' big brother grin at Margaret, and a smile flickers briefly across her face. Nancy returns with the ibuprofen Margaret requested, and after handing it to her daughter, she sits on the edge of the bed. Margaret eyes her mother over the edge of her juice glass as she swallows the pills. She's wearing an apron, and Margaret realizes the house is filled with the smell of freshly baked bread. Her mother may not be an overly affectionate or emotional woman, but she has always spoken her love through fresh baked goods. Margaret drinks slowly, soaking up the scene before her: mother, daughter, brother, together in love and support. It brings Margaret back to the time her dog had been run over by the mail truck.

Margaret and AJ had been fishing off the shore when a lone dog wandered out of the woods and onto the rocky lakefront beach. At fourteen years old, Margaret instantly fell in love with the scruffy mutt, his tongue lolling playfully out of his seemingly smiling mouth. She spent all afternoon playing with him in the sun, feeding him leftover chicken she found in the fridge, and showering him with belly rubs and ear scratches. And while AJ constantly told her not to get attached to the stray, she ignored him and decided to name the scruffy mutt Watson. When her mother pulled into the drive after work that evening, Margaret didn't even try to hide Watson. She ran up to her mother, the dog and his wagging tail following at her heels, and used one big breath to explain how Watson arrived in their yard and begged her mother to let them keep him.

It wasn't that she didn't like dogs. Nancy was actually very fond of animals, dogs in particular. But it was still a hard 'no' from her mother. "We can't, Margaret. I can't afford feeding and taking care of a dog. No. Now leave him be, before he *thinks* this is his home." She started walking into the house, leaving Margaret and Watson standing in the drive. "And don't feed him *anything!*" Nancy shouted over her shoulder, just as the front door shut behind her.

When the sun set that night, Margaret reluctantly said her goodbyes to Watson, and trudged into the house, wondering where Watson would end up tomorrow. But when she awoke the following morning, she found the dog laying in the sun on their back porch, as if waiting for Margaret to come out and play. Her mother had already left for work, and Margaret quickly dressed, grabbed some lunch meat from the fridge, and went out to greet her new best friend. Margaret spent all summer with Watson. His sudden appearance into her life was good timing too. She had just finished her last year of middle school, and it had been her most brutal school year yet. When you're the child of a single parent, life isn't always easy. Her hand-me-down clothes never fit quite right, and they were certainly never the same name-brand clothes the other girls in middle school wore. The teasing and tormenting had progressively grown worse, culminating her last year with tears on an almost daily basis. Watson came when Margaret's heart was a broken mess, and she spent that summer healing with a new, loyal friend by her side.

She had some savings from odd jobs around the community—raking leaves, shoveling sidewalks and driveways—and she used what she had to buy Watson real dog food (so her mother would stop snapping at her for sneaking food from the fridge) and some toys. While Nancy was adamant that the dog stay outside because she was not bringing a dog into the family, Watson never left. He spent his nights sleeping on the porch, and Margaret was greeted every morning with that drooping tongue hanging happily out of his smiling mouth.

Margaret's birthday was the end of August, always signaling the start of a new school year. That summer, for her fifteenth birthday, with her freshman year of high school looming right around the corner, Margaret sat on the porch with her mom and brother, Watson laying at her feet, opening her small pile of presents. After opening AJ's gifts (Margaret's favorite candy bar and a woven bracelet), she picked up the present from her mother. It was a relatively small box, wrapped in old newspaper, the colorful comics section. Margaret tore at the paper and lifted the lid off the box. Her breath caught in her chest when she saw a bright blue dog collar folded inside. She slowly lifted the collar and observed the shiny silver tag hanging from the front: WATSON was engraved on one side, with their home address on the other.

Margaret jumped from the table, squeezing her mother in one of the rare hugs the two of them shared. "Thank you! I really get to keep him? Thank you! Thank you!"

"Well it doesn't look like he's going to go anywhere, and the mutt will freeze come winter. He's going to need a warm house to stay in," Margaret released her mother, her eyes beaming with excitement. "He is 100% your responsibility," Nancy lectured her daughter. Margaret didn't appear to hear her mother. She was too busy kneeling beside Watson, putting his new collar around his neck. As soon as the collar was on, the pair bounded toward the house, Margaret eager to show Watson his new place on her bed. If Margaret had taken the time to turn around and give her mother one last glance before running excitedly into the house, she would have seen Nancy's hard exterior melting, discreetly brushing her eyes to keep any tears from falling.

Watson stayed by Margaret's side for the next four years. All through high school, Margaret always came home to Watson sitting expectantly at the end of the driveway for her arrival. It was early May of her senior year, she had just three weeks left of school, when the bus dropped Margaret off at home and Watson was not at the driveway waiting for her. She ran to the house calling for him, thinking maybe he was busy chasing squirrels or had fallen asleep on the porch. But instead of finding Watson on the front porch, she found a letter stuck in their front door.

I am so sorry, I hit your dog with my mail truck. I am bringing him to the animal hospital in town.

She grabbed her bicycle and peddled to the local animal hospital as fast as she could. "Hi, I'm Margaret," she explained to the receptionist, trying to catch her breath. "My dog was hit by the mail man, and he said he brought him here. His name is Watson." The face of the receptionist darkened.

"Oh yes, Watson. Take a seat over there, dear, and I'll let Dr. Tanner know you're here."

Margaret and the butterflies swarming in her stomach took a seat in the waiting room, her foot tapping busily on the floor. It was only a moment before the vet entered the room.

"Margaret? I'm Dr. Tanner." Margaret shook his hand, staring into his eyes to try to decipher the news. "I'm so sorry, Margaret, but Watson's injuries are extensive. I've made him comfortable, but I'm afraid he's not going to make it. Would you like to sit with him?"

Margaret hadn't realized she was crying until she felt a drop land on the hands folded in her lap. She nodded slowly at Dr. Tanner. He helped her up and led her to a room where Watson was found on a giant pillow, bandages around three of his legs and his head. His tail wagged limply as Margaret entered. She immediately fell to the floor beside her best friend, burying her face in his scruffy fur. He died not long after she arrived.

The bike ride home was slow and painful, as Margaret's constricted, aching chest made it hard to breathe. She collapsed on her bed and cried her heart out. Later, when her mother and AJ came home from their jobs, they found her broken in her room. Each of them sat on the bed with her, as she sobbed about what happened. AJ had held her tightly while her mother brought her a fresh batch of chocolate chip cookies and rubbed her back. At eighteen her world had caved around her, and she walked through the biggest heartbreak of her young life.

And now, nearly twenty years later, her heart was breaking in her chest again, though the pain she felt today was exponentially higher. And still her mother and brother were there, always there, to take care of her breaking heart.

"We have things we need to do today," Nancy's voice is all business now. "There are phone calls to make and things to prepare." Margaret doesn't move from the safety of her brother's arms. Nancy rises from the bed. "When you're ready, Margaret, come out to the kitchen table and we can get started."

When I'm ready, Margaret repeats to herself. *I'll never be ready.*

The door closes behind Nancy, and Margaret hears her voice mingle with Odette's down the hallway. AJ loosens his grip on his little sister and rises from the bed himself. "I know it's unbearable," he begins, fresh tears swimming in his eyes. "Take your time coming out. It's just the three of us out there. No pressure." AJ closes the door behind him, leaving Margaret in the empty room filled with suffocating silence.

After a few deep breaths, she reaches for her phone. As expected after sending her text to Carrie last night, there's a barrage of text and voice messages waiting for her attention. Carrie (or maybe it was AJ) must have spread the news of yesterday's events. She resolves that she doesn't have the energy yet to deal with her friends, so she puts the phone back on the table and rises from the bed, preparing herself to begin the business of death.

Margaret shuffles down the hallway to find her mother, Odette, and AJ sitting at the table, all three of them nursing steaming cups of coffee, their eyes looking as tired and raw as her heart feels. It appears she isn't the only one who had a sleepless night. Odette is the first to notice Margaret enter the room. "Oh! Margaret, you're up. Let me get you some coffee, love."

Margaret gingerly sits down at the last remaining seat of the table, facing her brother. Her mother wipes away a stray tear hugging the corner of her eye before getting down to business.

"Okay, there is a long list of calls that need to be made, things we need to do. Last night I drafted the obituary; I need you to review it so we can get it to the paper for tomorrow. I already called your school and told your principal the situation. You are going to need to call Austin's work. You need to talk to the HR over there to get his benefits sorted out. Did you guys have a financial adviser? I always told you get one, but you never listen to me, so I wouldn't be surprised if you never did have one. But *if* you were smart enough to get yourselves a financial adviser, they would be able to give you all the information you need for any extra financial accounts Austin may have..." Margaret has stopped listening to her mother, her stomach in knots, as Odette places a warm mug in her hands. She stares down into her mug, appreciative of the rich, dark liquid's stable comfort.

"...Margaret, are you even listening to me?" Nancy's voice cuts through the air.

"Mom, let her breathe. Let her wake up. She just stepped out of the room." Margaret shoots a weak, appreciative smile at her brother, as she takes a sip of her coffee. The liquid's warmth trickles down her throat, spreading to her chest. It helps her hollowed chest feel a little less empty. *It's the simple, dependable things, in life,* Margaret thinks to herself.

"I'm her *mother,* AJ. I am helping my daughter, that's my job. And we need to get things in order. We need to get all the legal stuff settled, and we also need to plan the funeral."

Margaret's stomach drops. *She's my mother.* She slowly sets her coffee on the table. *I need to call his mother.*

Nancy and AJ's bickering ceases, their eyes turning to Margaret, as she rises from the table.

"Where you are going?" AJ asks.

"I need to call his mother. She doesn't know yet." Her voice cracks, as she makes her way back to the bedroom to retrieve her phone.

Margaret feels bile rising up her throat as she treks outside, her phone feeling extra heavy in her hands. Odette has a passion for gardening, and has built an elaborate garden of varying trees, shrubs, and flowers in the back corner of their yard, with a sitting area centered in the middle, beneath an overhang of blossoming young trees. Margaret slowly lowers herself on the bench beneath the foliage, dreading the call she's about to make. She closes her eyes, and inhales deeply. It's late morning in early June in Minnesota, and that means the air is just beginning to warm up from the crisp evening, and it fills her lungs refreshingly. The sun beams warmly on her face, promising her a day of blue skies and sunshine. Birds are singing their hellos, and the young leaves above her rattle ever so gently in the soft summer breeze. Her bare toes are wet with the morning's last remaining dew drops still kissing the cool grass.

How can today be so beautiful after such an ugly yesterday? Margaret fights to hold off the tears as she contemplates the unfairness of it all. Finally, she opens her eyes again and turns her attention to her phone. More texts and calls have come through since she last checked, but she bypasses them all and calls her mother-in-law.

The phone rings three times, and just as Margaret is planning out what to say in a voicemail, a woman's voice answers.

"Hello?" Margaret can't find her voice. "Hello?" the woman repeats.

"Hi, Carolyn. It's Margaret."

"Hi, dear. To what do I owe this rare phone call this morning?" Carolyn's voice is melodic, yet formal. And for the first time in a long time, Margaret's heart yearns to have had a stronger relationship with her husband's mother.

"Carolyn, it's about Austin."

"Austin?" her tone becomes dark. "What about Austin? Is everything okay?"

"And the kids."

"The kids? And Austin? What's going on?"

Margaret tries to form a coherent sentence in her brain. "There was a storm yesterday, a tornado. Austin was driving the kids home from daycare and there was an accident. They're...gone."

The invisible line connecting Margaret and Carolyn becomes so heavy, Margaret can feel the weight of it through the phone. The tension is tight, as Margaret waits for any response from Carolyn.

"They're...dead?" Carolyn's voice cracks. "All of them?"

Margaret squeezes her eyes and pinches the bridge of her nose. Tears begin to fall fast and hard. "Yes," she musters. "All of them." Her chest cracks, and she rocks back and forth on the bench, hugging herself and gripping the phone forcefully as a torrent of grief washes over her. Carolyn clears her throat, and Margaret catches a subtle sniffle come from her mother-in-law.

"Margaret...I...my goodness. We'll be down right away. When is the funeral?"

The funeral. Just the thought of a funeral for her family makes Margaret's nausea uptick a level. "I don't know yet. Probably later this week."

"Okay. Well, I'll tell David, and we'll be on our way soon."

"Okay. Let me know when you'll be in."

"Yes, of course. And keep me updated on funeral details."

"I will."

A pause hangs between the two women, almost strangers to each other, yet connected through a very thin, invisible rope.

"Margaret," Carolyn pauses, and after no response from Margaret continues. "I'm so very sorry. This is devastating. Please, please let me know what I can do."

Margaret nods, then realizes her mother-in-law can't see her. "Yes, okay, I will. Thank you." And Margaret hangs up before another word can be spoken. A sudden wave of anger begins boiling in the pit of her stomach, its tendrils rolling and reaching throughout every inch of her being. She's so very angry. Angry at all the years and memories they missed. Angry that her children never truly knew their grandparents. Angry that her husband always questioned their love for him. Angry that she was never able to form a relationship with his parents or hear stories and see pictures of Austin's life as a child. So much anger is suddenly flooding Margaret's veins that she clenches her fists and lets out an agonizing, furious scream.

AJ comes running through the back door at the noise and finds Margaret pacing along the back fence of the yard.

"Margaret, what on earth? Are you okay?"

"No! Of course I'm not okay! How the *hell* would I be okay, AJ? None of this is okay. None of this is fair." Margaret is sobbing uncontrollably, her words spilling out of her mouth and into the summer sky, as she fumes back and forth across the yard.

"I know. I know it's all unfair. I know it all hurts. I know. I'm so sorry, Margaret. This hurts for all of us."

Margaret stops pacing at those last words and looks up at her brother. Her sweet brother, who has always been there for her. Who was the best uncle to her children. And a wonderful friend to her husband. Her heart swells with love for him, and she sees in his pink, wet eyes that his heart is breaking along with her own. She walks up to him and wraps her arms around his torso. They stand in the sun for a moment, before AJ leads her wordlessly back into the house, his arm around her trembling shoulders.

Margaret drops herself onto the couch, as AJ walks back in the kitchen toward their mother. Odette is clinking around in the kitchen, making Margaret realize she is quite hungry, having never touched the bagel her brother passed her way. She glances down at the phone in her hand, but as she's debating if it's time to respond to any of her friends yet, AJ and Nancy walk into the room. AJ takes a seat next to Margaret, and Nancy makes herself comfortable in a chair across from her children. A notebook and pen sit ominously in her lap.

"Margaret, I know you're hurting, we're all hurting with you, but we need to get this stuff done." Nancy pauses to make sure her daughter is attentive. "Officer Garrison and another officer stopped by again last night, after you had gone to bed. They brought your car, as well as left us with all the information regarding where the bodies have been transferred to." Margaret winces, closing her eyes and inhaling deeply through her nose. Nancy continues, stiff and mechanical. "I've called the local funeral home, and they are able to do a service this Friday, at 4pm. But that means we need to let the morgue know *asap* what to do with the bodies." Margaret's stomach recoils at the word 'morgue,' and she's suddenly lost her appetite again. She closes her eyes and tries to imagine being anywhere else but here, having this conversation.

"Margaret," Nancy's brisk voice snaps Margaret back to reality. "We need to tell them what to do. What do you want to do? Did you and Austin ever talk about this stuff?"

"Yes," Margaret begins, her voice soft and fragile. "We both talked about how we would both want to be cremated. Donate whatever we could, then cremate the rest." Margaret begins fidgeting with her wedding ring, spinning the sapphire around her finger.

"And the kids? Is that what you want to do with the kids as well?"

Margaret's stomach lurches violently, as she envisions the bodies of her children lying in a morgue somewhere, waiting for her to give the direction on how to properly handle them. She pushes herself off of the couch and runs for the bathroom, arriving to the toilet just in time to empty what little coffee and bile there is in her knotted stomach. She grabs some toilet paper nearby to dry her mouth, then flushes the toilet. Sliding onto the bathroom floor, she rests her head on the cool tile, closes her eyes, and wills the room to stop spinning.

As she's resting her head against the cool porcelain of the toilet, Odette enters the room. Margaret turns to look at her beautiful sister-in-law, a bitter jealousy brewing in her chest. Envy swirls in angry waves as Margaret's eyes land on Odette's swollen, expecting belly and her mind wanders to the conversations she and Austin had shared over adding a third child to their family. She glares with jealousy at the diamond ring her very-much-alive husband gave to her. And to top it all off, the woman was literally a super model.

But the storm brewing in Margaret calms a bit, as Odette takes a seat on the tile next to Margaret's head. She rests a cool, damp cloth on Margaret's forehead, and begins stroking her hair, her soft sniffles echoing off the walls. "There, there, love." It's only three words, but those three words melt Margaret's resentful mood, and she closes her eyes, letting her sister-in-law take care of her. "You take your time, sugar. Take all the time you need." Margaret lets out a wail, and

Odette shifts their bodies so her head is resting on her long, tanned legs. As she cries, Margaret feels her head shaking ever so slightly and realizes Odette is crying with her, her body trembling beneath her own. The gesture only makes Margaret cry harder, realizing Odette's love for her family ran as deeply as AJ's. Time passes, and their tears slow and their steady breaths return.

"Okay." It comes out as a croak, and it's all Margaret can muster.

"Alright then. Come on, sugar. Let's get those toes on the ground. They ain't gonna take you anywhere unless ya make them. One foot in front of the other. One step at a time. That's all we need, love. We'll do it together."

Margaret walks with Odette back to the couch, clears her throat, then locks eyes with her mother. "The same for the children."

Nancy nods with a sniffle and writes something in her ominous notebook. "Alright. I'm gonna go call the morgue and the funeral home and pass on that information. I'll do as much of this planning as I can, Margaret. You shouldn't have to do it all. Nobody should have..." Her voice breaks and her eyes shift to the floor. She coughs, clears her throat, and rubs at her eyes, leaving Margaret to wish her mother didn't feel the need to hide her emotions. "So-" cough "-I'll do most of the planning and organizing, but Margaret, I need you and AJ start planning the layout of the service. What do you want it to look like? Music? Picture boards? Videos? Guest book? I'll figure out what we should serve for food after the service. And here's the obituary I drafted," Nancy places a sheet of notebook paper on the coffee table before Margaret. "Read it, make any changes you want, then give it back to me and I'll send it in." She rises from her chair to start making calls in the other room. AJ and Margaret sit in silence beside each other.

Margaret takes the paper and begins skimming over the words, taking in the standard storytelling of situations like these: "...a loving father...bright-eyed child...terrible accident...survived by wife and mother..." She pushes the paper back on the table.

"I'd like to help too, if that's okay?" Odette's soft voice trickles through the still air. Margaret looks up at her sister-in-law, a warm smile creeping across her face.

"Of course, Odette. I'd love your help." A large, beaming smile makes its home across Odette's porcelain face, as she reaches across the coffee table and gives Margaret's hand a squeeze. "I guess we should go back to my house? We can start sorting through pictures over there."

"AJ, why don't you ride with Margaret to the house, and I'll swing by the craft store on my way over. I'll pick up some poster boards, glue, tape, all that stuff, and meet y'all at the house."

"Yeah, okay. Thanks, honey," AJ rises to give his wife a peck of gratitude on the cheek, then walks towards the front door and starts putting his shoes on. Margaret begrudgingly rises from the couch, taking the paper that houses the obituary with her to the kitchen. She tracks down a pen and scrawls "looks good" across the top, then joins her brother at the door. She finds her shoes sitting next to a plastic bag with her clothes from yesterday folded neatly inside. The keys to her minivan sit expectantly on top of the clothes. She puts her shoes on in silence, and follows her brother out the front door, into a world that no longer makes sense. A world that refuses to stop turning, even for just a moment, to allow Margaret to catch her breath. Earth is selfish like that.

"Are you good to drive, or do you want me to take the wheel?" AJ asks as they trek down the driveway.

"I can drive, it's fine."

The drive to Margaret's house is filled with country music and heavy hearts, brother and sister filling the air with nothing more than a grim silence. They pull into the driveway, and Margaret turns the ignition off. She doesn't want to open the garage door and see its empty shell. Her hands fall limp in her lap, as she stares at the house before her. For that's all it is now. No longer a home, just a house. The space tucked safely behind that brown vinyl siding used to be her favorite place in the world. Within those walls live all the memories that mean the most to Margaret, and her heart catches in her throat as she realizes that is all she has of her family anymore - memories. She steels herself, and exits the car, making her way toward the front door, AJ right behind her. She realizes she's holding her breath as she unlocks and slowly opens the heavy door.

The entryway of the house has a few jackets and sweatshirts hanging on hooks by the door. An abandoned baby doll lies face-down on the floor by the garage door. A memory flashes before Margaret's eyes, as she relives telling Izzy she couldn't bring the doll in the car with her to daycare that morning. Izzy stuck out her beautiful pink lips in a pout, but obediently left her doll behind. Margaret's heart fills with regret, wishing she had let Izzy take the doll. What had it mattered anyway?

Margaret kicks off her shoes, and treads slowly into the house. AJ hangs behind, letting her roam at her own pace. The kitchen sink is still full of mixing bowls and dishes, the counter scattered with the food Margaret had started to prepare for dinner after work. She passes the kitchen and walks into the living room. Jackson's ninja turtle blanket hangs on the arm of the couch from where he sat watching cartoons before school. Margaret picks it up and scrunches it to her face. She closes her eyes and inhales deeply, the sweet scent of her little boy intoxicating her veins. She doesn't fight the tears that begin to fill her eyes, and they spill onto Jackson's soft blanket. She continues her journey through the house, clutching his blanket to her aching chest as she goes.

She peers in the main bathroom and finds two little toothbrushes hanging over the edge of the sink, accompanied by a pink glob of bubblegum toothpaste stuck to the counter's marbled surface. Her eyes catch the streaks of water and flecks of toothpaste on the bathroom mirror, and she laughs internally at how frustrated she would get with the state of the kids' bathroom. It always irritated her that they could never keep toothpaste off the counter or smudges off the mirror. *How meaningless that seems now*, she thinks to herself, as she contemplates never washing that mirror again, just so she can have a piece of them in there forever.

She enters Izzy's room next. Bright rainbow colors are splattered across the room of her vibrant child. There are bright pinks, purples, yellows, and red everywhere you turn. A giant stuffed unicorn lays upside down on the floor beside her bed. *Must have fallen off the bed while she slept.* Margaret walks over and places the unicorn on Izzy's pillow. In the far corner of the room, a tall floor-length mirror stands next to a decorative chest filled with dress-up clothes. Margaret had been crafty with the mirror, sanding and painting the wood around the glass, then embellishing it with encouraging phrases. She had wanted her daughter to grow up confident, so she had decorated the mirror with sayings such as, "I am strong," "I can do hard things," "I am smart." Staring at her own reflection in the mirror, Margaret reads those words to herself and tries to believe them.

After a moment's pause, she continues onto Jackson's room. The floor is littered with Lego pieces and toy cars. A sad smirk creeps across Margaret's tear-streaked face as her eyes find a pile of dirty clothes *next* to his laundry basket, rather than inside it. She lays his blanket back in its place on his bed, her hand lingering for a moment on the soft, velvety fabric.

She ends her trail around the house standing in the doorway of the bedroom she and Austin shared. The bed is unmade, the tips of its wrinkled sheets brushing the carpeted floor. A few family pictures decorate the tops of their dressers, and a large wedding picture hangs above their king-sized bed. Austin's towel from his morning shower sits in a heap by the entrance to their master bathroom. Margaret enters the room, stepping slowly towards the towel. Gingerly she picks it up, reliving all the times she nagged him to stop leaving his wet towels on the floor, and hangs it on the rack in the bathroom. She traipses around the room, the tips of her fingers brushing the various picture frames, her chest growing tighter with each ragged breath she draws. She drops onto the unmade bed, hugs her knees, and rocks back and forth, as she cries over the memories she'll never get to create with her family. After several anguished minutes crawl by, she composes herself and makes her way back downstairs to her brother. She finds AJ cleaning up last night's prepped dinner still sitting out in the kitchen and takes a seat on one of the wooden stools at the counter.

"So, what do we do now?" Margaret whispers, picking at a smudge of dried jelly on the counter.

"Now, we spend some time combing through the good memories of some of my favorite people to ever walk this earth. And we try to put something together for the rest of the world to remember them by."

Margaret looks up at her brother. His back is to her, as he washes the dishes in the sink.

"I don't print pictures. I don't have things like that to go through. They all live on the cloud."

"Alright, then we spend the afternoon combing through your cloud. We'll pick our favorites to send for print and then make a video slide show of the rest. Come on, sis, make yourself useful. Bring the rest of the dishes from over there." Margaret begrudgingly rises from the stool and brings some more dishes to her brother. She has just finished wiping down the counter tops as her phone buzzes in her pocket, and she's reminded that she has yet to respond to any of the texts or calls she's been inundated with. She pulls the device out of the sweatshirt she's wearing. Carrie has messaged her again.

Margaret, please, please call me. Or text. Tell me what I can do.

Margaret opens her phone completely and reviews all her messages: a total of forty-two texts, nineteen missed calls, and four voice messages. She types a generic text message to all who sent her texts or called her.

Thank you for reaching out. It means a lot to me. There's a lot going on right now as we prepare next steps. The service will be Friday at 4:00.

Just as she finishes pasting her message into the last text, Odette walks through the front door. "Hey y'all," her voice chimes down the hall. "Can someone come help me with these bags?" Margaret sets the phone down and joins her at the door.

"Here, let me take those. Are there more in the car?"

"Thanks, hon'. Yes, I've got the posters in the car yet, plus I picked up some lunch, since all you've had today is coffee and juice and that ain't okay," Odette's smile is warm and soft, but her cheeks are flushed and her eyes are painted red, leaving Margaret to assume she had been crying on her way over to the house. Margaret brings the bags into the kitchen, setting them on the freshly cleaned counter. Odette stumbles into the kitchen closely behind her, juggling a few poster boards and a couple of bags of fast food. The intoxicating smell of hot, greasy fries hits Margaret's nostrils, sending a growling rumble through her stomach.

"Sorry, it's not the healthiest lunch," Odette huffs, her breathing slightly impaired from the growing baby pressing on her lungs. "But I thought some greasy, comforting, fast food is just what we all needed." She winks at Margaret as she starts unloading the paper sacks. AJ hungrily growls his approval as he pecks Odette's cheek and grabs a paper-wrapped burger for himself.

"Thanks so much, Odette. This is perfect," Margaret smiles at her sister-in-law, appreciating her more with every passing minute. The trio all grab a seat at the dining room table and eat their lunch in a warm silence that Margaret appreciates. The sounds of robins chirping to each other flow through the open kitchen window, adding chatter to the house that the grieving family cannot.

As they all finish their lunch, AJ claps his hands and breaks the silence. "So Mags, let's start reminiscing on these good times. We need some smiles and joy, what do you say?"

"Yeah, okay. I'll get my computer. I can hook it up to the TV so we can see everything nice and big and all look together." Margaret rises from the table. The sound of crinkling, plastic burger wrappers tells her the other two are cleaning up the lunch.

She sets up the laptop to display on the TV and is just getting logged into her cloud account when AJ and Odette take their seats on the couch. The first image that pops up is the last picture Margaret had taken on her phone: Izzy and her frizzy bedhead is sitting on Austin's lap on the edge of their bed. Her daughter's face is tilted up towards Austin, a sleepy, yet bright smile beaming in the morning sun, as Austin is leaning down toward Izzy, eyes closed, lips puckered, a breath away from kissing the top of her head. The last moments Margaret had laid eyes on the pair of them together, the two of them blissfully content in their last hours on Earth.

Margaret's heart begins to race erratically at the site of her beautiful daughter. The daughter she'll never hold again. She looks at AJ with tear-filled eyes, her voice catching in her throat. "I can't do this."

"Yes you can, Mags. We all can. We're going to do this together. We're going to remember all the great things about Austin, Jackson, and Izzy. And we're going to share those great things with others who loved them and who love you. So that their greatness can be remembered and cherished. Here," AJ moves to take the laptop from Margaret. "I'll drive. You tell us about the pictures, and what ones you want to put in a video slide show, and what ones you want printed for display boards at the service."

Margaret nods as AJ clicks through to the next image. Margaret begins telling stories of all the things she's documented through photos.

There's a photo of Jackson holding his first tooth he lost earlier that year.

One of Izzy and Jackson sitting cross-legged on the floor together, a pile of cars between and around them.

Austin and Margaret dressed up for a date night.

The family on a pontoon, all holding fishing rods, Jackson with a small sunfish hanging off his hook.

Izzy napping in her car seat.

Jackson playing with the neighbor's dog.

Margaret tells story after story as they dig through her collection. The tears never stop, as the three family members ebb and flow between laughing tears of joy recalling warm memories and shedding tears of grief and pain at the reminder that these are all the memories they will ever have with her family. She's retelling a story about the time Jackson wanted to be a dinosaur, so he tucked a dish towel in the loop of his pants and spent the rest of the day roaring and stomping through the house and jumping off the furniture, when Nancy walks through the front door.

"Hello?" her voice echoes off the walls.

"We're in the living room," AJ shouts in her direction, wiping tears of laughter from his eyes. Nancy enters the room carrying a stack of papers and her ever-ominous notebook. She looks at the picture of Jackson with the towel in his pants, roaring at the camera, and a smile spreads across her face. "I remember that phase," she whispers warmly. Margaret notices the pink rims around her mother's eyes.

"Hey, mom. Take a seat," Margaret instructs.

"Yes, okay. Hi," Nancy makes herself comfortable. "Okay, Margaret, I brought some stuff for us to go over." Margaret's muscles stiffen, and she readies herself for dealing again with the business of death. "I submitted the obituary to the paper, and it should be printed in tomorrow's edition. I also talked to the funeral director, and we've got all the details squared away. We'll start at four o'clock, and there will be an hour of visitation. After the visitation hour, everyone will move to the ceremony room, and we'll do the memorial service. Which means, we need someone to do the eulogy. I'm assuming you want to do that, Margaret?"

A large lump forms in Margaret's throat. "I don't think I can do the eulogy," she turns to her brother. "AJ, maybe you should do it."

AJ clears his throat with a rough cough. "I can if you really want me to, Mags. But think about it, okay? I think it should really come from you. You knew them best and loved them the most."

Margaret nods slowly. "Okay, I'll think about it."

"Okay, I made a checklist of what you need to do, Margaret. You need to finish the pictures, decide on music for the service and a couple of speakers, and choose urns for their ashes. Also, we need to figure out the food for after the service."

Margaret spends the rest of her day in her living room with her mother, AJ, and Odette, planning the memorial service for her family. The same room where just a few days ago, she was snuggled up with Jackson and Izzy watching *Frozen* is now the room where she is planning their memorial service. She chooses sandwiches and salads for the refreshments, and resigns to giving the eulogy, with an 'open mic' type setting beforehand, where those who have stories and memories to share can come forward and share.

"I want it to be a celebration of their lives, not a mourning over their deaths," Margaret explains.

"That sounds lovely," Odette agrees with a warm smile.

After hours of planning out the memorial service, placing the catering order for that day, browsing through more pictures, and choosing urns, AJ, Odette, and Nancy make their way toward the front door, preparing to leave the house. The sky is a canvas of velvet black, extra dark, as the moon and stars are not even bothering to make an appearance, hidden behind a thick blanket of clouds. A wave of exhaustion flows over Margaret. Her shoulders feel as heavy as the heart turned to stone sitting deep within her chest.

Nancy pulls Margaret in for a hug at the door. "Sleep well, Margaret. You're already getting circles and bags under your eyes. Worse than you normally have them. You don't want everyone seeing that come Friday." Margaret clenches her jaw, refraining from a sharp retort as she realizes that this is the first hug from her mother since the accident. "Work on that checklist I left, and I'll call you in the morning." She releases Margaret and turns her attention to Odette and AJ. "Goodnight, dears." She pecks them each on the cheek. "Love you both." Margaret watches her mother walk out her front door, noting how she didn't say "love you" to her, and wondering how the woman keeps such a solid composure when the world seems to be crashing down all around.

"Hey, don't dwell on Mom," AJ begins as he pulls Margaret in for a hug. "She means well."

"Yeah. I know."

"Are you okay here tonight? You're more than welcome to stay at our house. Really."

"I know, thanks. But I'm going to try staying here by myself. And I just really want to be alone." Margaret's eyes are already filling with the tears at the thought of being alone, but she inherited her stubbornness from her mother and wants to try to be independent.

Odette sweeps up Margaret from AJ, giving her a firm squeeze. "Oh Margaret, I love you so much. Please call if you need anything tonight. We're not far." She releases her sister-in-law, flashing one last reassuring smile before following AJ out the door.

Margaret stands on the front step, watching them all leave. The sun has set beyond the horizon, reminding her she has survived her first full day in a world that no longer makes sense. She wanders aimlessly through the deserted house, the silence deafening. She trudges up the stairs to her bedroom, but once there, she can't cross the threshold. Staring at the empty bed in the middle of her room sends her heart racing. The thought of getting into that bed after Austin's death makes her stomach clench. She walks into Jackson's room and takes the ninja turtle blanket off his bed. Then she makes her way to Izzy's room and finds her unicorn. She lumbers down the stairs to the living room, and lays down on the couch, draping Jackson's blanket over herself. She buries her face in the unicorn and lets the dam she's been fighting to hold up all day finally break.

Her agonizing wails fill the empty house, her grief bouncing off the walls in anguished echoes. Her chest aches, and it feels as if her hammering heart is sending shards of glass through her body with each erratic beat. She lets herself succumb to the pain and exhaustion of the day. Eventually, her world turns black as she drifts into another night of broken sleep.

Chapter Nine

Thursday, June 14, 2018

Margaret wakes easily the next morning. Excitement tingles through her veins, and she's not entirely sure if it's excitement to see the dolphins or to see Will. Maybe it's a little bit of both.

She throws the blankets off herself and heads into the bathroom. She fusses over how to wear her hair that seems to grow thicker and wilder with each passing day in the aggressive humidity of the island - should she wear it down? In a ponytail? Do a bun? In the end, she decides to do a ponytail - most practical for being on a boat out in the ocean. Margaret shoots a text over to her brother, telling him she's going on a dolphin tour. She checks that her bag still has all of her stuff in it: a book, sunglasses, a sweatshirt, a water bottle, and some of her Hawaiian snacks. She takes some time to lather on some sunscreen, then tosses the bottle in her bag with the rest of her belongings. She takes one last assessing look of herself in the mirror, fidgeting with her ponytail a bit. It's the most time she has spent in front of the mirror since her trip began, and it doesn't go unnoticed on her. She shimmies the butterflies out of her stomach, then heads out the door to go meet Will.

As she steps outside, a light, refreshing breeze floating off the ocean sweeps across her skin. The sun is already shining, hanging low in the sky. A chorus of birds fills the morning air, and Margaret notices she's walking a little bit faster than normal. And is that a spring in her step? She smiles to herself. The island truly is intoxicating in the most positive way.

As she comes around the corner up to the Huli Huli Hut, she sees Will sitting at a small table outside with a cup of coffee, reading a magazine. The carefree spirit Margaret was enjoying quickly vanishes, replaced with anxious butterflies fluttering in her stomach. Why is she nervous and stiff all of a sudden?

Will looks up from his magazine to take a drink from his steaming mug and catches Margaret coming his way. His one-dimpled smile stretches broadly across his face, and he looks genuinely happy to see her approaching. The sight of Will smiling her way instantly eases Margaret, and she can feel her muscles begin to relax.

"You owe me for making me get out of bed early when I'm on vacation," Margaret playfully jabs as she approaches the tiny metal table he's claimed for his morning coffee. Will's smile grows at her words, and he closes his magazine, setting it on the table beside his mug. "I'm guessing we're going so early because dolphins are more active in the morning or something?" she questions.

"No idea," Will smiles. "The tour isn't until nine. I just wanted breakfast with you first, but I knew if I asked you to breakfast, there's no way I'd get you to agree to a dolphin tour as well." Will looks smug with his plan, but Margaret's heart immediately starts to race. Breakfast? Just her and Will? Like a date? Panic starts to course through her veins, and her muscles stiffen, freezing her on the spot.

Will must be able to read her change of mood. "Margaret, it's just breakfast. As friends. I just don't like the idea of you eating all your meals alone. Have breakfast with me. Please?"

"Have you ever thought maybe some people like to eat alone?"

Will's eyes soften as he looks at Margaret. "So do you want to eat breakfast alone, then? And just meet at the shuttle in a bit?"

Margaret's stubborn side wants to say *yes*, just for the sake of saying it. But she does really enjoy Will's company. "No, let's have breakfast together. You're right, it will be nice to have a meal with a friend."

Will's smile grows back on his face. "So I'm a friend?" he says, as the two walk up to the Huli Huli Hut window. Margaret just grins and throws him a side-eye glare.

"Aloha, my friends! Howzit this beautiful morning?" The same large, tattooed man that took Margaret's first order here is working the window again today.

"Aloha!" Will replies enthusiastically. "Can I get the eggs and spam platter?"

"You got it, my brother. And what about for the pretty lady?"

Margaret smiles. "I'll have the same. And a glass of pineapple juice, please."

"Comin' right up. Take a seat on the lanai and enjoy the beautiful sunrise this morning. I'll bring it out when it's ready."

"Mahalo!" Will waves. Margaret leads the way to a table on the edge of the patio, right up to the sand. As she sets down her bag, she catches sight of a crab scurrying its way towards the morning waves. An albatross sweeps over the rolling waves.

"So!" Will exhales, as he takes his seat. "What shall we talk about this lovely morning?"

"The picture," Margaret blurts out, surprising herself, as she didn't even realize it was on her mind.

Something shifts briefly in Will's eyes, but he keeps his boyish smile on his face. "What about the picture?"

"Why did you take it? Why did you send it?"

"I took it because I liked the way you were soaking up the moment. And I sent it because I wanted you to see yourself lost in that moment. You looked light and happy. And I just had a feeling it's probably been a while since you felt that way, so I thought I should capture it."

Margaret stares down at her lap as Will explains, twirling her wedding ring.

"Was that not okay?"

"No, no, I mean, yes. It was okay. It was...lovely, actually. Thank you." An awkward pause hangs in the air, and Margaret finds herself wishing the Huli Huli Man would come out with their food and break the tension.

"Ask me anything," Will finally says.

"What?" Margaret looks up.

"Ask me anything. You've done a lot of talking the past couple days. And I appreciate it. I'm honored you'd share so much with me. Now it's my turn. Ask me anything you want to know about me." Will's face is serious, his ice blue eyes piercing into Margaret's. As Margaret debates what to ask Will, the Huli Huli Man appears around the corner, bearing their steaming breakfast plates.

"Here you are, my friends. Enjoy! Mahalo!" He is beaming with genuine joy and happiness, leaving the air a little lighter when he leaves.

"Okay," Margaret begins, as she takes up her fork and knife and begins to enjoy her breakfast. "Are you a dog or a cat person?"

"Starting simple," Will smirks, taking his first bite of egg. He chews a moment, before pushing his egg to his cheek to answer. "Definitely a dog. I would want a pet that's actually happy to see me when I get home."

"Good answer," Margaret replies, smiling. "Okay, in honor of being on a tropical island, it's time to play the desert island game." Will smiles, knowing what's coming. "What three books would you want if you were stuck on a desert island?"

Will grins, and turns his eyes to the sky, clearly pondering his answer. Margaret enjoys some more bites of her Hawaiian breakfast as Will takes his time coming up with a response. "Okay," he finally starts. "I would bring *The Martian* by Andy Weir, *1984* by George Orwell, and *The Things They Carried* by Tim O'Brien."

Margaret is impressed with his choices. "So you're a reader?"

"Yup. Not as avid of a reader as a certain someone I know, but I like to read," he grins playfully at Margaret, who smiles back, enjoying the banter.

The two finish their meal together, filling the air with easy, innocent conversation. Margaret enjoys the lighthearted chat, a nice change of pace from what seems to be all of their other conversations. The time passes as easily as their conversation, and too soon they need to end breakfast.

"Oh man, I didn't realize what time it is," Will states. "We should head over to the shuttle terminal." Margaret nods her agreement, and the friends walk away from the sandy beach. She feels as warm and light as the Hawaiian morning sun as she takes pleasure in the delightful feeling of having a friend at her side.

It's a short shuttle ride over to the marina, where an array of boats, yachts, kayaks, and other marine vessels are tethered to the many docks, rocking and swaying in rhythm with the waves. Margaret's eyes scan the various vehicles, awing at the range of sizes, colors, and shapes. The boardwalk she traipses across with Will's family is weathered and faded from the burning rays of the sun and the salt of the sea. Her steps fall in rhythm next to Kara, and the two make small talk about the wedding as they head toward the docks.

Harbored at the dock is a bright yellow speedboat with the word *Atlantis* written in turquoise across its hull. The speedboat glistens in the sun, rocking along with the waves. It pulls tight against its ropes, as if already itching to go chasing after some dolphins in the wide open blue. Margaret peels her eyes away from the boats and looks up ahead at Will. His t-shirt is tight across his back, accentuating his broad shoulders.

"...you know what I mean?" Kara finishes. "Margaret? Earth to Margaret?"

Margaret snaps her attention back to Kara. "Oh, sorry, I zoned out for a minute." Kara shifts her eyes up to her big brother ahead, then returns her gaze to Margaret.

"Mhm," she smirks. "I was saying I couldn't very well wear a ball gown on a beach for my wedding, so obviously I opted for a more functional, soft and flowy choice."

"Yes, of course, that makes sense."

While Margaret found Kara to be a sweet, spunky young woman, there was only so much she could listen to about wedding details from someone she didn't really know. Then again, she found the young girl's excitement about her upcoming day charming, and had grown to be excited for her.

"So, do you feel ready for the big day tomorrow?" Margaret asks.

"Oh yeah. I'm not nervous at all. I've known I wanted to marry Christopher since I was fifteen. And being on vacation for our wedding makes it even less stressful. There's not all the big fuss about all the tiny details. There aren't hundreds of guests I barely know that I have to make small talk with. It's like a big beach party with my closest friends and family. Easy peasy." She beams in excitement at Margaret, and Margaret can't help but smile back.

The group approaches the waiting yellow speedboat along with a few other groups of tourists, and Will repositions himself next to Margaret, smiling down at her. "So, how'd you like all the wedding talk?" he grins.

Margaret smiles an easy smile back at Will. "It was lovely. Your sister is a sweet girl. Charming. And very much in love."

"Yeah, she most definitely is. To all of the above." The tour guide introduces himself to the small crowd and explains the rules of the boat and the sea. He reviews the safety precautions, explains where to find the life jackets, and then allows everyone on the boat. Margaret quickly shimmies herself through the crowd toward the very front of the boat, determined to get a prime viewing position to be able to scan the open waters for her favorite animal. She jumps when she feels a hand grab her own from behind. She glances over her shoulder to see Will's shining eyes through the crowd, a soft smile planted on his face. He gives her a short nod, as if urging her to keep going. She turns back around, trying to ignore the electric current suddenly pulsing through her veins, from the tips of her fingers and up her arm. She finds a seat at the bow of the boat and pulls Will into the seat next to her.

Will has a goofy smile on his face. "Man, you were pretty set on getting a good spot, huh?" he chuckles. Margaret smiles and turns her eyes from Will. There's a warmth growing up her neck toward her cheeks, and she can't tell if it's from the sun or from Will's electric touch moments ago. The pair gazes out into the rippling ocean as everyone gets settled into their seats and the captain readies the boat. The rest of Will's family has taken seats at the back of the boat, and Margaret feels a ping of guilt for bringing Will up here with her. But then she remembers it was *him* who grabbed *her* hand, and suddenly she's feeling flushed again. The engine of the boat kicks to life, and the vessel slowly peels itself away from the dock, beginning to make its way out to open sea.

As the captain steers the crew of tourists out to sea in search of wildlife, Will decides to make some small talk. "So tell me about dolphins. You obviously love them, you're so eager to see them. Why?"

Margaret doesn't peel her eyes off the blue expanse stretching before them, afraid to miss the peek of a dorsal fin slicing through the waves. "They're my favorite animal. They're so elegant, to begin with, the way the just glide through the water. And I love their family structure. Family is very important to them. And they're so social! They talk to each other, tickle each other, play. And they can feel emotion, did you know that? They're known to mourn and grieve, but also express joy and happiness. They're like humans in so many ways." She takes her eyes off the ocean to glance at Will as she finishes her rant, and finds his eyes staring intently at her, a soft smile hanging on his face. "What?" Margaret says a little too defensively. Will barks out a deep, booming laugh from the pit of his stomach. The sounds relaxes Margaret, and she turns back to the ocean.

"The way you talk about dolphins...you're just very passionate about them. It's fun to see. I haven't seen this side of you yet." Margaret can feel his eyes on her, and she focuses on staring only at the water.

"Yeah, I guess I am. When I was a kid, I wanted to be a marine biologist. I actually wanted to be a dolphin trainer. But I lived in Minnesota and there aren't a whole lot of dolphins in Minnesota," she laughs. Will's soft chuckle is barely audible over the roar of the boat and the waves.

And then Margaret sees it. Off in the distance to her right, she swears she saw a dorsal fin break the water. She feels the boat turn that direction and assumes the captain has seen it as well. Sure enough, a moment later, two more dorsal fins break the water side-by-side, this time much closer to the boat. Margaret squeals, jumping out of her seat to lean over the railing.

The captain's voice cackles over the speaker on the boat as he slows the engine down. "Ladies and gentlemen, we're coming up on a family of dolphins off to our right, looks like they're making their way toward our boat to check us out." He continues teaching the tourists about how a group of dolphins is called a pod, and other facts about the marine mammal. More and more fins begin to break the surface, and Margaret feels like a young kid in a candy shop. Will stands up next to her, leaning to get a good look as well. His warm arm brushes against her own, sending another electric current crawling across her skin. She glances up at him, but he is focused on the pod out ahead, a large open smile painting the scruff on his unshaven face. She turns her attention back to her favorite animal, and watches as they dance and glide in the water around the boat. They're so close to the boat, she's sure she could touch them if she reached out a hand. As they swim near and under the boat, the water is so clear and the dolphins are so close that she can make out their scratches and scars on their backs from their exotic adventures in the ocean. *There must be a hundred of them*, she marvels to herself as she gazes below. She debates taking her phone out to grab some pictures of the beautiful creatures but decides she doesn't want to experience this moment behind a lens. She wants to be *in* it. So she watches with her own eyes, trying to sear every moment into her memory forever.

Eventually the dolphins appear to grow tired of the boat, and they start to dance and glide away from the group, but not without a show. A few of the dolphins leap and jump out of the water, as if saying goodbye to the humans above their home.

The captain announces that the time has come to change directions and head back to the marina, but they'll continue to keep their eyes peeled for wildlife as they go. Margaret is more relaxed on the drive back to shore, having seen what she had dreamed of seeing today. A warm, content feeling floats in her belly. Will has seemed to move a bit closer to Margaret after they rejoined their chairs, his arm brushing hers with every bump and toss the boat tackles on the waves.

"That was something, wasn't it?" he asks.

"Absolutely magical. A dream," Margaret sighs happily, smiling up at Will.

"Yes. It definitely was," Will confirms. His eyes capture hers, holding her gaze. Margaret can't turn away. She feels a magnetic pull into his charismatic charm, his comforting presence. She stares into the ocean of his eyes, her heart racing. The boat lurches violently as it clashes course with a rather large wave, and the jolt snaps Margaret from the intimate moment, sending her sailing from her chair. Will jumps up and grabs her arm, but it's slick with ocean spray from the violent waves, and his grip slips, making Margaret fall back on the wet floor of the boat. The two start laughing hysterically, and eventually Will is able to help Margaret back into her chair. She's laughing and brushing the hair out of her face when she glances back at Will. He's laughing with her, running a hand through his shaggy hair. His laugh softens as he slowly reaches a tentative hand out to brush a strand of her hair clinging to her face. His finger softly traces across her cheek, burning her skin in its wake. *I can't.* The words flash at the forefront of Margaret's mind, and she briskly turns her gaze out to sea, breaking the magnetic pull of Will's gaze.

The pair spends the rest of the boat ride back to the marina in silence, but not the comfortable silence Margaret has grown accustomed to in their friendship. She's afraid to look at Will, so she continues browsing the ocean waters for signs of sea life. Too soon, and *The Atlantis* is gliding into the marina, where the captain ties her to the dock. After thanking the guests for traveling with him, the crowd slowly clambers out of the rocking vessel. As the group thins out, Margaret and Will stand, Will gesturing for Margaret to take the lead. As she climbs out of the boat, she spots his family gathered at the foot of the dock, waiting for the two of them to join.

"What did you guys think? Wasn't that just wonderful?" Mary asks.

"Oh, I think Will and Margaret definitely had a wonderful time," Kara answers, winking at the pair. Margaret glances at Will, who is glaring at his little sister. Kara must have spotted them during their intimate moment on the bow of the boat. She feels her cheeks turning red and starts digging in her bag to avoid making eye contact with anyone.

"Yeah, it was a great time," Will says casually. The group starts to walk towards the shuttle bus, and Margaret is grateful for the eyes of the group to no longer be on her. Will gently pulls on Margaret's arm to make her walk at the back of the group, just the two of them. "Let's go parasailing when we get back to the resort."

"Parasailing?" Margaret repeats.

"Yeah. I saw some signs for it in the resort lobby. The boats go out like every half hour. Have you ever been parasailing before?"

"No, I definitely have not. That's a little too adventurous for me. I have to pass."

"Come on. Let's do it. You can go in pairs so you won't be alone. We'll be up there together."

"I'm afraid of heights. I can't do it."

Will assesses Margaret, his eyes piercing. They arrive at the shuttle bus with the rest of the group, and everyone loads in, Margaret and Will sitting together at the back of the bus. "You did fine up on the crater. That was high." Will continues their conversation.

"That was different. There was a railing, and our feet were planted firmly on the ground," Margaret retorts.

"The view will be spectacular. It'll be a sight you'll never forget."

"I bet it would be…if I did it. But I'm not going to."

Will just huffs and drops the subject. The bus pulls into its port at the shuttle transit at the resort, and the travelers empty out.

"Anyone wanna grab a bite?" Jack asks his family.

"Sorry, dad. Margaret and I are going to squeeze in some parasailing before the rehearsal dinner." Will looks down at Margaret, a huge dopey smirk on his face. Margaret just glares back. *Food sounds a thousand times better than parasailing,* she mumbles in her mind.

The family members say goodbye and go their separate ways, and Will grabs a hold of Margaret's hand and leads her down toward the beach before she has time to protest.

"Okay, first of all," Margaret begins, pulling her hand free from Will's strong grasp. She stops advancing down the path towards the beach, forcing Will to stop and turn to face her, a smirk hanging on his face. "I said I'm not parasailing. And even if I *did* go parasailing, which I'm not going to, I don't have a suit on *and* my stomach is empty. And I don't like it when my stomach is empty."

"Okay, you're right," Will concedes. "We should eat first. Let's reserve a time, and then we'll eat and change. Sound good?"

"No, I'm not doing it. I'm serious, Will. I'm terrified of heights."

The corners of Will's mouth dip down, as he frowns at Margaret. "Margaret. You're really missing out on something spectacular if you don't try it. Please. We'll do tandem, so I'll be up there with you. And if you really can't handle it when you're up there, we can give the boater a signal to bring us down early."

Margaret folds her arms tightly across her chest and chews on the inside of her cheek, analyzing Will's words. *Being up there with someone does make it less scary,* she thinks to herself. *And having a signal is a good idea. I can come down whenever I want.* "Fine," she concedes. "I'll try it. But only if we absolutely, positively, with one hundred percent certainty can give the driver a signal."

"You got it," Will's smile is the biggest Margaret has seen yet this week, and she can't help but smile back. They restart their trek to the shack where excursions are reserved and pick a time slot.

"So," Will claps his hands and looks around. "What do you want to do for lunch today?"

"Well, I haven't tried poke bowl yet, and I heard that's a must."

"Great idea. Let's go find some."

The two meander over towards the food lounge and settle in at the Waikiki Eats cafe. Margaret glances up at Will over her menu, studying his face as he studies the menu. His vacation stubble has grown into a vacation beard running along his chiseled jaw line, and the faintest of crow's feet wrinkles can be seen collecting in the corner of his eyes. His brow is slightly furrowed as his attention is focused on deciding his next meal. Will glances up from his perusing, catching Margaret's eyes for just a moment before she snaps her focus back to her own menu, heart palpitating with embarrassment at getting caught staring.

They both get poke with ahi tuna, but Will tops his with a spicy mayo sauce, and Margaret choose a sweet ponzu sauce. The server leaves their table to input their order, and Margaret starts fidgeting with her wedding ring as her eyes peruse the restaurant. Will's eyes glance toward her spinning ring.

"So, what are your three desert island books?" Will inquires. Margaret stops spinning her ring and returns her eyes to Will. His trademark warm, one-dimpled smiling comforts Margaret, and she smiles back at her new friend. She takes her time thinking, she and Will smirking at each other as she does so.

"It's so hard to only choose three. But I would probably settle on <u>The Guardian</u> by M. J. Stowell, *Britt-Marie Was Here* by Fredrik Backman, and The Harry Potter series."

"Whoa, you can't do a whole series. That's cheating the system," Will laughs.

"Oh come on, yes you can."

"Nope. You gotta pick one or none."

Margaret bites her lip as she thinks some more. "Fine. *Harry Potter and the Deathly Hollows.*"

"I can't believe you're picking Harry Potter as one of your books. What are you, twelve?"

"Hey now! Don't be hating on Harry Potter. J.K. Rowling practically raised me with those books. Plus, they have a wonderful message."

"Sure, sure," Will smirks playfully at Margaret, hands in the air. "Whatever you say, Miss Maggie."

Margaret's heart falls to her stomach, her breath catches in her throat. Her sudden change of mood must be reflected on her face, because Will's playfully sparkling eyes turn steel, eying Margaret with concern.

"I'm sorry, did I say something?"

Margaret starts spinning her ring again, staring at a scratch in the table's wooden surface, avoiding the look on Will's face. "No. I mean, yes. It's just..." she feels tears begin to gather, and she fights with all her might to keep them from falling, tired of crying in front of Will. "It's just, Austin. Austin used to call me Miss Maggie when he was being playful."

"Oh, Margaret, I'm sorry. I didn't know. It just came out. It felt natural. I am so sorry."

"Don't apologize, you didn't know," Margaret glances up from the scratch, trying to smile softly at Will. "I'm sorry I am such a yo-yo. I came to Hawaii to escape my family, and somehow I can't stop talking or thinking about them." Margaret shrugs her shoulders, trying to shake of the sadness that has suddenly fallen on her shoulders. "You're supposed to help distract me."

Will stares at Margaret, silent. She stops fiddling with her ring and finds the courage to return Will's gaze. A tension hangs in the air, and she can't decipher if she's created something negative from her reaction, or if it's something else hanging between them. The server breaks the tension when she arrives with the poke bowls.

"Poke bowls for the lovely couple," the beautiful woman says. "Can I get you two anything else?" Margaret's stomach flips again at the use of 'lovely couple,' but she doesn't bother correcting the server.

"No, I think that's good. Thanks," Will speaks for both of them. Margaret's hands dive toward her poke bowl, looking for an excuse to not fiddle with her ring. The two begin their meal in a heavy silence.

"I don't know why you are so adamant on escaping them or not thinking about them," Will begins as he swallows a mouthful of food. He moves his eyes from his to bowl to look at Margaret. "I would think you would never want to escape them. That you would want to talk about them to keep their spirit alive."

Margaret refuses to look up from her bowl. "It hurts too much. I feel too many things. But mostly, I feel angry at the unfairness of it all. The unfairness for me, the unfairness for Austin, and the unfairness for my kids. And I turn into an ugly, angry person when I think about them." Salty tears leak from her eyes, trailing down her cheeks, dripping from her chin onto the table.

"And now you read. Because when you read, you don't have to feel the pain and anger."

Margaret nods, dripping more tears from her chin. A silence hangs over the table once more. She looks up from the small puddle of tears clinging to the table's surface, and finds Will's concerned eyes drinking her in. He reaches across the table and takes her hand. His firm grip is comforting, warm. "Margaret," Will begins. "Can I say something bold? About your situation?" Margaret nods, wiping her wet face with her free hand.

Will smiles sadly, and squeezes Margaret's hand. He takes a deep breath, as if preparing himself for what he's about to say. "I think you need to stop hiding from your family. I think you need to stop trying to escape this pain in your life. I think you need to face it head on." He gives her hand another squeeze and doesn't let go. "I don't think you're ever going to recover from this pain if you keep running from it, hiding from it. And you're missing so much. Right now...right now you're just surviving. But life is so much more than just surviving. Life is about *living*."

Margaret inhales deeply, as her heart yearns for it be her husband's hand she's holding across the table, aches for her children to be sitting beside her. She closes her eyes, focusing on the inhaling and exhaling of breathing. When she opens them again, Will's brow is creased over eyes that have turned pink and damp.

Margaret's heart catches in her throat, at the sight of tears pooling in his eyes. She pulls her hand away, and resumes eating her poke bowl. An awkward silence descends upon the table, and the two finish their lunch with no words.

As they exit the cafe and walk out into blazing sun, Margaret stops under a canopy of giant flowers hanging from the vines overhead. She closes her eyes, and inhales deeply, savoring the intoxicating floral aroma. The scent relaxes her, and she opens her eyes and looks at Will.

"Thank you, for your advice," Margaret smiles at Will. She doesn't know what else to say. The thought of accepting a life without her family seems impossible. Will doesn't return her smile and just eyes Margaret with his concerned eyes. "I am going to go back to my room and change into my suit before we hit the boat. Meet you at the rental shack?"

Disappointment flickers across Will's face before he paints on a smile that Margaret can read is forced. *Was he expecting me to talk more about what he said?* She thinks to herself.

"Sounds like a plan. Just don't bail on me." He winks at Margaret before turning on his heel and sauntering away, leaving Margaret alone and confused with her thoughts.

Back in her room, Margaret stares at her reflection. She notices her face has become sun-kissed over the past couple of days, leaving her cheeks a soft pink. She spreads out her swimming suit options before her - one-piece or bikini? Unfriendly, self-conscious thoughts fill her mind, so she slips into the one-piece. She looks at herself in the mirror again, assessing the new honey glow of her skin. "No," she announces to herself. "I'm in Hawaii. I am bold, adventurous, and going freaking parasailing." She strips out of the one-piece and replaces it with a black bikini. Standing at the mirror, she glides her fingers over the shiny scars on her belly that mark her identity as 'mother.' "This is for you two," she whispers, a soft tear escaping her eyes. "You were here." She lets her mind wander to Izzy and Jackson for just a moment, bringing their faces before her eyes, and mentally hugging their tiny bodies. She pulls her windswept hair into a messy ponytail, slips a bright, flowy cover-up dress over her suit, takes one last glance in the mirror, and nods her approval at what she sees. "Let's do this." Her voice is strong and confident, an unfamiliar sound to Margaret, and she smiles at her reflection. She grabs her belongings and walks out the door with her chest puffed out and head held high, ready for another adventure.

·♥·♥·♥·♥·♥·

Margaret finds Will at the excursion shack, and he tells her it's going to be about fifteen minutes. The pair make themselves comfortable on the white sand near the surf, the bubbly edge of the waves kissing the tips of their toes as it ebbs and flows before them.

"How are you feeling? Not going to lie, I was half expecting to be stood up." Will's playful one-dimpled smirk is hanging on his face as he interrogates Margaret.

She lets out a nervous chuckle. "Not going to lie, I almost did bail," she says with a playful smirk. "I'm okay. I mean, don't get me wrong, I have about a million butterflies swimming in my stomach right now, but I'm going to go through with this." She smiles determinedly at Will.

"Perfect. Now, on a totally separate note: you should come to the rehearsal dinner tonight. I could use some company."

"Some company? It's your family. How could you use company with your own family?" Margaret laughs.

"It would be nice to talk about fresh stuff with a new friend. Not the same old, same old family interrogations, you know? Asking about jobs, relationships - the same things they ask you every time they see you."

Margaret suddenly realizes she knows nothing about Will's relationship status. "No. Thanks but no. That's too awkward. Going to a stranger's rehearsal dinner? I can't. I'm not that extroverted to be brave enough to intrude on something like that."

"You wouldn't be intruding, my family knows you. Kara loved talking with you. It was actually her idea to have me invite you."

Margaret mulls this over in her head, wondering if Will is telling the truth. "I don't know, it still feels weird." Will leans over and playfully shoves her with his shoulder.

"Come on, Margaret. Please?"

"I'll think about it," she states, standing up and brushing the sand from her sun-kissed legs. "Come on, looks like they're ready for us." She reaches out a hand to help Will lift himself off the sand, and they walk over to the boat.

"Aloha, my friends!" The Hawaiian man's warm smile helps to calm the simmering butterflies in Margaret's stomach. "Ready for some fun today? The sun is shining, the wind is in our favor. You're going to have a great time. I am Makoa, welcome to my boat!" He reaches out his hand to Margaret. "Beautiful lady, let me help you in." She returns his contagious, bright smile, and takes his hand. It's as warm as his eyes. "There you are, lovely." Will climbs in behind Margaret, and Makoa begins to instruct them with the standard safety procedures.

"Okay, we're going to drive out a little way before we get you up in the air. You will take off from sitting in the boat, but when it comes time for landing, you land in the water, and we bring you back into the boat from the water. That sound okay?" Margaret and Will both nod, and Makoa smiles back at them. "Alright, let's go!"

As Makoa steers the boat, a young man begins assembling their harnesses and contraptions. "Okay, we're going to get you strapped in. So whatever you don't want getting wet, take it off and leave it in the boat." Margaret puts her sunglasses into her bag, then slides her cover-up dress over her slender arms. As she finishes pulling it over her head and stows it in her bag, she catches Will eying her from the other side of the boat. She forgets all about the nervousness of being hoisted high into the air, and instead all her thoughts are focused on how suddenly exposed she feels, as she second-guesses her choice of bikini. She ignores the rush of heat running up her neck and tries her best to act confident and sure of herself. As she bends down to pick up her flip-flops, she catches a flash of her stretch marks, and her heart swells. *I will forever and always be your mom,* she thinks to herself, a new-found confidence flowing within her.

Will removes his shirt and shoes, and the young man begins to hook the two of them up to their harnesses. Makoa slows the boat, bringing it to a stop, and it lops back and forth in the rocking waves. "Okay, who's excited?" He beams eagerly at the pair. Margaret begins to feel sick, as the anxious butterflies reclaim their territory within her. She feels Will's eyes on her, watching from the seat beside her.

"You're going to be okay, Margaret," he softly soothes her.

"Uh-oh, do we have someone who is nervous?" Makoa asks, looking at Margaret with concern.

"Just a little," Margaret tries to sound nonchalant. "I'm just not a fan of heights."

"Oh, my lady," Makoa begins. "I understand, it can feel scary. But I promise you: when you get up in that sky, and the wind is blowing your hair, the sun is hugging your skin, I promise you will feel nothing but joy. It is spectacular up there. Did you hike up a volcano yet?"

"Yes."

"And was the view breathtaking from up at the top?"

"Of course, but—"

Makoa cuts her off. "Yes, yes, your feet were planted on the ground there. But lovely, listen to me: you thought the view from the top of the volcano was the most beautiful view you had ever seen. Well, it does not even compare with the view you are about to see from the sky." He smiles warmly at Margaret, taking her hand. "You're going to be okay, I promise." Makoa's pep talk has dissipated some of the butterflies in Margaret's stomach, and she feels a little bit better. She smiles warmly at the man, trying to put on a brave face. "Okay, let's fly!" he announces. "I'm going to start the boat, and this time when we get going, you will float up into the sky and join the clouds. Margaret, do not close your eyes, okay? Do not live in fear. Eyes open, and take it all in, okay?"

Margaret nods, and reaches for Will's hand, squeezing it tightly. He squeezes back, looking down at Margaret with a comforting smile. The rev of Makoa's engine makes Margaret's stomach churn, and she squeezes her eyes shut, trying to focus on her breathing. The boat begins moving slowly at first, then picks up speed. As the boat speeds up, so does the wind, and in a flash, it catches the colorful wings of the parasail and starts lifting the pair out of their seats on the boat. Margaret squeals at the sudden feeling of weightlessness, and she hears Makoa's voice as her feet leave the boat, "Open your eyes!" Will gives their clenched hands a little shake, urging Margaret to do so.

She slowly peels her eyes open, and her breath catches in her chest as she watches the boat become smaller and smaller beneath them. The bright red rope connecting them to the boat flows beneath them, the sight of it comforting to Margaret - something tethering her to safety. Will lets out a "Whoop!" beside her and she looks over at him.

Will's shaggy hair is whipping around him, and his face is positively childlike. He's wearing the biggest smile Margaret has ever seen, and his eyes are wide and sparkling with delight. He gives her hand another squeeze. "Isn't this amazing?" he asks with glee.

Margaret turns her eyes from Will to the ocean, and her stomach lurches to see how high they have ascended in a matter of seconds. Will is laughing beside her. The silky, musical sound of his laugh relaxes her, and a smile begins to creep onto her face. She closes her eyes, letting the wind caress her face, tickling her hair. She feels weightless, free. She drops Will's hand, and stretches her arms out before her, imagining she is flying.

"Open your eyes, Margaret. You're missing it!" Will shouts beside her.

Margaret lowers her arms and opens her eyes. The sun casts a honey reflection on the surface of the bluest water Margaret has seen. *How does the water look so different from above than from the shore?* Margaret thinks to herself. It's an unnatural blue, a turquoise sheet of glass beneath them. Margaret grips the straps of her harness as they continue to fly, her eyes scanning the scene around her. Surfers decorate the shoreline as if they are tiny little polka dots floating in the water. The sand is a brilliant, blinding white, running along the coast. Up ahead in the distance, Margaret sees another island, its tropical landscape the most vibrant of greens standing stark against the cloudless blue sky. Will shouts and points at a spot to their right in the water, and Margaret sees it - a huge pod of dolphins breaking the surface of the water. They're so far from the shore, there's no way anyone on the beach sees the beautiful creatures. But from their vantage point up above, Margaret and Will watch the family dance and play in the water below. Margaret's heart is racing, but the adrenaline she feels is exciting and wild. Gone is any nervous energy that plagued her before their ride. She tilts her head to the heavens again, breathing in the air and salt around her. She turns her attention back to the water and catches the tail of a humpback sliding back under the waves. "Will! Look over there. Watch!" she shouts over the wind.

Will finds Margaret's hand again, and together they watch as the giant sea creature breaks the surface of the water again, exhaling a puff of air from its blowhole, the spray creating a rainbow effect the air. Margaret turns to Will, beaming with excitement and glee. She feels like a little kid, unable to contain her excitement, a giant smile shining brightly at Will. He laughs, smiling just as broadly back at her.

The experience is over all too soon, and Margaret feels the rope being reeled back into the boat, bringing their sail closer and closer to the water. First their toes drag along the surface of the water for just a moment, then they're crashing in, the buoy of their life jackets keeping their heads above waves. Margaret can't stop giggling, and she beams up at Makoa as he brings the boat over.

"Well, my friend, looks like you enjoyed yourself!"

"That was amazing, Makoa. And you were right - doesn't even compare to the top of the volcanic crater."

Makoa smiles warmly at Margaret as he reaches out his arm and helps her into the boat. Will climbs up after her, shaking his head like a dog before grabbing his towel. Makoa and his assistant help the two out of their harnesses, as Margaret retells everything they saw while up in the sky.

"Yes, truly beautiful right? It's like flying to heaven." Makoa responds, as he makes his way back to the wheel to the take the pair back to shore. Margaret thinks about what she would give to truly fly to heaven, her mind suddenly elsewhere than the beautiful adventure they just embarked upon.

When her feet touch land again, Margaret gives Makoa a warm hug, and thanks him for the adventure. "Come back again sometime, my dear. I will fly you to heaven any time you want." She gives a small wave as she desperately wishes that were true. She takes her place beside Will, and they begin the trek up the beach towards the resort.

"You seem like you enjoyed it, just a little bit," Will begins with a smirk.

Margaret gives him a playful nudge and smiles back. "That was amazing. I've never experienced anything even remotely like that before. Thank you. Thank you for pushing me, once again, to do something out of my comfort zone."

"You're welcome. And since you seem to enjoy stepping out of your comfort zone, why don't you step out of your comfort zone and come to my sister's rehearsal dinner tonight. We're having a traditional Hawaiian pig roast. It'll be great."

Margaret takes a few steps in silence, debating her choice before her. "I can't, Will. It just feels too awkward. I barely know your family."

Will exhales, and Margaret can sense the disappointment in her decision. "Okay, I'll stop pushing. I gotta head back to my room though and get ready." He stops walking and turns to Margaret. She's sucked into those ocean-blue eyes, and feels a longing pouring out of them, though she can't tell what it is that he longs for. His gaze is intense, and after a moment, Margaret has to look away, unable to hold it any longer. Will takes a step forward and reaches out, softly taking her hand in his. "Margaret," he begins, and butterflies fill the pit of Margaret's stomach again, though these feel different than the ones that had accompanied her on the boat moments ago. "I really want to see you again. I truly enjoy spending time with you. I get it if you feel awkward coming to the dinner tonight, but," he trails off, seeming to try to form his words. "Can we meet up again? After the dinner tonight? Can I call you?"

Margaret's heart is racing in her chest, and she's certain that it is beating so strong and loud that Will must hear it as strongly as she can feel it. She looks down at the hand he is holding, words tumbling around in her mind as she tries to form something to say. "Okay," is all she manages to get out. Will smiles, his thumb tracing patterns on Margaret's palm, stirring the butterflies.

"Great," he smiles down at her. "I am going to call you later tonight." Margaret returns a smile, giving his hand a small squeeze. "Bye Margaret. I'll talk to you later." And he turns to walk back to his room, leaving Margaret standing in the sand and the sun, wondering what she's gotten herself into.

When Margaret returns to her room, she decides to take a shower to wash the salt from her skin. As she steps out of the shower and towels off her hair, she yearns to call her brother to talk about the day's events with him. Glancing at the clock, she sees it's about nine o'clock back in Minnesota, so she knows he'll still be awake. Her heart is racing, and she realizes she is nervous to tell him about her adventures, though she's not sure why.

AJ picks up on the third ring. "Hey, Mags. How's it been going?" Margaret feels the muscles in her whole body relax at the sound of her big brother smiling on the other end of the phone. A smile crosses her own face.

"Hey, AJ. I had a wonderful day today."

"Yeah? That's great. What did you do?" Margaret wanders around the room in her bathrobe as she dives into all the details from the dolphin tour to the parasailing experience, savoring the opportunity to relive the moments in her mind. She feels like a giddy schoolgirl on the best field trip of her life. AJ does his part providing commentary and asking questions, and Margaret can tell he's genuinely interested in all that she has experienced on the island. She ends her retelling with a happy sigh and plopping herself on the bed. AJ's chuckle flows through the phone, making her heart ping ever so slightly with homesickness.

"That sounds like an amazing day, Margaret. I'm glad you're enjoying yourself. You sound really great, really happy." And Margaret realizes she *is* effortlessly happy for the first time in a very long time.

"I am, AJ. I am really enjoying myself. In fact, I've only been able to finish four books so far."

AJ laughs at her comment. "That's four more than I would have, Mags. So, uh, you doing all this stuff by yourself?"

Margaret bites her lip, debating how much she should tell her protective big brother. "No, Will's been keeping me company. The guy from the hike." She listens intently, trying to grasp any sound her brother might make so she can gauge his response. He is silent on the other end.

"I wish I knew who this Will guy is," AJ huffs out. "I just hate the idea of you halfway across the world with a stranger."

Margaret rolls her eyes behind the security of the phone. "AJ, he's fine. He's nice. You'd like him. He's a good guy." She pauses, again trying to hear his thinking. "He's in Hawaii for his sister's wedding. Half the stuff we've done his family has been there too."

"Yeah, well, I still don't like it. You're in a vulnerable state, Mags." Margaret flinches at the words 'vulnerable state,' hating the idea of herself as some weak, timid woman.

"Anyway," Margaret begins, trying to sidestep the strife beginning to brew between them. "I'm back in my room on my own now, and I'm going to go down to the beach and enjoy the sunset with some cocktails and my next book."

"Cocktails with this Will guy? Watch your drink. I mean it."

"You know, AJ, I was really excited to call my big brother and tell him all about the fun I've had today, but he's kinda ruining it by putting down everything I'm doing," Margaret huffs into the phone. "If I wanted to feel bad about myself, I would have called mom."

AJ lets out a sigh, and a heavy pause passes between the two siblings. "Look, I'm sorry, Mags. I care about you. I want you to be happy, but I also want you to be safe." Margaret doesn't say anything, letting the air hang heavy. AJ continues, "It makes me so happy to hear how much you are enjoying yourself. Really, it does. That's what this trip *should* be for you. I'm glad you're living it up over there."

"Thanks," Margaret mumbles.

"I love you, Mags." Margaret can't help but smile.

"I love you too, AJ."

"And hey, speaking of mom, you should check in with her. She keeps asking me for details about your trip and if you're still alive, because Lord knows it's too hard for her to ask you herself." Margaret rolls her eyes but concedes.

"Yeah, okay. I'll check in with her after we hang up."

"'Kay. Enjoy the rest of your night, Mags. And hey, Margaret?"

"Yeah?"

"Tomorrow's your last full day there, right? Keep making the most of it." Margaret's stomach does a small, anxious flip. She didn't realize how fast the week had gone, and she suddenly doesn't want it to end.

"Yeah, it is. Guess I better, huh?"

"Yeah. Love ya, Mags. Night."

"Love you too, AJ." Margaret hangs up the phone and stares at the ceiling, thinking about the past couple days. She smiles to herself, as she recalls the adventure she's had and the beauty she's seen. After a moment, she remembers she promised AJ she would check in with her mother.

Nancy picks up on the first ring. "Margaret! Well it's about time I've heard from you. The only reason I knew you weren't dead somewhere was thanks to your brother. Seems you love *him* enough to talk to him on your trip, but not your own mother." Margaret bites the inside of her cheek to keep from saying something she'll regret.

"Hi, Mom. Sorry I haven't called until now."

"Yes, well, anyway. How's the trip so far? Enjoying yourself? Getting lots of reading in on the beach?"

"Well, I was. Then I made a friend who has been making me take adventures all over the island. It's been really fun, actually."

"Oh, thank heavens. It makes me feel better knowing you're not spending an astronomical amount of money just to take your library to the tropics. What a waste. I'm glad to hear you're actually doing something with your time there instead of moping around in your books when you can mope around here at home for free."

Margaret can feel the temperature of her skin start to rise, and it takes all her self-control to sidestep her mother's comments. Instead, she begins to retell her adventures again, this time to her mother. Her mother doesn't ask about this mysterious friend she made, and for that Margaret is thankful.

"Alright, well I'm glad you're enjoying yourself. And that you're not spending all your time alone."

"Thanks, mom. And no, I'm definitely not alone."

"Okay, well, that's it then I guess. Next time don't wait so long to call your mother. Bye, dear." Margaret hangs up the phone and again her eyes focus on the ceiling. Her mother has never been an affectionate woman. It's never been easy for her mother to say 'I love you' or give Margaret or AJ hugs or kisses when they were kids. She supposes it has something to do with the amount of stress and work her mother was always under as a single mom.

Margaret lifts herself off the bed to get dressed for the beach. As she stands before the bathroom mirror drying her hair, her mind wanders to Will. She replays how his strong grip on her hand comforted her at the beginning of their parasailing adventure. She thinks about the spark of the electric current that coursed through her when he first touched her skin. And then there's his smile. His easy, one-dimpled smile that hangs effortlessly on his face. How differently her vacation would have gone had Will not come up to her at the beach bar, and she smiles to herself, genuinely happy to have let Will mess up her vacation plans.

Margaret's bikini-clad body is stretched across a towel on the sand, the evening sun still strong enough to warm her skin. She lays on her stomach, her book propped open on the sand, a daiquiri propped in the sand beside her, beads of sweaty condensation trickling down the cool glass. Her eyelids start to feel heavy, threatening to close and seduce her into a welcoming nap. But just as she lets her eyelids fall, she is forced awake by the ring of her phone. Looking at the screen, she sees Will's name, and her stomach does a little dance.

"Hey, Will." She uses the most casual voice she can muster.

"Hey, Margaret. What are you up to?"

"Reading. On the beach."

"Of course." Margaret can hear the smile in his voice. "Wanna grab some shave ice with me and take a walk? We can walk to the pier and watch the sky change."

Margaret's heart warms at the idea of another adventure with Will. "Yeah, I'd love to. Give me some time to change. Where should I meet you?"

"I'll just come with you, looks like you're going to need help carrying all your stuff back to your room." Margaret's head whips around, and she sees Will walking her way, his face now clean of his vacation beard and his usually shaggy hair tamed neatly with hair product. Margaret suddenly feels very self-conscious laying stretched out in her bikini. She hangs up and jumps up from her towel, working hard to remain cool.

"Why hello, stalker," she says as Will approaches. Will's deep laugh gives her goosebumps. He looks into Margaret's eyes with sparkling playfulness dancing in his own. Margaret starts cleaning up her towel, books, and snacks, Will joining in to help her out. Once everything is packed up, he takes the bag from her, and together they walk up towards Margaret's bungalow.

"I liked the beard," Margaret confesses, as they walk side-by-side.

"Yeah, I think I did too. Unfortunately, Kara did not."

Their conversation is easy and casual, with Will filling in Margaret of details from the dinner: the menu, the speeches, the wedding party gifts. "You know, everyone asked where you were."

Margaret's head snaps up to look at Will. "Seriously? Why would they expect me to come?"

"They like you. They've enjoyed your company. And come on, it's a Hawaiian wedding. Go big or go home, right? The more the merrier. All that jazz," Will explains. "In fact," he continues. "Kara said she better see you at the wedding tomorrow."

Margaret can feel her face flush, embarrassed at the way Will's family seems to feel. "I can't go to Kara's wedding. I don't even know her."

"Sure you do. You two chatted forever the other day. She likes you. Plus, my mom said she wants to see you at the wedding too."

"Will, it's one thing to tag along on a hiking trip or dolphin boat ride with your family. It's a totally different thing to crash a *wedding.*"

"You're not crashing, you're invited," Will continues to press.

They get to Margaret's bungalow, and as Margaret lets them inside, she realizes how second-nature it was to have Will come back to her room with her. Will tosses the bag on the bed, and Margaret goes straight to her dresser to grab a change of clothes. Will refuses to let the conversation die. "So what do you say? Come with me to my sister's wedding. You'll have a great time. The ceremony is on the beach, and then after the ceremony, the reception is a traditional Hawaiian luau. You'll love it. You can't come to Hawaii and not attend a luau."

"I need to change," is all Margaret responds, taking her clothes with her into the bathroom. She closes the door behind her, grateful for an excuse to escape the conversation and take a moment to think. She takes her time changing out of her bikini, trying to gather her thoughts before returning back to Will. But the problem is, she can't figure out what to tell him. The idea of attending a luau sounds really fun and intrigues Margaret. But the idea of attending a wedding, especially with the company of a man she just met, makes Margaret feel slightly queasy. She hasn't been to a wedding since the accident, and the idea of watching someone else get married when her own husband was taken from her makes her stomach somersault. But every 'adventure' she's taken with Will these past several days has turned out to be memories she'll never forget. Her heart is torn. She's still chewing on her thoughts when she exits the bathroom to find Will out on the patio.

She walks out to stand beside him, gazing out at the bright Hawaiian sun that is just beginning to kiss the horizon. After a moment, Will turns to look at Margaret, and the two lock eyes. Her skin tingles as Will's gaze pierces through her. He takes a step toward her, and her heart picks up its pace, threatening to break through her chest. "Let's go get our shave ice," Margaret announces, breaking whatever electrifying emotion was hanging in the air. She turns and walks back in the room, releasing the breath she didn't realize she had been holding. Will follows, and the two make their way toward the trolley cart that sits at the entrance of the pier and offers Hawaiian shave ice to resort guests.

Margaret orders a shave ice drizzled with a rainbow of fruit juices and topped with mochi balls. She dives into her cool, refreshing bowl and is pleasantly surprised at the flavorful concoction. "This is so much better than a snow cone," she affirms to Will. He is smiling, as he devours his own cup of frozen goodness. "It's so much softer, silky almost. Snow cones back home are crunchy, ya know?" She scoops another bite into her mouth, purring as it slides deliciously down her throat.

Will chuckles. "Nice, huh? Let's walk down the pier while we enjoy our treats." Will leads the way down the pier, and Margaret falls into stride beside him. Their usual comfortable silence fills the air between them, and Margaret ponders the fact at how quickly a new friend can feel like an old friend. It's one of life's sweetest gifts. The sun has now fallen completely behind the water, replaced by an expanse of stars that decorate the night sky.

As they near the end of the pier, Margaret is scraping the bottom of her bowl with her spoon, trying to get every last morsel of the sweet, refreshing treat. Will stretches out his hand, a smirk painted on his face, waiting for Margaret to hand over her empty bowl. She glares up at Will but resigns herself to the fact that her delicious dessert is gone, and begrudgingly hands it over. As Will walks over to the waste bin in the corner of the pier, she makes herself comfortable crossing her arms and leaning on top of the wooden wall of the outstretched dock. She rests her chin on her arms, and peers out over the now black water, listening to the rhythmic crash of the waves against the legs of the pier. Will idles over from the trash can and makes himself comfortable next to Margaret, resting his hands on the ledge, his arm grazing her own. Goosebumps climb up Margaret's arm, and she doesn't know if they are from the soft breeze blowing off the waves or from the electric current coursing up her arm from Will's touch.

"So, about the wedding," Will begins. Margaret stiffens and avoids looking up at Will, still torn on what to do about tomorrow's lingering invite. "Have you given it any more thought? I really think you'd have a good time."

Margaret chews the inside of her lip, trying to figure out what she wants to say to her new friend. "I don't even have anything to wear to wedding."

Will nods, thinking. "It's a beach wedding. In Hawaii. You don't need a formal dress or anything."

"All I packed are bikinis, jean shorts, and pajamas. Not wedding attire, even for a beach wedding."

"Well I've seen tons of tropical sun dresses in the gift shop." Will presses. Margaret is quiet, focusing on the point in the horizon where the sky and the water melt together. She clenches her jaw as her mind races a mile a minute. She feels Will looking at her, assessing her. "Look, I don't mean to push or make you uncomfortable. I'm just saying, if attire is your excuse, there are solutions for that. But if it is something else keeping you from wanting to come, well, then that's something else I guess."

Keeping her eyes focused on the horizon, Margaret chooses her words slowly and carefully. "The idea of watching someone else marry the love of their life, when the love of my life was stolen from me...it's just - that's not something I think I can stomach." Will lets out a sigh, and crosses his arms across the ledge, turning his gaze from Margaret's blowing hair to the stars sprinkled across the sky.

"What if," Will begins, but pausing, seeming to think carefully about his words. "What if, instead of thinking about the situation from a sort of 'unfair' viewpoint, you tried to view it differently." He pauses, watching Margaret for a reaction. When she gives none, he continues. "So instead of thinking about how it's unfair that someone else gets to marry the love of their life while your husband, and whole family, was taken from you, what if you looked at it as a celebration of all that person is about to gain? Think about your own marriage. From what I can tell, it was a pretty great one. Think of all the memories and love and wonderful life you built together while you had the chance. And now someone else gets to experience all those things too. That's something to celebrate, not be jealous of."

Margaret's heart is racing as she battles a myriad of feelings coursing through her veins. Unfortunately, the emotion boiling closest to the surface is anger. *How dare he try to tell me how to feel*, Margaret thinks to herself. *How dare he keep pushing when I said I'm not ready*. Margaret clenches her teeth to keep from lashing out, but her chest threatens to explode from the force of her angrily beating heart. As broken as it may be, it still puts up a fight in her chest.

"You have no idea how I feel," Margaret begins, her voice barely above a whisper. "You have no idea what this past year has been like, what was taken from me. I lost everything. Everything!" Her voice rises to match the ferocity of her emotions. She stands up straight, turning to face Will. Will pushes off the pier's ledge, straightening himself as well. His brow is furrowed, his eyes swimming with concern and sadness. He doesn't try to interrupt her. "It's not as simple as 'thinking about it differently.' It's my entire life, my entire being." Margaret is yelling now, her fists clenched tightly at her side. Angry tears well in her eyes, threatening to spill over. "You're just like everyone else. Everyone thinks I'm being dramatic, that it's time to move on. I just need to 'get over it' and put the past behind me. Well maybe I don't want to! Maybe the idea of a future without my family isn't a future I want to think about!" Margaret realizes she's shaking, and the tears escape aggressively down her cheeks. She heaves in heavy, ragged sobs. "You're just being selfish. You only care about yourself and what you want - you want company at this wedding. You don't care about what it will do to me to watch someone else live the happiest day of their life when I am still trapped in the worst day of mine. You just push. Like you've been pushing all week. Well I've had enough pushing. I said no. Leave me alone, Will. I'm not going to the wedding tomorrow, and I don't want to talk to you again."

Margaret storms off, stomping down the pier with a heaving chest and clenched fists, leaving Will watching her as she goes. She's sobbing openly now, the tears coming strong and free. Her heart pounds aggressively in her chest, reminding her of how bruised, broken, and battered she feels. As she opens the door to her bungalow and takes a moment to breathe and collect her emotions, a wave of guilt washes over her for the way she yelled at Will and left him standing on the pier. A new wave of tears flows through her, and she collapses on her bed, burying her face in her pillow.

She lets her emotions roll over and through her. She cries in agony for her family taken away from her. She cries in anger of the unfairness of their lives ending too soon. She cries in sadness for a world that lacks the joy her children once brought in it. And she cries in regret, for treating the one friend she's made this past year like dirt. Eventually her body grows tired, and she drifts off to the sweet release of sleep.

Chapter Ten

Wednesday, June 14, 2017

It's almost ten in the morning when Margaret finally pushes herself off the couch, her head throbbing just behind her eyes. As she scans the room to gain her bearings, her eyes catch the paper with the "checklist of death" her mother left for her.

"I can't deal with that right now," she announces to the empty house. She walks into the kitchen and turns on the coffee pot then digs in the cupboard for some ibuprofen, grabbing a glass for water while she's in there. Her phone, plugged into the wall and charging on the counter, starts ringing. She glances over and sees Carrie's face light up the screen. She ignores the call, and instead swallows her pills, then reaches for a mug from the cupboard and pours herself a cup of coffee.

She tries to sit at the kitchen table enjoying the warm brew in her hands, but the silence is unbearable. So instead she rises and grabs the vacuum. "Vacuums are loud," she justifies to the room. She starts vacuuming the living room, then moves to dining room, loving the ease with which her vacuum switches from carpet to hardwood. "It's the little things," she smiles to herself. She brings the vacuum upstairs and starts cleaning the hallway. Her heart jumps to her throat when she reaches the door to Jackson's room. She stands in the doorway, and the vacuum's growls fill the house as she assesses the smattering of toys throughout his bedroom. Slowly, she starts leading the vacuum through the door and around the maze of toys. Heavy tears begin to stream down her face as she walks around Legos, plastic animals, and superhero figurines that she refuses to pick up. Because once they're picked up, they'll never be taken out again, and she's not ready to admit there's nobody left in the house to play with them.

She continues through the bedrooms, her tear-filled wails intensifying with each room she enters. When she's vacuumed every room in the house, she grabs her dusting mitt and begins dusting everything in sight. But dusting doesn't make any noise, so she turns on her favorite country radio station, and blasts the music through the house. After dusting, she washes the walls. And the appliances, the tables, the baseboards, the floors. The whole time it's just the music and her tears to keep her company.

She's on all fours scrubbing the legs of her kitchen table when she notices two feet standing in front of her. "Alexa, stop," she announces to the smart device. She looks up into the eyes of Carrie, a mix of concern and sadness blanket her face. "Hey," she says weakly to her unannounced friend. "How'd you get in the house? Did I not lock the front door?"

Carrie holds up a brass key. "I found your key under the mat," she explains, tossing it onto the table. Margaret rises to meet her friend's eyes. "Margaret I've been worried sick about you. I want to help you. How are you doing?"

"I'm fine," Margaret lies. "What did you come over for?"

"I came over because you're my best friend and I wanted to make sure you're okay. And because I brought you some food." Margaret notices a couple of paper bags sitting behind Carrie's legs.

"Thank you."

"What are you doing?"

"Cleaning."

Carrie gives Margaret an assessing look, taking in her swollen, pink eyes and damp cheeks. "Do you want help?"

"No, I'm done. Let's put away that food. Thanks for bringing it." Carrie brings the bags into the kitchen, and the two work in silence emptying the contents. When the groceries are put away, Margaret pours them each a glass of water, and they take a seat at the table.

"We're all worried about you, Margaret. How are you?"

"What a stupid question," Margaret mumbles. Carries sighs and reaches for friend's hand across the table.

"What have you been doing these past couple days?"

"I've been at AJ's mostly. And here, I guess. We've been planning the memorial service, getting things in order. I woke up this morning and couldn't stand how quiet the house was. And I didn't know what to do with myself. So I just started cleaning. And then you came over unannounced," Margaret smirks at her friend, who returns a playful, yet sad smile.

A silence falls between them, and Carrie addresses the elephant in the room. "I can't believe it, Margaret. I just can't wrap my head around it. I'm so sorry." Margaret feels her heart rate begin to increase, and she avoids contact with her friend, trying to stave off the tears that have begun to well in her eyes. "How can they be gone?" Carrie's voice, heavy with emotion, cracks. "Do you want to talk about it?"

At those words, a storm starts to brew in Margaret's chest, the dark, angry cloud working its way through her veins. "No, I don't want to talk about it," she spits out. "What on earth would I want to talk about? How my entire family is dead? How I don't get to watch my babies grow up? Or how I don't get to grow old with my husband? Or maybe we can chat over coffee about the fact that my heart *physically* hurts so much, that I wish I could rip it out of my chest and tear it to shreds just to put it out of its misery." Margaret glares at her friend, unable to control the raging monster taking form inside her.

"Margaret, I know you're hurting—" Margaret pulls her hand from her friend.

"Hurting doesn't even begin to describe how I feel." She watches the tears falling from her friend's eyes, but instead of finding comfort in a friend grieving alongside her, all she feels is jealousy. *How dare she cry when she still has everything.* "It's indescribable what I feel, Carrie. You can't put it into words. It's unfathomable. Everything, *everything*, I loved most in this world is gone. Everything that defined the core of my being is gone. Everything I found worth living for is gone. What the hell am I supposed to do now? How is this real life?"

"You didn't lose *everything*, Margaret. You still have me, your mom, AJ and Odette. You still have people who love you." Margaret glares at the table, angry that her best friend just doesn't get it. A heavy cloud of anger is released as

Margaret lets out a sigh, her shoulders relaxing. *There's no point in trying to explain it to her. She will never understand,* Margaret thinks to herself.

"Thanks for the groceries, Carrie. I really appreciate it. And I appreciate you coming over to check on me." Carrie gives her hand a squeeze. "But I think you should go. I just want to be alone right now."

Carrie stares intently at Margaret, trying to assess her true emotions. "You sure? I don't mind staying. We don't even have to talk. I can help you clean." Margaret thinks about the offer, trying to decide if company could be a good thing.

"Okay, I could use some help cleaning." Carrie smiles gladly, letting the tears welling in her eyes fall as she embraces Margaret in a strong hug. When she is finally released from the iron grip of her friend's hug, Margaret rises from the table, Carrie following suit.

"Cleaning supplies are in the hall closet. Just do whatever, anything would be helpful."

"Okay, sure." Carrie turns to head to the closet when Margaret's voice cuts through the air.

"But *don't* clean up the bedrooms. Leave those untouched."

"Of course," Carrie's sad eyes linger on her friend a moment before turning to collect her supplies. Margaret resumes the music throughout the house and resumes washing the legs of the kitchen table. A few songs pass before she realizes she should offer Carrie a snack or a beverage while she works. She sets her cloth down and leaves the kitchen looking for her friend.

She finds Carrie scrubbing the bathroom counter. "What are you doing?" Margaret doesn't even recognize the guttural, screaming voice coming from her own body. Carrie jumps in surprise, her eyes wide in panic.

"I'm cleaning the bathroom. There was toothpaste all over the counter."

"No," her voice becomes a mourning wail, filling the room with its agony. "No, no, no. What did you do?" She runs her hands along the spotless counter, touches the crystal-clear glass of the mirror. Heavy tears stream down her face, as she thinks about how bubblegum toothpaste will never litter this counter again.

"Margaret, I'm sorry. I was just cleaning. It was a mess in here."

"Leave. Now." Margaret refuses to look at Carrie, her anger boiling dangerously close to the surface.

"I'm so sorry. Please, Margaret, let me stay. I can keep helping. I want to be here with you. For you." At that moment, Carrie's phone starts ringing. The two friends lock eyes, as Carrie pulls the phone from her pocket. "Ugh, it's Tyler," she mumbles under her breath. The monster of anger and grief rolling in Margaret's chest breaks free, and all she feels is a furious jealousy.

"Get out!" Margaret bellows, making Carrie jump. Carrie scurries out of the bathroom, Margaret on her heels. She stops at the front door, turning to face Margaret, who refuses to lock eyes.

"Margaret, you're my very best friend. I can't possibly comprehend the pain you're feeling, but that doesn't mean I can't help you. I'm only a phone call away. No matter how loud you scream at me, I'll always be a phone call away." And with those words, Carrie steps out of the house, closing the door behind her.

Even with the upbeat country music swarming through the air, the house feels deafeningly quiet, and Margaret's head and heart are spinning with a whirlwind of feelings she can't control. Her palms grow clammy as her heart picks up speed, dread flooding her veins at the thought of another night alone in this house. She grabs her phone and calls AJ.

"Is everything okay?" Concern fills her brother's voice.

"No. I can't be here. I can't be in this house. Can I come over?"

"We both had to go into work for a little bit today to wrap up some things before taking time off, but go on over. Make yourself comfortable, you know where the hide-a-key is. I'll bring something home for dinner when I'm done with work."

"Okay, thanks."

"Call me again if you need anything, Mags. I'm here for you. Let me know if you want me to come home, and I'll leave here in a heartbeat."

"Thanks, AJ." She hangs up the phone and gathers a small bag of clothes and toiletries. She takes Jackson's blanket and Izzy's unicorn. From Austin's closet, she takes his favorite sweatshirt. As she's walking out the door, she remembers the checklist her mother left her, and grabs that as well. She pauses as she's pulling the car out of the driveway and looks up at the house before her. "Is this my life now?" she wonders out loud. "Unable to be at home in my own home?" She curses at the morbid irony, the angry monster brewing inside her again. She switches the car into reverse and begins her drive to her brother's house, doing her best to keep the monster from coming alive.

When Margaret enters AJ and Odette's home, she's met with the same unbearable silence she was trying to escape. "I need something to do," she thinks aloud. Her mind flutters to the checklist folded in her purse, but the idea of handling the business of death makes her stomach squirm unpleasantly, so she starts to wander the house, looking for something to do, anything to take her mind off life as she knows it.

She walks down to the basement, thinking she'll turn on the TV and make herself at home on the couch, but her attention is drawn to the giant bookshelf that covers the entire back wall of the room. It's filled with trinkets and decorative things, but there's a decent selection of books tucked in its corners as well. *It's been so long since I've sat down and read a book.* She runs her fingers gently along the spines as she skims the titles; some she recognizes, others are books she's never heard of before. Margaret plucks a thick book with a picture of a wishing well on the cover. *The Guardian* is written in gold scrawl across the cover. According to the blurb on the back of the book, it is a story of a woman living in Germany back in the 1940s and her role in hiding dozens of Jews during World War II. *Perfect,* Margaret thinks. She always enjoyed historical fiction.

She makes herself comfortable on the couch and begins reading. Almost immediately, she's transported to a different world, leaving her current pain and grief behind.

The sound of the garage door slamming shut snaps Margaret out of the pages of the story and back to present day. "Margaret?" AJ's booming voice floats down the stairs.

"I'm in the basement. I'll be right up." She walks into the kitchen to find AJ unloading bags of Chinese takeout onto the table.

"Hey, sis. What are you up to?"

"Found a good book downstairs, so I've just been reading."

AJ grins sideways at his sister while elbow deep in a paper bag, lifting the last box of food from the sack. "Nice. Odette's gonna be home any minute. Can you grab the plates? What would you like to drink?"

"I'll just have water," she decides as she sets the table. A moment later, Odette walks through the door.

"Hey y'all!" she shouts from the entryway.

"Hey honey," AJ calls back. "We're setting up dinner in here."

"Oh perfect, I'm famished. It smells wonderful. Hey, Margaret," Odette grabs Margaret in a warm hug as she enters the kitchen. They all take a seat at the table, and Margaret listens passively as they discuss the daily happenings of their job.

AJ changes the topic, putting Margaret on the spot. "So what did you do today, Margaret?"

"Me? Well, I cleaned the house top to bottom. Carrie came over for a bit. Then I came here and read for a handful of hours."

"Oh that's nice Carrie came by. I bet that felt good to see her."

"Yeah, I suppose."

"Did you get anything done on that list mom gave you?"

Guilt creeps into Margaret's gut. "No. I just couldn't yet. We have the service figured out, everything else can wait." Margaret feels AJ's eyes on her, but she refuses to look up from the sesame chicken she's picking at with her fork.

"That's alright, sugar. Don't let AJ bully you into stuff you ain't ready to do," Odette pats Margaret's hand. "You take your time."

AJ lets out a big sigh. "Yes, of course, take your time, Mags. But, you do have to get the eulogies written. Those actually *do* have a due date. At least try to focus on that tomorrow, okay?"

"Okay," Margaret dutifully agrees. They fill the rest of dinner talking about anything but Margaret's family, and she can't decide how she feels about it. She appreciates not having to talk about it, yet doesn't want to pretend as if the world is fine. So she lets AJ and Odette fill the majority of the conversation, as she picks at her rice and chicken. When they finish eating, they all clean up dinner and AJ suggests the three of them enjoy a movie to take their mind off things before calling it a night.

"No, I don't want to intrude on your time. I just couldn't be in my house anymore," Margaret explains. "I'll just head back downstairs and keep to myself. You guys do whatever it is you do on a typical Wednesday night. Thanks for letting me crash here."

"You sure?" AJ presses.

"Yes, I'm sure," she confirms, wrapping her brother in a hug. "Goodnight you two." She gives Odette a hug as well, before heading back to the couch in the basement. She picks up *The Guardian* and resumes her reading, immediately falling back in time to war-torn Germany, far away from twenty-first century Minnesota.

There is a large puddle of tears on the pillow Margaret had been sleeping on when she wakes in the middle of the night, her heart pounding furiously in her chest. Her body trembles as she sits up and wipes her face. "I don't know what's worse," she contemplates to the dark room. "Living in the empty reality of the day or reliving the horrors each night." She wraps her arms around herself, sobbing into her chest, and praying for any sort of relief.

When her tears have dried, she decides to walk upstairs to get some water for her parched throat. *Was I screaming in my sleep?* The house is blanketed in darkness, but Margaret refuses to turn any lights on, afraid of disrupting the still house and waking its occupants. But a light at the end of the hallway catches her eye, and she stops in tracks. Loud, heavy sobs escape through the cracks of the master bedroom resting at the end of the hallway.

"...so unfair, all of it. I think of those kids, those beautiful kids no longer here, and it makes me sick. I miss them so much already."

"I know, love, I know. I do too. I miss those beautiful babies too." Odette's voice is shaky and cracks, chipping a bit of Margaret's heart with it.

"And Margaret. I don't know what to do for her. What the hell am I supposed to do?"

Margaret doesn't hear a response, only the sound of Odette and AJ crying heavily together. Her stomach knots and her legs tremble beneath her at the sound of her brother's grief. She shakily takes herself back to the couch in the basement, completely forgetting about her parched throat. Her pillow welcomes her tears again, as she cries for AJ, cries for Odette, and cries for herself. But mostly, she cries for a life that once was and all the people that are hurting because of the life that now is.

Chapter Eleven

Friday, June 15, 2018

Margaret awakes the next morning deliciously buried in the luxurious pillows and blankets of the resort, yet groggy and with a raging headache. She pulls herself up to a sitting position against the headboard and groans when she recalls how the night before ended. She realizes her headache must be from all the crying that escaped before sleep washed over her. She closes her eyes, rests her head against the wall, and focuses on breathing. After a few minutes of some breathing exercises (the only exercise Margaret believes is worth doing), she opens her eyes and searches for her phone. It's still buried in her bag from the night before, and as she turns on the screen, she sees two texts.

The first text she opens is from Odette: ***Enjoy your last full day! I hope you found what you were looking for. Can't wait to hear about it. Xxx*** Margaret smiles warmly and sends a heart emoji back to her sister-in-law. She makes a mental note to be sure to bring back a souvenir for her.

The second note is from AJ: ***Keep up the momentum on your last full day. Go do something fun and make the most of the day. Love you.*** Warmth and longing flood over Margaret as she yearns to hug her brother. Her eyes begin to swim with fresh tears of guilt as she thinks about the way she treated Will last night, who was just trying to help her make the most of the her time on the island.

Margaret tries to brush it off and pushes herself off the bed. She desperately needs some ibuprofen for this pain throbbing in her head, so she quickly changes into some fresh clothes, grabs her bag, and makes her way to one of the shops on the resort.

Once in the store, she immediately makes a beeline to the medical supplies, grabbing a travel size bottle of ibuprofen and bringing it to the register. The smiling woman rings up her purchase, and Margaret swallows two pills with the water bottle in her bag. She stows the bottle back in her tote and takes her first true look around the store. Various products line the shelves and racks, from Hawaiian sweets and treats to clothing to souvenir knickknacks. She strolls leisurely through the aisles, searching for goodies to bring back to AJ, Odette, and her mother.

She comes across the clothing section, and Will is right: the store has plenty of beautiful Hawaiian sun dresses for Margaret to choose from. She runs her fingers along the racks, perusing the different colors, patterns, and styles available. One dress catches her eye, and Margaret pulls it from the rack to take a closer look. It's a beautiful flowing, bright yellow dress, painted with large, colorful tropical flowers in pinks and purples, that ties around the neck in a halter-top style fashion. Margaret takes the dress into the fitting room to try it on.

Once she has the dress on, she twists and turns in front of the mirror in the changing room. The white of the dress amplifies the sun-kissed skin she has developed during her stay, and the cinch at the waist accentuates her hips, hugging her curves in all the right ways. The pleated skirt fans out beautifully when Margaret twirls around the room and makes her feel like a little girl. She stops spinning and looks up, smiling at herself in the mirror. She changes back into her own clothes and drapes the dress over her arm. After grabbing some gifts to bring back to her family, she carries all the items up to the register to purchase. Margaret's mind wanders to Will as the woman packs up her purchase.

"Mahalo," she thanks the woman, as she takes her bag and steps back out into the Hawaiian sun. She pulls out her phone to check the time: it is almost nine o'clock. She walks with her bag over to the beverage hut near the beach and orders herself a cup of Waialua coffee. She keeps thinking about Will, unhappy and guilty over how she treated him. She pulls out her phone to send him a text.

Hey. I'm sorry about last night. Can we talk?

After hitting send, she sets the phone on the counter beside her, and pulls her book out from her bag. She figures she'll sit and enjoy her coffee and a book while she waits for Will's response.

After twenty minutes, she is still on the first page of book. She keeps glancing at her phone to see if Will has responded yet, only to be disappointed each time. She closes her book in a huff, unable to concentrate. The last dregs of her coffee are drained from her cup, then she climbs off her stool, gathers up her belongs, and trudges back to her bungalow.

Once back in her room, Margaret tosses the bag from the shop on her bed and walks out to the patio. She takes a seat on the wicker chair, and her mind wanders again to Will. Her stomach turns to knots as she worries about the idea of Will completely ignoring her and leaving last night as the last things she said to him.

Suddenly, her phone pings, and her heart drops to her stomach. She looks at the screen and it's Will. She opens the text, her heart racing with anticipation.

Hey. Yeah, we can talk. I don't have much time because of wedding stuff. Meet me at the Huli Huli Hut at 11?

Relief floods Margaret's heart.

Sounds perfect, she responds. Now to just kill time until eleven.

Margaret makes her way across the resort towards the Huli Huli Hut, her stomach in knots at the thought of seeing Will again. She tries to guess how mad he is at her, but that just makes her stomach churn, so she decides to focus on what she'll say instead. As she comes up to the hut, she finds him sitting on the lanai, a cold glass of water dripping condensation onto the table beside him. He's staring out at the waves flowing steadily on the sandy beach, seemingly deep in thought.

Margaret stops in her tracks and watches him for a moment, preparing herself. "Hey," she tentatively begins, as she takes the chair across him at the table. Will just nods and flashes a half-smile across the table. It's missing his one dimple. Margaret starts nervously spinning her wedding ring, trying to think about where to start. She decides to start where it's easiest.

"I'm so sorry for the way I reacted last night," Margaret begins. "I just..." she struggles to find the right words. "I just couldn't control all my emotions. It's been a long, exhausting - but fun - week, and I got angry and defensive and I'm really sorry. You've been so nice to me, and I was so rude." She moves her eyes from the sapphire spinning on her finger, to Will's face. His eyes are pouring into her, something raw and fierce burning behind his stare, and Margaret feels goosebumps growing up her arms. He doesn't make any attempt to add anything to the conversation, his jaw clenched as something fierce brews deep within his eyes. "I'll go. I'm sorry. I just wanted to say I'm sorry. Especially because you've made this trip mean so much more than I thought it would. So thank you. I'm sorry, and thank you." The words flow fast and furious out of Margaret's mouth, as she skittishly rises from the table to excuse herself, feeling foolish. Will's arm flashes out and grabs her wrist as she passes his chair. She stops in her tracks and slowly turns her gaze to him. He stands from the table, not taking his eyes off hers.

"Let's walk. Do you want a cup of coffee first?" His sudden willingness to be a part of the conversation throws Margaret off guard.

"No, I don't need a coffee. But I'd love to take a walk with you."

Will releases her wrist and leads the way down the path toward the beach. They walk in silence along the sand, the mid-day Hawaiian sun hanging high in the sky, its rays radiating heat on Margaret's shoulders. Will leads them to a shaded tide pool, secluded in the corner of the resort, and she is grateful for some relief from the scorching sun. He sits himself on a rock, turning his gaze out to the ocean waving before them. Margaret takes a seat beside him, her heart pounding nervously in her chest. Will inhales deeply, and breaks the silence, keeping his eyes on the blue water.

"Margaret, you're not the only one who knows unbelievable pain." He pauses, and Margaret swallows, turning her eyes to look at Will. His jaw is clenched, his focus hard on the horizon. "I was engaged. Her name was Emily," a slow, soft smile crawls across his face, replacing the scowl that previously hung in its place. "She was amazing. She was so smart, smart as a whip. And sassy. But in a fun way, you know? God, she was fun. She was always up for adventures. We'd go hiking and camping every weekend. She loved being outside. It didn't matter if it was raining or crappy weather, she was always wanting to hit up the state parks and hike around. She was fearless. She was - Emily. My Emily." A darkness falls over his eyes, and his jaw begins to clench again.

Will looks over to Margaret and locks his smoldering eyes with her own. His eyes are flooded with an ache she can feel in her own bones. "I always hated when she hiked alone," he continues. "Like I said, she was fearless. She thought the only other people out hiking were fellow nature enthusiasts." His voice cracks, and although his focus is burned into the ocean before them, she can still read the anger and anguish flashing across it. "It took them a week to find her body." Margaret reaches over and grasps his hand firmly in her own. Will returns the gesture with a light squeeze but doesn't move his eyes off the water.

The two sit side-by-side in silence, the crash of the waves the only sound in the air hanging between them. Will turns to look at Margaret, the light in his eyes replaced with swirling gray clouds of pain.

"You had a life Margaret. You built a life together with your husband, made memories with your children. You got to achieve plans you had made. I know not all of them, and I know you had a million more. I know, because I had a million plans too. The only difference is I didn't get to make any of my plans a reality." Will shifts his eyes down to Margaret's hands encompassing his own, and he begins to trace his thumb along her skin, as he struggles to find words. "I know it's hard. Believe me, I know it's hard when your whole world is taken away from you unexpectedly, when you don't get to finish your plans. But Margaret," His voice and thumb stop simultaneously, "I also know how important it is to keep living. After Emily died, I was a wreck. I was so angry at everyone, everything. I wanted to find the guy who did it and kill him myself. I actually spent multiple days combing that same park, looking for the creep that did it."

"Oh Will..."

"But then one day on one of my treks through the park, I came up to this bluff. It was spectacular. Absolutely breathtaking. I was up a couple hundred feet on this cliff, with this sparkling lake below that I swear was bluer than the ocean in front of us. And the sky. Not a cloud in the sky, just blue as far as the eye could see. There was a pair of eagles calling to each other as they circled in the air. It was just…it was like something out of a movie, you know? Almost like it couldn't even be real, it was so beautiful. And it just hit me: this is why Emily loved to be out in nature. I sat down, right there on the cliff, and I just listened. And breathed. And thought."

Will looks into Margaret's eyes, energy and light returning. "I realized, as I was sitting on that cliff, that if there was one thing Emily did well it was making the most of every moment she had. She loved to squeeze everything she could out of every day. And that's when I decided I would do the same. For Emily." Will rises from the rock, pulling Margaret up with him, their hands still clutched together. "And it saved me, Margaret, it truly saved me. I was going down a dangerous hole, but changing my perspective, saved me. I stopped thinking about all that I was missing and would never get to experience with Emily. Instead, I thought about all that I could do *for* her. Emily wasn't able to explore the world anymore, but I could. So I did. And I never say no to any opportunity. You need to try to do the same."

Margaret opens her mouth to protest, but Will stops her. "You need to keep living *for* your family, Margaret. You need to stop hiding behind books, trying to escape life. Your family wouldn't have wanted you to do that. And you're such a wonderful person, Margaret. You should be shining bright for everyone to see, not hiding behind a book all the time. You have so much to bring to this world." He runs his fingers through his shaggy hair. "It's been almost five years since Emily was taken from this world. I still miss her. I still think about her every day. Like you, there's something in every day that reminds me of her. That doesn't ever go away, it just gets…easier to manage. As we keep living, the pain takes up less of our world, because our world keeps getting bigger."

Margaret shifts her gaze to the sand, her toes tracing circles in the soft earth, unsure how to respond to all that Will has told her. "Will, I am so sorry that happened. What happened to your Emily…that's awful. Thank you for sharing your story with me." Margaret fumbles with her thoughts, trying to decide what to say next. It's a nice idea, Will's proposal on how to handle her grief, but it just seems so much easier said than done. She rests her head on his chest, suddenly heavy with a million thoughts running through her mind, and Will mimics the action, placing his cheek atop her hair. "I don't even know how I would start doing that," she confesses.

"You already have." She feels a small smile creep across the cheek laying softly atop her frizzy hair. A smile spreads across her own face as well, as she realizes Will is right; she has lived so much this past week, and her family has been a part of every moment. Her thoughts fixate on all that she has experienced in just the past couple days, and all the possibilities that still lie before her.

"I'd like to come to the wedding, if the invite still stands. I bought a dress." His head snaps up, his one-dimpled grin flashing at Margaret, making her feel relaxed and comforted.

"You bought a dress, huh? What if I say the invite has been rescinded?" His smirk is playful, his eyes shining again.

"Then I'd say be on the lookout for a wedding crasher, because I'm going to a luau tonight," Margaret smirks back.

Will's sparkling blue eyes stare straight into Margaret's soul, while something shifts on his face. Her heart begins to race as she feels the air around them change, growing heavy with emotions Margaret hasn't felt in a long time. Will takes a step toward Margaret, as her heart threatens to crack her ribs.

"Didn't you say you had a lot to do before the wedding?" Margaret asks, breaking the heat that has suddenly filled the air.

Disappointment flashes across Will's face. "Yeah, I should be getting with the guys. They'll be getting into their outfits any minute, and pretty sure my sister's sending a photographer to capture every moment." He doesn't take his eyes off her own, burning her with his gaze.

Margaret decides to start the momentum, so she turns on the spot and starts to walk back the way they came, holding her flip flops and relishing the silky, warm sand between her toes. She feels Will follow behind her but doesn't turn around to look at him. As they come to the point where sand meets grass, he pulls up alongside her, taking her by surprise when he slides his fingers between hers. The feeling of her hand interlocked with his sends butterflies fluttering around her stomach. They stand together, eyes locked for a moment before Will speaks.

"I'll text you the details, where to be and when," he informs her. His eyes comb her face intently, making heat rush up her neck to her cheeks.

"Okay," is all Margaret is able to whisper, her voice and her words tangled in his.

Will's thumb traces circles around Margaret's palm, sending pulsating electric currents from her fingers to her palpitating chest. She watches his face as he watches their hands, and she catches his brows come together ever so slightly in thought. A part of her yearns to reach out and touch his conflicted face, but her own conflictions fluttering within her keep her free hand hanging loosely at her side. Eventually, Will drops her hand, reconnecting his gaze with Margaret's.

"I need to go," his eyes speak more than his words, and Margaret nods as he flashes a quick smile goodbye and makes his way back to his room. She spends a moment watching him leave before making her own trek back to her to bungalow, trying to decipher her own emotions along the way.

The first thing Margaret does when she enters her bungalow is call her big brother. She curses when he doesn't answer, assuming he must still be at work. Just as she's about to toss her phone on the bed with her bag, the device pings, and Will's name lights the screen. She clicks open the message to find instructions for the evening.

The ceremony starts at 5:30 down on the south end of the beach. Just walk along the beach, and you'll see the chairs set up and everything. I'm a groomsman, so I won't be able to sit with you, but I'll find you after the ceremony. Luau starts at 6:30, but there's no assigned seating, even for me, so I'll find you after the ceremony and take you to the luau.

Margaret reads the message three times over, second-guessing her decision to attend at all. Her phone pings again.

I'm so happy you're coming.

Well, that doesn't help settle any of the nerves she feels coursing through her veins, but it does help her decide not to cancel. Margaret grabs a book off the counter, a bottle of water from her fridge, and heads out to the balcony. *Getting lost in a book sounds like the perfect way to kill time and not think about tonight,* she tells herself. Margaret plops herself down on one of the wicker chairs on her patio and uses the other chair to prop her feet up. She turns her gaze out to the ocean. As she listens to the waves rolling on the shore in the distance, she closes her eyes, relishing the feel of the wind softly blowing across her skin. A flicker of sadness passes through her heart as she thinks about how this time tomorrow, she'll be traveling back home. But she shakes the thought away, determined to enjoy her last full day on the island. She opens her eyes to the blinding Hawaiian sun, flips her book open to where she last left off, and begins to lose herself between the pages.

Margaret stands before the mirror, cursing at her reflection for not packing a curling iron. "What the hell am I supposed to do with this mop?" she questions to the empty room. Her long brown hair has grown wild from fierce humidity, the salty sea air, and windswept days exploring the island. Thinking she would spend all day every day on the beach reading, Margaret had opted to leave all hair products and tools at home. This means her natural curls and waves have made a dramatic appearance. And while it definitely matches the whole "beach vibe" she has been showcasing the past week, it definitely doesn't meet her expectations for "wedding approval."

Margaret begins to pull the strands upwards, attempting to pile them in a messy, yet elegant bun atop her head. She pulls a few strands out of the hair band, letting the curls frame her face. The Hawaiian sun has gifted her with a subtle, glowing tan across her cheeks, so she is not at all upset that all she brought for makeup is the lip gloss in her purse. After glossing up her full lips, she slips into her flowered dress from the resort shop. When she looks into the mirror again, she feels satisfied that she looks like someone who would be a guest at a beach wedding, and smiles at herself.

"It will be fun," she affirms. She gives herself an encouraging nod, stuffs her phone in her purse, and leaves the safety of her bungalow to attend a stranger's luau wedding on the beaches of the Hawaiian islands. She doesn't take a single book with her. Margaret chuckles to herself as she thinks about where she stands today, the absurdity of her reality in this moment. Her walk slows as the wedding seating comes into view. A small group of about thirty people mingle about. Margaret stops in her tracks, nervously watching the group hug each other and laugh together. It's very clear Margaret is intruding on an intimate family affair, and she begins to second guess her decision. Just as she's about to turn around and cancel her plans, Will walks into view.

Margaret watches him from a distance, his wide, one-dimpled smile hanging easily on his face as he walks around offering hugs and handshakes to various guests. She is surprised to see him wearing a floral Aloha shirt with khaki shorts and sandals. As she takes in his Hawaiian attire, Margaret realizes everyone wandering around the seats is clothed in soft, summery Hawaiian clothing, and she suddenly feels silly for stressing so much about what she would wear. *Of course this is what a Hawaiian beach wedding would look like,* she thinks to herself, smiling at the sight before her. Her eyes find Will again, as he nods along to a conversation with a young couple. He glances around the small crowd as he listens, and his eyes catch Margaret. His quick sweep over her body is not missed by her, and it causes a sudden rush of heat to flood her through her body. When his eyes lock onto her own, his gaze his smoldering. He grins happily her way, excuses himself from the conversation he was participating in, and strides over to Margaret.

Her nerves flare up as he approaches, and she instinctively starts to spin her ring. Without any words, Will's arms wrap around Margaret in a firm hug. After the initial shock wears off, Margaret leans into her friend, enjoying the embrace. She closes her eyes and inhales Will's sultry cologne. Austin's face flashes before her eyes - Will's cologne smells exactly the same as Austin's. She works hard to push him from her mind, trying to focus on the excited energy radiating from Will's embrace. He pulls away from Margaret, beaming.

"I'm so happy you came."

Margaret returns his infectious smile. "Me too." And even though the thought of sitting with strangers at the wedding of someone she just met three days ago makes her feel slightly unsettled, she realizes she is genuinely happy to be standing here before Will.

Will takes her hand and leads her over to the small crowd of guests. He takes a few minutes introducing Margaret to a few of his relatives—some cousins, aunts, uncles—and then he recommends she take a seat. "We're going to start in a few minutes, so I have to get back to the rest of the wedding party. Don't wander when the ceremony finishes, okay? I want to find you again." Margaret swears Will's smile is the biggest she has seen it since she first laid eyes on Baggage Claim Man, and she returns the smile warmly and easily.

"Okay, I won't wander, or abandon the big event," she confirms playfully. Will gives her hand a quick squeeze, leaves her in her chair, then walks to the front of the crowd to announce everyone take their seats. As he makes his way away from the guests and back towards wherever his sister and the rest of the bridal party are hiding, he flashes one last toothy smile her way, awakening a whirlwind of butterflies fluttering in her belly.

Margaret fidgets with her wedding ring as everyone takes their seats around her. Beautiful Hawaiian music begins from somewhere behind her, the sound of ukulele chords floating on the tropical breeze. The guests face the ocean as the honey sun begins to dip closer to the horizon, its rays bouncing off the rolling waves. In front of the guests sits a simple wooden archway, donned in huge, vibrant tropical flowers matching the pattern of Margaret's dress. Twisting green ivy snakes up the sides of the arch, working its way between and among all the flowers. As her eyes comb the beautiful flowers in front of her, an older gentleman passes along her side as he makes his way toward the flowered archway. When the man reaches the archway, he turns to face the crowd, and Margaret immediately recognizes Keith's leathery yet regal face, and she's transported back to her flight down to this amazing island, his warm hand gently patting her own. Her mind starts whirring, trying to make connections on how the kind man might know Will's family.

As her mind is spinning, Keith nods at something behind Margaret, and soon she hears the soft plod of feet trekking through the sand as the bridal party begins to make its appearance beneath the archway next to Keith. As the group makes its way down the aisle, Keith's eyes roam the crowd of guests, smiling leisurely as he combs those in attendance. His smiling eyes catch Margaret's and stop, holding her gaze. He gives Margaret a wink, which she returns with a shy smile, curious to know how Keith is connected to Will's family.

After the entire wedding party is standing beneath the arch, the ukulele changes its song, sounding just as beautiful as it did with the first tune. Keith's strong voice booms out over the crowd. "Please rise," he announces, raising his hands in motion with his words. The guests all shift to a standing position and turn their eyes to the back of the chairs as Will's sister begins her descent down the aisle, her father's arm locked around her own. Kara is absolutely radiant. Her sparkling white teeth shine through her very large, open smile, obvious joy and excitement shining from her eyes. She seems to be pulling her dad down the aisle more than her dad is walking her down the aisle; her eagerness to get to her soon-to-be husband is a stark contrast to the leisurely stroll her father seems determined to maintain, as if soaking up the last of these moments of his baby girl as his own.

As Jack passes Kara's hand over to Chris upon reaching the alter, he wipes the first of his tears from his eye and kisses his daughter softly on the cheek. Margaret's heart catches in her throat, as a rush of emotions begin to flood her. She recalls AJ walking her down the aisle of her own wedding, giving her away to Austin. She's suddenly, once again, very homesick for her big brother.

Keith smiles warmly at the young couple and welcomes everyone in the crowd to the ceremony on this beautiful Hawaiian day. Margaret sits attentively, her heart pounding in her chest. She begins spinning her wedding ring, eyes focused on Keith, trying to avoid looking at the young, happy couple radiating love, hopes, and dreams, as conflicting emotions begin to battle for space within her mind.

"Love. That's why we're all here today, right? To celebrate love. But what is love?" begins Keith. "People often ask that question and over-complicate the answer. But I'm a farmer, a simple man, so I'm here to talk to you today about love in the simplest, most relatable thing I know - farming." Keith's eyes twinkle as he reaches into the pocket of his Levis and pulls out a small, glass bottle. Inside the bottle rattle two barely visible seeds. "Seeds are my life. As a farmer, I dedicate my days to making sure my seeds have everything they need to grow and flourish.

I first make sure my soil is fertile and ready to grow my crops. Then, when the weather doesn't cooperate, I irrigate. I fertilize. I pull weeds. I make it my priority to take care of my seeds so they can grow into the sturdy, fruitful crops they're meant to be. Because when my farm is flourishing, I am flourishing.

That's our job as a spouse. Kara, look into the eyes of your soon-to-be husband. Chris, look into your bride's eyes. To have a successful marriage, you need to make taking care of your spouse a priority in your life. Nurture them. Care for them. Provide them with all that you can to help them be successful. Because when your spouse flourishes, so will you. Your love for each other will grow.

But there's two important things to keep in mind as you take care of your 'seed.' First, the soil you plant your seed in is one of the most important parts of being a farmer. If your soil is not healthy, it is virtually impossible for your seed to grow to its full potential. The same is true for your marriage. You cannot nurture your spouse if you do not also nurture yourself. Second, a farmer can't control the weather. Our crops are exposed to the elements: wind, rain, sun, all of it. Your marriage is also exposed. As much as we sometimes would like to, we can't live in our own little bubbles. Outside forces will affect your marriage, some for the good, others for the bad. Sometimes it will be people, other family members. Other times it will be finances or work or kids. Life will be hard. It will be messy. It will get crazy. There's no avoiding it. The storms are going to come, the wind is going to howl, and the rain is going to pour. But the sun always comes out again. Always. That I can promise you." Keith pauses, his eyes shining warmly on the couple before him. But Kara and Chris have eyes only for each other. Their smiles radiate in a way that makes an almost-stranger in the crowd feel genuinely happy for their future.

The happy couple share their vows for each other, and Keith moves on to the giving of the rings. Margaret's cheeks are wet with tears as she watches, her heart breaking with the happy memories of her own wedding day. She recalls the giddy joy making a bounce in her step as AJ walked her down the aisle, Austin standing at the altar, smiling down at her with tear-filled eyes. She remembers the feel of his hands holding her own as the priest spoke to the crowd, slightly clammy, shaking just a tad. In their vows, she spoke of hopes and dreams for the future, and Austin declared his fierce love, devotion, and admiration for the woman standing before him. She remembers lying in bed with him that night, after all the commotion had been swept away, and falling asleep to dreams of all that their future would hold. Soft tears escape her eyes as she recalls all those feelings and fantasies; so many fantasies that will never come to life.

Margaret wipes at the tears in her eyes, a flurry of mixed emotions swirling in the pit of her stomach. All at once, her heart breaks for her family gone, yet rejoices in the memories they made together. She rises as the new bride and groom make their way down the aisle, clutching each other's hands while the bounce in their steps carry them along the sand. The rest of the wedding party follows, and Will flashes Margaret a smile as he passes on his way to join his little sister at the back of the seating area. Keith remains standing at the arch, watching the rest of the participants exit the archway. After the last member of the bridal party passes the chairs, the guests follow suit and make their way to pay their congratulations to the newly married couple. Margaret instead makes her way to straight to Keith, not tearing her gaze from the piercing amber eyes staring back at her.

"Miss Maggie," Keith smiles at Margaret as she approaches. "Fancy seeing you here. I almost didn't recognize you."

"Keith," Margaret begins, extending her hand. "I suppose I look different all done up for the wedding." Margaret smiles. Though she only spoke with Keith briefly on the plane, there's something about him that makes her feel as if she is catching up with an old friend. There is so much comfort offered in his kind eyes.

Keith chuckles. "No, no, it's not that. Though you do look beautiful, if I may admit so." His smile is warm. "Hawaii looks good on you. You're absolutely glowing."

Margaret feels herself blush. "Really? Glowing? Must be my tan." She tries to laugh off the compliment she wasn't prepared for.

"No, it's your eyes, my dear. Your eyes are shining in a way they weren't almost a week ago." Margaret stares into the eyes of the old man, as he takes her hands in his. He brings his face close to her own, and Margaret notices the specks of gold within his eyes. "It's okay to be happy, Miss Maggie," he whispers, patting the top of her hand. "You don't need to feel guilty about it." Margaret's breath catches in her throat, just as Will finds his place beside her.

"Keith!" Will happily announces, as Keith drops Margaret's hands from his grasp to be replaced with Will's. "I see you've met Margaret." Keith shoots Margaret a sparkling glance and turns his attention to Will.

"Yes, a woman who gives the beauty of this island a proper contender," he winks at Will.

Without looking at Margaret, Will affirms his assessment, "That she certainly does." Margaret feels heat rising up her neck and turns her attention again to the sand beneath her feet. "Great ceremony, Keith. Absolutely lovely. As always, you have a wonderful way with words."

"Well, decades of experience often lead to an abundance of stories and words with which to tell them."

"Your experiences are priceless. You had the room in tears, thank you." Margaret looks up to see Keith smile humbly at Will. "But on that note, I actually came over here to steal Margaret away from you, if that's okay?"

Keith pins his eyes on Margaret, and Margaret gets the uncomfortable feeling he's assessing her. "Of course. Margaret, I'm glad to be reacquainted. I do hope I'll have the chance to talk some more before the night is over."

"Yes, I'll make sure to find you and continue our chat," Margaret smiles. "So where are you taking me?" she asks as she turns to Will. Will takes her hand as if it's the only natural thing to do and starts leading her toward the foamy surf crashing along the shore. Margaret feels Keith's eyes on the two of them as they wander, but she keeps her focus forward facing. She's hyper-attentive to the feel of Will's fingers laced between her own, noting how the act feels both foreign yet natural at the same time.

"Just on a quick walk before I have to be at pictures. I feel like I haven't had as much time with you today as I've gotten used to and just wanted to see you again." His sapphire eyes hold her gaze, and she swears those beautiful blue eyes hold the universe, as if everything that ever was and ever will be can be seen in his eyes. Margaret's heart flutters at his words and the feel of his thumb tracing circles on her hand. They stroll along the shore in silence, listening to the rolling waves and watching the fire of the sun slowly dip closer to the horizon.

Eventually, Will breaks the silence. "Keith used the word 'reacquainted' when he was speaking to you. How do you two know each other?"

"Oh, I don't really *know* him, know him. He sat next to me on my connecting flight down here. We chatted a bit, that's all."

"Ah."

"How does your family know Keith?"

"Oh Keith is an old family friend. Before my dad's manufacturing company took off, he actually worked on Keith's ranch. Keith has several hundred acres of land, and he's got a bunch of animals. Mostly cows, but some horses, pigs, and goats and things too. Keith was like an uncle to me growing up. As kids, we were always going with my dad to the ranch. We'd run around and play while my dad and Keith and the others worked. We did some chores around the ranch too, of course. And then my dad started his business manufacturing farm and ranching equipment. Keith was his very first customer, for obvious reasons. Anyway, he's just always been a part of our family, it feels. Kind of like an extra uncle or grandpa." Will stops their progress on the beach and glances back toward the wedding. "Actually, speaking of family, we should probably head back. I'm sure Kara and Chris are done with their separate pictures, and it'll be time for me to get in on the action." Margaret's heart sinks a little as they make their way back toward the archway. She has come to savor her time with Will as something treasured and healing.

At the entrance to the luau stand two beautiful Hawaiian women in grass skirts, each holding a pile of leis for the incoming guests. The event is set up like a large outdoor picnic. Round, wooden tables are spaced throughout the grass, and long buffet tables draped in floral cloth rest behind the tables. Margaret assumes the tables will soon be stacked full with food and desserts, and the thought of some Hawaiian cuisine makes her mouth water. In front of the tables sits a simple wooden stage. On the left of the stage stands a row of ornate drums. Behind the stage, the glowing Hawaiian sun dances across the crashing waves of the Pacific.

"Aloha!" The melodic voices of the beautiful Hawaiian women ring out in unison. The woman on the right drapes a lei around Margaret's neck, as the woman on the left decorates Will. She rubs the velvety flower petals, admiring the soft, smooth sensation on her fingertips. After receiving his lei, Will turns smiling to Margaret.

"Okay, I have to go join my family for pictures. Are you going to be okay until I get back?"

"Yes. I'll be fine. I'll just go sit at the bar and try to make small talk with people."

"Okay. Promise you won't pull out a book and miss the fun?" Will smirks at Margaret.

"I didn't even bring a book tonight," Margaret proudly retorts.

Will's eyes sparkle playfully as he smiles proudly at her. He lifts her hand to his lips, and brushes a soft, quick kiss on the back of her hand, before turning to go find his sister. Margaret is left standing breathless, the air in her lungs having left her when Will's lips electrified her skin. She subconsciously rubs the back of her hand where his mouth grazed as she makes her way to the bar in a daze. She finds an empty stool and orders herself a glass of ice water, not wanting to dive into drinking too fast. The last thing she needs tonight is getting too intoxicated and making a fool of herself in front of people she just met. The clinking of glasses and bottles behind the counter is met with the sound of the wooden stool beside her scraping along the ground. Margaret turns to see Keith pulling himself a seat alongside her. Immediate comfort floods over Margaret, and the flash of Will's lips on her skin fades from her mind.

"Hello, stranger," Margaret smiles at Keith.

"Hello, beautiful. I'll just take a water," Keith gestures to the bartender. "So you've met Will, I see." He's turned his attention to Margaret, but she doesn't say anything. She sips from her glass, waiting to see where Keith decides to take the conversation. Keith laughs boldly, the deep sound emanating from the pit of his belly. "Don't be shy, Margaret. Like I said earlier: it's okay to be happy."

"Why do you say things like that to me? Like, 'it's okay to be happy' and on the plane, all that talk about running away. What makes you think to say those things to me? Do I look unhappy?"

Keith takes a long draw from his glass, seeming to buy time before answering her. "I told you on the plane: I have run away before too. I know what a runner looks like." He watches as Margaret begins to spin the sapphire on her finger. After a moment, he places his leathered hand on top of her fidgeting hands and waits for her to look his way. She takes a deep breath, then looks into those piercing golden eyes. "I'm not gonna ask what it is you're running from, that's not my business." Margaret exhales a sigh of relief, grateful she doesn't feel obligated to retell her story to another stranger. "But can I ask - has Hawaii given you what you came for?"

Margaret thinks on his words a moment. "I don't know. I don't even know exactly what I expected. I mean, have I had a good time? Of course. Yes. Thanks almost entirely to Will." Her voice trails off as she thinks of all of their adventures these past few days, and a faint smile creeps across her face.

"Margaret, this world is a big place, and we're just tiny specs on this Earth. And we're only here for the blink of an eye," he pauses to look at Margaret. "Though something tells me you already know that." She refuses to look at Keith and turns all of her focus on fighting the tears that are suddenly biting at her eyes. Keith sighs and places his hand on top of Margaret's once more. "Don't waste the time you have, Margaret. Grief is okay. Pain is inevitable. But don't let those things keep you from enjoying this life you're given...even if it seems unfair to be enjoying it." Margaret looks up at Keith, her eyes swimming.

"Oh, my dear," he gives Margaret's hand a squeeze and lets out a heavy sigh. "I lost my wife almost forty years ago. Beth died of cancer, and I ran. I ran away from life and into the bottom of the bottle. She was my best friend, the most beautiful woman in every room. She was my Beth. And I watched her get sicker and sicker, completely helpless to do anything to stop it. She died, and I ran to the bottle."

Margaret watches the lines on Keith's face shift and move as he recalls his story, and her heart breaks for him. His face still reads both pain and love for his wife after all these years.

"It took me a long time to stop running," Keith continues. "A long time. But I just woke up one morning, sick of running. Sick of hurting. Sick of feeling sorry for myself. Sick of this pit I had dug myself into. So I turned around, and I started running in a different direction. I started running back to my roots." Keith stops to take a long drink from his water. "It wasn't easy. It certainly wasn't a straight and narrow journey by any means. And it wasn't fast. But eventually, I found my way back home, back to happiness."

Margaret sips her water, thinking about Keith's story. She looks at him, and, surprisingly, finds his eyes sparkling with joy, rather than grief from reliving his darkest days. "How did you make it happen?" she whispers, suddenly aware she's moved to the edge of her seat.

"I bought a ranch," Keith's belly laugh rings out again. "I gave myself something else to live for. I had animals. And my animals needed me. I couldn't lay in bed drunk all day, I needed to get up and tend to my ranch. The physical labor was good for my soul. The animals were therapeutic. All of it was good."

Margaret goes back to spinning her sapphire, thinking about Keith's words.

"You two found each other again." Will's voice sneaks up from behind Margaret, making her jump out of her thoughts. She spins around on her stool, and smiles up at Will, happy to see him again.

"How were the pictures?" she asks, grateful for a new topic of conversation.

"Ah, fine. Glad they're done so I could come find you again." Will's face is radiating, and Margaret's heart flutters at the sight of someone so genuinely happy to see her. Keith clears his throat, breaking the air between them.

"Well, Miss Maggie, it was a pleasure chatting with you. I'll leave the two of you be." Keith stands from his stool and takes his water from the bar. "Have fun tonight, kids." Keith winks at the pair and wanders off to mingle with other guests.

Will laces his fingers with Margaret's and leads her to a table close to the stage. "Let's grab a good spot for the show before they're all taken."

As Margaret takes a seat at the table, Will continues to stand. "I'll grab us some drinks before it starts. What can I get you?"

"Tell them I want to try something local. Surprise me!"

Will flashes a smile at Margaret and nods, as he turns to head to the bar. Margaret hasn't been sitting alone for more than a minute before Will's parents come up to her. "Margaret!" Mary happily exclaims. "It's so good to see you here! Will mentioned he was going to see if you were free to come."

"Yes, thank you so much for letting me tag along. The ceremony was beautiful."

"Wasn't it? I think I was a puddle of tears the whole time."

"You and me both, Mary," Jack adds. Margaret smiles warmly at the proud parents.

"Would you two like to sit with me and Will?" Margaret invites.

"Oh you're so kind. We'd love to, but the parents, the bride, and the groom are all at the center table over there," Mary explains.

"Ah, gotcha. Speaking of bride and groom, where are Kara and Chris? I've been keeping my eye out for them to wish them congratulations, but I haven't seen them."

"Oh they're probably wrapping up the last of their pictures with their photographer," Jack explains. "They should be here any minute I would think. We're supposed to get started in about ten minutes or so."

"Okay, well I'll keep my eye out then." Margaret smiles.

"It's so nice to see you, dear," Mary pulls Margaret in for a squeeze. "But we're going to get settled at our table now. Have a wonderful time."

"Thank you, again, for letting me tag along." The couple give a nod and smile at Margaret as they wave goodbye to head to their table, stopping to visit with others along their way.

Will makes his way back to Margaret, setting a frothy, white beverage before her. The drink has a tint of yellow to it, and a chunk of pineapple and a cherry have been speared together with a toothpick, resting on the top of the foam. Margaret clasps her hands around the glass and inhales the tropical, fruity scent. "Mmm. Smells delicious. What is it?"

"It's called a *chi chi*, apparently. It's pineapple juice, cream of coconut, sugar, and ice.

"This is delicious," she whispers, eyes closed, relishing the cool, refreshing taste. "Good choice."

"Well thank the bartender. I told him to surprise me with a taste of Hawaii."

Margaret laughs. "Well if I had to give a taste to Hawaii, this would definitely be it." Her eyes close again as she takes another long slurp from her straw. When she opens her eyes, she sees Will watching her with his one-dimpled smile planted on this face. She tries to act nonchalant, pretending that his burning eyes don't set her heart on fire. "So, I have a *chi chi*. What did you get?"

Will holds his glass up, showing off a blend of bright red and white foaming swirls. "It's called a lava flow. It's got strawberries, bananas, rum, pineapple..." his voice trails off and his eyes shift from his glass to Margaret. "I wanted a little taste of Hawaii too," he smirks in her direction.

Margaret giggles at Will, flashing him a playful smile.

"What's so funny?"

"I mean, it's kind of a froufrou drink, isn't it?"

"Froufrou? It's lava! I mean, does it get any more masculine than lava?"

Giggles bubble uncontrollably from Margaret. Will watches her with adoration in his eyes, and she feels her skin grow hot, a feeling occurring more and more frequently it seems, and only leaving Margaret more and more conflicted each time. Will assesses his drink before him and joins in with Margaret, the pair's musical laugher floating from the table. Kara and Chris enter the luau, both radiating happiness, hands tightly intertwined. "Oh!" Margaret exclaims, rising from her seat. "I've been waiting for those two to make their appearance. I need to tell them congratulations quick before the luau starts. I'll be back in a minute." Margaret takes off for the newlyweds, leaving her glass and Will at the dinner table.

"Kara! Chris!" Margaret waves as she approaches. "Hey. I just wanted to come over and say, first of all, thank you for letting me crash your wedding."

"Margaret!" Kara squeals, pulling her in for a quick hug. "Will told me you might be coming. No thanks needed, I'm glad you could join. There's plenty of food and fun to go around."

"Thanks. The ceremony was absolutely beautiful. And I can't wait for this luau! Sounds like it should be a fun change of pace from all of the other wedding receptions I've been to."

"Yeah, should be fun," Kara agrees. "After the show, we'll still do a DJ and dance and cake and all that fun stuff. We're actually having pineapple up-side-down cake for our wedding cake, 'cause, you know, Hawaii, right?" Kara laughs, absolutely beaming with joy.

"That's fantastic, I love it," Margaret agrees. "Well, I am going to get back to my table before this thing starts. Thanks again, guys. You both look so happy. Congratulations!"

The three new friends give quick hugs, and Margaret departs to reclaim her seat next to Will. A few more guests have joined their table, and Will is deep in a conversation with a young man and woman sitting beside him. He looks up from the couple as Margaret sits back down beside him. "Margaret," Will begins with a smile. "I'd like you to meet my cousin Trevor, and his wife Julianne."

"Hi," Trevor reaches across the table to shake Margaret's hand. "Will was just telling us how you two met."

"Oh he was, was he?" Margaret grins at Will.

"Yeah - apparently you had some trouble at the baggage claim?" Will starts laughing, and Margaret shoots him a glare, feeling her face go red.

"Oh *that* first time we met. I thought maybe he would start at the tiki bar on the beach," Margaret says, as she gives a giggling Will a nudge with her shoulder.

"Now that wouldn't be the first time we met, would it?"

Margaret just glares at Will, fighting the smirk growing on her face. She's about to bite back a retort when the lights go down and music begins flowing into the party.

A Hawaiian man ascends the stage at the front of the room. He is adorned in a crimson skirt starkly decorated with deep black swirls and ribbons. Matching black swirls are tattooed across his sculpted tanned skin, and large bands of long green grass wrap around his thick wrists and solid calves just below his knee. "Aloha!" the man shouts energetically out to the guests. "And welcome to this very special edition of The Hibiscus Cove Luau!" The small crowd begins cheering and clapping.

"My name is Mano, and I'm going to be leading our big event this evening. Tonight, as you all know, we are celebrating a very special day for a very special couple. Everyone please give a special round of applause for our most exclusive guests, Mr. and Mrs. Kara and Chris Bernard!" The crowd begins clapping again, as the newlyweds stand from their table and wave energetically to their family and friends before them. "Come on up here, lovebirds." Kara and Chris take hold of each other's hands and make their way up to the stage, each of them beaming as warmly as the setting sun.

Mano wraps his arm around Chris and pulls him in for a side hug. "Congratulations, you two," he says warmly into his microphone for all to hear. "You two are absolutely radiant, and I think I speak for everyone in this room when I say it's obvious that you are very much in love." Kara gazes adoringly at her new husband beside her. "In Hawaii, we have a special saying that I want to share with you: '*No Keia La, No Keia Po, A Mau Loa.*' It means, 'From this day, from this night, forever more.'" A light sigh weaves through the crowd. "And that's what I wish upon you two tonight, this very special night. May the love you feel and radiate today last forever more." The guests clap in agreement, and Chris pulls his new wife in for a deep kiss, dipping her elegantly on the stage.

Margaret looks on fondly, a mix of both deep yearning and genuine happiness mingling in her veins, as she thinks about Mano's words - love living on forever more. She thinks of Austin and her children, how she loves them as fiercely and deeply now as she ever has before, and how she always will.

"Alright, alright," Mano chuckles into his microphone. "You two can take that back to your table now, because it is time to feast! No luau is complete without an abundance of delicious, mouth-watering Hawaiian food! The imu has been smoking some of the best food you'll have during your stay on this magnificent island. We've got *poi*, kalua pig, *laulau*, and an array of delicious Hawaiian desserts. Plus there's an entire table dedicated for you to build your own poke." Murmurs of excitement fill the room, as heads turn to try to see the buffets set up at the back. "We'll let the bride and groom and their table help themselves first, then it's a free for all! Once you all have your fill of delicious foods, the *real* party starts." A wide smile spreads across his face as he winks at the crowd before him.

He sets the microphone back into its stand on the stage, then gestures towards to Kara and Chris, signaling they can get the buffet line started. The sound of chairs scraping against the floor and voices resuming their conversations fill the air, with light island music floating around the room. Margaret follows Will up to the buffet table, her stomach rumbling in anticipation as the various aromas filter through her senses. Assorted meats are wrapped in large, green banana leaves. Mounds of rice are piled into bowls throughout the table. Several types of fish Margaret has never seen before lie in platters, as well as something that Margaret thinks may be squid. Determined to have a true Hawaiian experience, Margaret scoops a little bit of everything onto her plate, and she watches as Will does the same. The far end of the table is piled with exorbitant amounts of fruit, which Margaret eagerly adds to her plate.

As she walks back to her table, she giggles to herself at the sight of her enormous platter of food. "Hungry?" Will smirks her way, as he pulls up alongside her.

Margaret laughs. "A bit. I just wanted to try everything!"

"Yeah, I hear you. Me too. That's why I got *two* plates." Margaret didn't notice at first because she was distracted by Will's oceanic eyes, but he is indeed holding two plates loaded with every food from the menu. A warm smile lights her face, and she feels better about her own plate.

The two friends make small talk with the cousins sharing their table while they all enjoy their Hawaiian cuisine, the sound of ukuleles and the crashing waves as their background music. Margaret finds she is thoroughly enjoying herself, though as an avid lover of food, it's hard for Margaret not to enjoy herself when she's eating. As her mind wanders to how she never thought she would be able to say she enjoys the taste of squid, the lights dim down low again, and the music amps up. Margaret's chest begins to vibrate in tandem with the booming drums that have begun to beat rhythmically throughout the room. A string of beautiful sun-kissed Hawaiian women flood the stage, their grass skirts floating on their hips with each step, seeming to sash and sway with each beat of the drums. They immediately flow into a choreographed dance, their arms flowing and waving through the air, their hips swirling and shaking with the music. As they continue their dance, several men stomp rhythmically onto the stage behind the women. Their attire matches Mano's, and they join the women in a ritualistic dance of stomps and chants. The performance comes to an end, and the dancers take a bow to the claps and cheers of the guests present. Mano comes out on the stage to introduce the next performance.

"Do you want another drink? I can get us some quick refills between per-formances," Will whispers. His warm breath on her neck tantalizes her skin, spreading goosebumps up and down her arms.

"Yeah, sure. I'll just have water this time around. Thanks, Will."

Will shoots her his signature one-dimpled smile and rises from the table to refresh their drinks. She watches him walk away, her heart and her mind sending her all sorts of mixed messages. She reflects on the growth of their friendship this past week. There's something about Will that makes him feel familiar and comfortable even though she barely knows him. She has grown to appreciate and crave his companionship, and their easy conversations make her feel as if she's in the company of an old, familiar friend rather than a new acquaintance. Yet as much as she considers Will a friend, there's a magnetic pull of something she can't quite name whenever she's in his presence. It's in the way she catches him watching her with his stark blue eyes, and the way her skin tingles with a simple brush of his fingers. It stirs feelings in Margaret that leave her both breathless and confused.

She turns her attention back to the stage as Mano announces the fire dancers are going to be making their debut. As he exits the stage, the pounding drums begin again, and a lone fire dancer walks onto the stage. The man is huge, his muscles threatening to rip the grass bands wrapped around his bulging calves. His broad, tanned chest houses pecs the size of dinner plates, and a smattering of symmetrical abs carve their way down his smooth stomach. Stark black tattoos decorate his bulbous biceps. In each saucer-like hand he holds a giant stick adorned with raging flames on each end. The dancer spins and twirls each blazing baton with ease, as if he's twirling a simple dancer's ribbon. The drumming intensifies, and more fire dancers line the stage. Will makes it back to the table with their beverages just as the line of fire dancers fall into their choreographed performance. Margaret is on the edge of her seat, enthralled by the spectacle before her. She glances at Will to gauge his reaction to the amazing show, but Will's not watching the fire dancers. His eyes are locked on Margaret, smiling at her child-like excitement.

Margaret feels her skin flush and quickly turns her attention back to the stage. A strange sensation burns in the pit of her stomach, something she hasn't felt in a long time. She tries to focus on the dancers and ignore the beat of her heart pounding for release from its cage.

Mano returns to the stage, microphone in hand, a beaming smile on his face. "How about that show, everyone? Let's give it up for our performers!" The guests respond with a wave of cheers and claps. "*Mahalo, mahalo.* What a way to celebrate this special occasion. Our traditional luau is over but that doesn't mean we have to stop celebrating the special couple. Refresh your drinks, grab some more desserts, and put on your dancing shoes. We're going to take some time to convert the stage into a dance floor and then keep the good times rolling." Whoops and shouts emanate from the crowd as some men come out and start disassembling the stage.

"I hope you're a dancer," Will begins the small talk as the transition takes place.

"I'm not drunk enough for dancing yet," Margaret defends bashfully.

"We'll have to test that theory then." His playful smile sparks a small flame in Margaret's chest, warming her from within.

In a matter of moments the area has been completely transformed. Tiki torches flare around the perimeter. Color-changing spotlights have been erected to shine on glowing dance floor that occupies the space where a modest wooden stage stood moments before. A black covered table has been planted at the back corner of the dance floor, and Mano has taken a seat behind a computer on the table, large speakers flanking either side of his setup. One hand holds a headset to his ear, and with the other, he grabs the microphone sitting before him. "Alright, alright. Let's get the second half of this celebration started. The bride and groom are going to take it away with a song they chose specially for their first dance as husband wife. Come on up, lovebirds."

Kara and Chris waltz their beaming faces toward the newly constructed dance floor, and Mano begins playing a smooth love song through his speakers. Margaret sighs as she reminisces on her first dance with Austin, a warm, soothing sensation stirring in her soul at the memory.

After a couple minutes of the newlyweds dancing solo on the floor, the music transitions to a livelier tune, and guests filter out onto the floor to join together in dance. Without a word, Will takes Margaret's hand and leads her out to the floor. His smile hangs easy and warm across his face, and she tries to relax and feel the music. She used to love dancing at weddings. She would spend all night out on the dance floor, barefoot and crazy, dancing just enough for her muscles to protest in the morning. Will takes her hand and starts spinning her in circles, and slowly Margaret lets the music and laughter floating around carry her self-conscious thoughts away. She lets a glorious, bright laugh roll out from her belly as the joy and happiness floating among the crowd permeates the tough armor she has worn the past year.

Margaret and Will spend the next two hours at each other's sides dancing and laughing more than either of them have done in a very long time.

Margaret collapses on a chair a ball of giggles, fanning her face with her hand. Will falls into a chair beside her, his chest heaving, flashing a large, toothy smile Margaret's way. "I can't believe how much I've been dancing!"

"Fun, huh?"

"I mean, I always love dancing at weddings, but usually it takes two or three drinks to get me out there. But here I am, too busy dancing to start even a second drink!"

"I can fix that for you. Want me to get you something?"

"I think at this point, I just need some water."

"Coming right up," Will pecks a quick kiss on her cheek as he rises from his chair to head to the bar, leaving Margaret's head spinning as she tries to assess what kind of kiss that was: intimate or platonic? He returns with their waters and a smile, but Margaret avoids eye contact, afraid of what she'll find there.

"Want to take these waters out for a walk and some fresh air? Cool down a little bit?" Will asks. "I found something yesterday, tucked in a corner of the resort, and I want to show you. I think you'd really like it."

"I'd love to."

Margaret stands and barely thinks twice when Will wraps his fingers between her own without a moment's hesitation. They make their way to the surprise destination in silence until they come upon a heavily flowered walkway.

"What is this place?" Margaret asks, releasing Will's hand and taking a step toward the invigorating, heavy aroma wafting from the plants before her.

"It's the resort garden. I found it yesterday and immediately thought of you. It reminded me about how you said the trees look greener here. Well, I think these flowers look brighter than anything I've seen at home. Want to take a walk through it?"

She turns back towards Will, smiling eagerly. "Yes, please!"

A wide smile forms on Will's face, and he walks toward her beaming. As they enter the jungle before them, it's Margaret who reaches for Will's hand, the act becoming an instinctive, comforting feeling for her.

They walk through the garden in silence, the only sound accompanying them is that of the wind tickling the leaves above and around them. Their stroll is slow and leisurely, and Margaret stops frequently to look at each flower's details and smell their petals. Even in the dark, with nothing but the light of the moon, stars, and a few sporadic lanterns to illuminate the foliage, the colors are tantalizing to the observer - from bright red, to honey yellow, to lush purple. Margaret snaps pictures of much of the flora, thinking her mother would love to see the exotic flowers. Every time she's finished snapping a picture, her hand instinctively finds Will's again, as comfortable as sliding into your favorite pair of jeans.

They reach the end of the garden where another archway indicates the exit, and Will pauses, his eyes focused on the trail ahead of them that will take them back to the wedding reception. "Well, it's getting late. Do you want to head back to your bungalow?" Margaret checks her phone: it's almost eleven.

"Are you kidding? It's my last night on this island and I was having a blast dancing the night away. As long as the music is playing, I want to stay at the party." The smile painted across her face is the biggest it's been since she first arrived on her vacation, and the midnight glow of the celestial bodies above highlight the joy radiating from her face. Will returns a giant smile and the pair begin meandering back to the rainbow glow of the flashing dance lights off in the distance.

Back at the reception, Margaret never leaves the dance floor, swaying, bouncing, and moving nonstop. Even when Will needs a break and heads back to their table, she stays on the floor, having made fast friends with the rest of Will's family. Will watches her from a distance, a woman so unlike the one he met at baggage claim just days ago. Once timid, shy, and reluctant to make eye contact, let alone conversation, that same woman is now blowing up a storm on the dance floor and charming everyone she talks to. Her smile, no longer hidden behind a book, lights up the room. She is almost unrecognizable.

Mano announces the last song for the night, a slow song, to send the newly-weds off with an extra dose of love. Margaret has used every slow song prior as an excuse to get some water and give her feet a break, but as she walks back to the table, Will rises from his seat, his gaze piercing. She immediately gets lost in his eyes, the eyes that hold the whole world.

Will clears his throat. "It's our last song together, will you share it with me?" Margaret's heart is pounding in her chest as she drinks in Will's pleading eyes. Will, the man who has been her strength and comfort in a whirlwind week. The man who has made her laugh and feel genuine, carefree joy again. She gives his hand a squeeze and places her other hand on his shoulder. A smile dances across Will's face, as he gently places his other hand on her waist, and slowly spins her out on the dance floor. They softly spin in circles, their eyes speaking the words their voices cannot. The song ends, but as everyone claps their 'thank you' to Mano, Will and Margaret only have eyes for each other. Margaret wonders if Will can hear her heart crashing against her ribs, as she tries to understand the dozens of emotions running through her veins. She decides to break the silence.

"I better go say my goodbyes and thank-yous to everyone." She lets her hand drop from Will's grasp as she makes her way over to Will's parents. Will watches her walk away, a dreamy look painted on his face.

"Thank you so much for letting me be a part of this night - and this week. Your family is so welcoming, I felt like I was dancing with my own."

"Oh my dear, I am so glad you were able to attend. It's been an absolute pleasure getting to know you." Mary wraps Margaret in a hug with her goodbye. She finds Chris and Kara and offers them one last congratulatory hug.

After all the well wishes and goodbyes, she makes her way back to Will and he laces his fingers between her own. They begin the walk back towards her bungalow, the air between them heavy with emotion. Their steps are slow and deliberate through the sand, each of them attempting to slow time and make the evening last longer than fate allows. Will's hand is strong and warm within her own, his thumb tracing its familiar circular pattern across her hand. Margaret's head and heart create a whirlwind of conflict and turmoil within her, Austin forever in the background of her mind.

The two reach the elaborately carved door to the bungalow, but she doesn't pull out her room key. She turns to face Will, her heart screaming in her chest, beating so violently against its cage that she is sure Will must be able to hear its erratic rhythm from within. His eyes shine like liquid pools of fire, piercing through her and igniting a desire deep in her soul she hadn't realized she'd been missing. His defined cheekbones are sharpened by his clenched jaw, as he appears to battle something within him.

Will's hand slowly rises towards Margaret's face, and her breath catches in her throat when his fingers brush against the sun-kissed skin of her face, sweeping a loose curl out of her eyes. His eyes are like pools of sapphires, drowning Margaret in their beauty. One hand rests gently on her cheek, the other finds her hip, and he slowly pulls her close. "Will," she whispers, resting her forehead against his, their warm breath mingling in the crevice between them. Will's lips find her own, his kiss soft, tentative. She closes her eyes and tilts her head to rest comfortably in his palm, enjoying the warmth of his mouth on her own. He is slow, careful and calculated. A hungry yearning crawls through Margaret's chest, as she opens her mouth to let him in. She wraps her fingers through his shaggy hair, pulling him close. Will responds by giving her hip a squeeze, pulling her tight against him. He pins her against the door and buries his fingers in her mess of curls. Margaret lets out a sigh, as his lips explore down her neck, nibbling on her collar bone.

She inhales deeply, Will's sultry cologne flooding her senses. Austin's cologne. Her eyes snap open, as a flood of images of Austin stream before her eyes. She pushes Will away from her, a torrent of emotions building within the cracking walls of her heart.

"Will, I can't." She stammers, her heart still hammering within her heaving chest. "I'm sorry. I'm so sorry, but I can't. Austin…" She trails off, locking eyes with Will, his eyes swimming with a longing Margaret feels in her bones. "I'm just not ready." She quickly turns on her heels, her dress fanning out around her, and lets herself into her room. The door slams tightly shut behind her, and Margaret lets the dam break. Her back hits the door, and she slides to the floor as a stream of tears escape her tightly shut eyes. Her heart's erratic rhythm is a mirror of the confusing thoughts and emotions flooding her soul, each one contradicting the next, making her tears flow even harder.

Will is comforting, easy, sweet. He sends electric currents through Margaret's veins and makes her skin tingle with desire. He makes her laugh in a way that helps her forget the world just as easily as her books do.

But that's part of the problem, isn't it? She cries to herself. Will makes her forget. And she's not ready to forget, not ready to replace. Kissing Will was electrifying and wonderful for those few moments she was able to forget. But then Austin swims back into focus, and she feels as if she's cheating on him or abandoning him. And her heart yearns for Will's touch but breaks at the thought of Austin never being the one to touch her again, the one to make her weak in the knees again.

She looks through bleary eyes at the digital clock beside her bed - it's just after one o'clock. The glowing green light of the clock on the bedside table is the last thing Margaret remembers before crying herself to sleep.

Chapter Twelve

Thursday, June 15, 2017

T he sound of AJ's footsteps echoing on the ceiling above her wake Margaret, and she rolls over to pick the book she had been reading up off the floor. At some point last night she had drifted off to sleep while lost in 1940s Germany. She walks upstairs and decides to start a pot of coffee for everyone. As the coffee brews, she pulls out her phone. The messages and calls have died down, but one catches her eye - it's from Austin's mother.

We'll be landing in Minneapolis at 8:10 tonight. We're staying at the Hilton. We'll be at the funeral tomorrow, but let me know if you need anything before then.

Margaret doesn't have the energy to deal with her in-laws so early in the morning, so she just responds with a simple ***Okay***.

"Morning, sis," AJ greets Margaret as he enters the kitchen. "Mmm...coffee brewing already. I like it." He pours some of the dark, rich drink into a mug for himself and takes a seat at the table, pulling up the local news station on his tablet. Margaret takes a seat opposite her brother and assesses him over her mug. After eavesdropping on his breakdown with Odette last night, she is left wishing her brother would break down to her, *with* her. What is it with him and her mother? Why can't they be devastated with her? Why do they feel the need to put on a front and go on with life as if everything is okay when clearly it is not?

Ugly anger starts to bubble in her stomach, so she takes her eyes off her brother and decides to continue skimming through the messages on her phone. She notices she missed a couple texts from her mother checking in yesterday.

Oops, Margaret thinks sarcastically as she continues scrolling, not feeling *too* guilty for having missed a lecture.

Odette enters the kitchen, wearing a pencil skirt and heels, her hair perfectly curled around her porcelain face. *She makes pregnancy sexy,* Margaret thinks to herself, envying her gorgeous sister-in-law. "Good morning, Margaret! How'd you sleep last night, love?"

"Oh fine. Much better than I would have at home," Margaret admits.

Odette smiles sadly at Margaret, as she joins them at the table with a glass of water and an orange. "Well I'm glad you came over last night. Stay as long as you want today. But, darling, please promise me if you end up spending another night here, that you'll at least use the guest room this time? I hate the thought of you sleeping on that lumpy couch down in the cold basement." Margaret smiles at her sister-in-law, her appreciation for the beautiful woman growing deeper with every passing day.

"Thanks, Odette. I'll keep that in mind. I think for now, I'm going to go home and try to get some stuff done before tomorrow."

"You sure? Odette and I are off now for the next week. You can stay here," AJ offers.

"Thanks, really, but mom is just going to nag me about this list, and I know I'll be more productive on my own."

"Yeah, okay. Well you know you can call or come on over whenever. Don't hesitate."

"Yeah, I know."

They say their goodbyes, and Margaret reluctantly climbs into her van to head back to the house. She's come to hate the minivan. It feels so giant and too quiet now that it no longer carries her children within its doors. She takes the time on the drive to check in with her mother. Nancy answers on the first ring. "Margaret? I've been trying to reach you. Thank God my other child kept me up to date on your whereabouts. Why were you at their house last night?"

Margaret sighs. "Good morning to you too, mom. I couldn't sleep in our bed last night, and I couldn't stand being alone in that house a minute longer." She hears her mother let out a long sigh on the other end of the phone, and Margaret smiles inside at how alike the two women are. *Maybe that's why we butt heads so much.*

"Are you okay? What are you doing today?"

"No, I'm not okay, mom. That's such a ridiculous question, and I'm so sick of everyone asking it. I don't know exactly what I'm doing today. I just left AJ's, and I'm heading home."

"Well I'll tell you what you're doing today: you're going to write those eulogies for your family, that's what you're doing today. When you get home, take a shower. I'll be there at noon. I have some stuff to bring over, and then I'll help you get those written."

Margaret rolls her eyes, regret for calling her mother beginning to roll in her chest. "Fine. I'll do that. Is that all?"

"Yes. See you at noon."

"Okay, see ya then."

"Margaret!" her mother calls, just as Margaret is about to hang up.

"Yeah?"

Nancy pauses on the line, only adding to Margaret's irritation. "I love you, Margaret."

Margaret's stiff, icy exterior melts slightly.

"I know, mom. I love you too."

Nancy hangs up the call, leaving Margaret gripping her steering wheel, wishing life were simpler.

Margaret steps out of the shower and tries to avoid looking at anything that belonged to Austin. She's flipped all the photos in the room down, and she removed the giant wedding picture from the wall, sliding it beneath their bed, so she is able to walk around her bedroom without her heart hurting any more than the consistent dull ache from the grief constantly rolling around inside her. She walks straight to her closet and chooses a simple t-shirt and jeans for the day.

She runs a brush through her unruly hair and decides to let it air dry. *The less work the better. Get through the day one step at a time.*

She's sitting on a chair in her living room, reading a new book she grabbed from AJ's house, when her mother walks through the door.

"I brought lunch!" Nancy calls from the threshold. Margaret hears her kicking off her shoes. "I figured you're probably not cooking anything, and you and I both need to eat. So I picked up something."

Margaret sets a scrap piece of paper in her book before setting it on the coffee table and joins her mother in the kitchen. Nancy is unloading burrito bowls out of a paper sack, and there's a large crate on the floor beneath the kitchen window holding three large boxes.

Margaret grabs some forks out of the drawer. "What's in those boxes, mom?"

"Oh I'll show you those after lunch. Let's eat." Nancy fills up two glasses with water and joins Margaret at the table. After a few moments of enjoying their meals, Nancy breaks the silence. "So, how are those eulogies coming."

"I haven't started them yet. I just got home not that long ago and showered like you told me to."

"Alright, well we can't let those fall by the wayside. What are you going to say in them?" Margaret stares at the bowl of rice before her, her jaw flexed. "Have you given it any thought at all, Margaret?"

"Of course I have. And every time I give it any thought, I want to throw up. What am I going to say? I can't get up in front of everybody and talk about them. I can't. It hurts too much." Margaret pushes her bowl away, glaring down at the table as hot, angry tears make their familiar path down her cheeks.

Nancy reaches across the table and takes Margaret's hand, giving it a squeeze. "Margaret. I cannot even begin to imagine the pain you're feeling. I think of the pain I'm in..." Nancy's breath catches in her throat as a short sob escapes through her quivering lips. "...when I think of them being gone from this earth so soon, it makes me so angry, and it absolutely shatters my heart. And I know your pain is a hundred times more than anything I am feeling." Margaret looks up to see her mother's eyes swollen with tears. She can't recall a time ever seeing her mother cry before, and the sight in front of her reminds her that her mother loved her family almost as much as she did. She thinks of how wonderful of a grandmother she was to her children, and feels some comfort in knowing that her children knew, without a doubt, that they were loved. "I know it's unbearable to think about, but the world doesn't stop turning for anyone. The sun will keep rising, the birds will keep singing, and everything will seem so unfair - because it is. It's so unfair what happened." Margaret's shoulders tremble at Nancy's words, as she pulls herself into her mother's arms, sobbing into the crook of her neck. The scent of Nancy's perfume transports Margaret to her childhood: she's suddenly six years old, curled up in her mother's lap after getting a scraped knee or a bump on the head. How big and painful those injuries seemed then. Why is it that as we age, we replace the numerous physical injuries of childhood with the numerous emotional injuries of adulthood? And how unfortunate for us, for our emotional injuries tend to leave us with deeper scars.

"I don't know how to live, mom. I don't know what to do with myself. I feel guilty that I'm here and they're not." Nancy sighs, petting her daughter's soft, still-damp hair.

"You'll figure it out. It might take you a while, but some day, you'll realize life *can* keep going. It's going to be a different life than you ever imagined. But it'll be there." The women sit together in silence. A mother relishing in feeling needed again. A daughter soaking up the childlike comfort of a mother's hug.

Eventually the women release each other and resume their lunch in that awkward silence that tends to follow the moment when stubborn adults reveal their vulnerability, unsure how to navigate the air between them.

Margaret is the one to break the silence. "Well, I finished my bowl. Thanks for bringing lunch, mom. Now will you show me what's in the boxes?"

"Yes, yes." Nancy quickly scoops the last couple of bites into her mouth, so as to finish and show Margaret what she brought. "Here," she hands her bowl over to Margaret. "You clean up the bowls, and I'll get these boxes out." Margaret does as she's told, and when she returns to the table, the three boxes are lined up waiting for her. "Go ahead. Open them."

As Margaret opens her first box, her heart catches in her throat. In her hands is the urn she picked out for Jackson. It's navy blue, with swirls of green and gold. His name, along with his birth and death dates are engraved on the front. Margaret shakily sets the urn on the table.

"What do you think?" Nancy asked. "I ordered the one you picked out, but I added the engraving. I thought it was a nice touch."

"A warning on what I was about to open would have been nice," Margaret mumbles, fighting to keep her nausea at bay. She gently runs her fingers across the etching. "But yes, the engraving is a beautiful touch. Thank you."

"Well, go on. See how the others turned out."

Margaret opens the second package. This one is for her Isabelle. Its base color is pink, with swirls of purple, gold, and silver marbled in. The same intricate engraving decorates the front of her urn as well. Margaret's hands are shaking uncontrollably by the time she gets to what she knows is Austin's urn. "Can you open it, mom?"

Nancy takes over without a word and pulls out Austin's urn. It's larger than her children's and very regal. The base color is a midnight black, with minimal swirls of gold and silver snaking around the urn. Etched in gold is Austin's name and the dates of his life. Margaret slowly lowers herself onto the chair.

"They really turned out lovely. I have to bring them to the funeral home today, but I wanted you to see them before I did. They'll be empty for the memorial service, we won't have the ashes back yet, but I still wanted to have them displayed."

Margaret can't take her eyes off the artifacts before her, silent tears falling fast and hard. "Mom, can I be alone for a minute?"

Nancy eyes Margaret from across the table. "Yes, of course. I'll be in the living room."

Margaret is staring at the three urns before her, when it suddenly happens. It feels as if something cracks in her chest, a physical break. Her heart begins to beat furiously and erratically, as if begging to be let out of its agonizing cage. Her lungs seem to have forgotten how to work, her breaths escaping in uneven, ragged succession. She wraps her arms around the three vessels, pulling them all close to her and buries her head between them. Anger, despair, and grief roll over her like the ominous, rolling thunderheads that ripped her family away from her just days ago. Her agonizing wails burst through the house that's not a home, riding on the summer breeze into an unforgiving world.

Nancy loads the urns into her car and says her goodbyes to her daughter. "I'll bring these to the funeral home, you try to work on those eulogies, okay?" Margaret just nods, her throat too sore to try to let words escape. Her mother wraps Margaret in a rare, tight hug, and whispers in her ear, "It *will* get better." She climbs into her car and drives away, leaving Margaret standing alone on her front step.

Exhaustion weighs heavy on her shoulders as he walks into the deserted house. She drops herself onto a chair in her living room and pulls out her phone. A low groan escapes her lips as she scrolls through more texts and messages. *I don't have the energy to talk to anyone,* she thinks to herself. So she puts the phone down and reaches for the book she took from her brother. She leans back in her chair, wraps herself in a blanket, and lets the book whisk her away to medieval England, where she's an apprentice learning the trade of a blacksmith.

She must have fallen asleep, because she bolts out of her chair at the sound of her phone ringing - it's Odette. Margaret glances at the clock above her fireplace and sees it's almost six. "Hi, Odette," she answers casually.

"Hi, love! Just checking in on you and seeing how you're doing. AJ's just 'bout to put some burgers on the grill - should we put one on for you? You wanna come on over for dinner?" Margaret bites her lip thinking about the offer. She would love the company of her brother and Odette, but she tells herself she needs to get used to being in her house.

"Thanks, Odette. I think I'm going to stay here tonight, have dinner on my own and work on these eulogies."

"You sure? We'd love to have you over."

"I'm sure, really."

"Alright, sugar. You call if you need anything, okay?"

"Of course. Thanks."

"Bye," Odette ends the call, leaving Margaret alone and second guessing her decision.

She walks into the kitchen and finds a notebook and a pen and sits down at the table. "Okay, let's get this done," she announces to the room, ready to finally write these eulogies. Except nothing comes out. Margaret sits at the table for ten, twenty, thirty minutes. She can't seem to put anything on paper. She can't seem to form any words in her head. "What am I supposed to say?" she thinks out loud. "The funeral isn't until four tomorrow. I can write this in the morning."

She pushes her chair from the table, walks back into the living room, and returns to medieval England. She stays there, far from reality, until sleep overcomes her.

Chapter Thirteen

Saturday, June 16, 2018

Margaret wakes up puffy-eyed and sore, the tropical sun greeting her warmly for her last morning on the island. There's a literal ache in her chest, and she wonders if it's from all the heavy crying she did last night or if her heart truly is broken, shattered one too many times. A glance at the clock tells her she has three hours until she has to be in a shuttle bus on her way back to the airport. She groans and flops backwards on the bed, closing her eyes tightly in an attempt to stop last night from replaying in her mind.

She flashes back to Will's fingers in her hair, his hand firm upon her hip.

Will.

Her eyes flash open as she remembers how she ended the night with him. Guilt bubbles up inside her. She digs under the cloud of blankets searching for her phone. She can't let last night be the last time she talks to Will. He deserves a proper goodbye.

"Aha!" She shouts to the empty room, rejoicing in her efforts. "Gotcha!"

She opens the screen to see she already has a text from Will. It was sent at 3:37 this morning.

Margaret's heart plummets to her stomach. She's scared to open it and see what Will has to say after last night. She inhales deeply, then opens the text. Her stomach knots when she sees the length of which he wrote:

Margaret, I'm so sorry. I feel like such a jerk. I shouldn't have kissed you like that. It was thoughtless of me, and I apologize. I hate that I made you upset. And I hate even more that your last night in Hawaii ended like that. Can I see you tomorrow? One last time? I would love to say a proper goodbye. I can't sleep knowing this is how our week together ends. I'm sorry.

She walks out to her balcony clutching the phone to her chest. She closes her eyes as she sits down and lets the warm Hawaiian wind rattle her hair and her senses. The tropical breeze carries salt, sunshine, and promises of a better tomorrow in its dance, but Margaret feels none of that, her mind too lost in the storm of emotions whirling within her.

It's six-thirty in the morning. *Is that too early to text him back? No*, she decides. **I'd love to see you one more time. Huli Huli Hut in an hour?** Her heart flutters about as she presses send. Barely a breath later, and she already has a reply.

Sounds perfect. See you in an hour.

Margaret jumps up from her chair, a new energy flowing through her veins. She's determined to pack up her room as fast as she can and get checked out of the bungalow, so she can spend every last minute with Will before she has to be on the shuttle to the airport. "Where do I start?" she assesses the room before her, her eyes landing on her collection of books shelved neatly in the kitchenette. "You," she declares to the ones who have been her best friends the past year. She scoops up an arm-full and stuffs them into her suitcase. "I don't need you anymore." Her heart races in her chest as she stares at the books resting in her luggage. But for the first time in a long time, it's a kind of racing that has her feeling exhilarated and free, rather than anxious and confused. She powers through the rest of her packing with a newfound energy.

"I'm going to be so early," Margaret mutters as she makes her way across the resort to the Huli Huli Hut. The familiar friendly face of the Huli Huli Man greets her at the window of the hut as she approaches, his smile as broad and sunny as the first day she met him.

"Aloha, pretty lady! Howzit today?"

"Aloha! It's a beautiful day."

"It sure is. What can I get for you today?"

"Can I have your strongest, richest Hawaiian coffee?"

"Coming right up, beautiful." The Huli Huli Man turns the corner of the hut, and Margaret leans against the ivy-covered wall, listening to the waves tell their story on the sandy beach. A moment later he comes back to the window, carrying a steaming Styrofoam cup. "Your coffee, pretty lady. You'll like this one. It's Kona coffee with hints of chocolate and macadamia and honey. Delicious. Enjoy!" He flashes his contagious smile, and Margaret thinks about how much she's going to miss that friendly, welcoming face when she leaves this place. She walks around the corner to find a table, and her heart skips a beat when she sees Will is early too, already perched beneath a palm tree, reading a book. Her heart and her face smile together, her soul happy to see him waiting for her.

"Hey," she smiles warmly his way as she takes a seat across from his earth-shattering eyes. His broad smile is warm and genuine, that lone dimple hanging on his cheek.

"Hi. I'm so glad you came."

"Of course I came."

Will closes his book with a sigh, the smile erasing from his chiseled face. "I wouldn't have been surprised if you said no. I felt horrible when I left last night. I can't believe I kissed you like that. It was thoughtless of me."

"Stop." Margaret puts her hand on Will's. "I...listen, I just need to dump everything that's jumbled in my brain out, and I just need you to listen, okay?" Will's sky-blue eyes pierce intently through her own as he nods his agreement. Margaret takes a deep breath, readying herself for the speech she's practiced all morning. "I like you. I like you a lot. You've been magical this past week. This past year, I was a zombie. I was going through the motions, just trying to survive. I'd work, eat, sleep, read. That's it. Reading has been my therapy, because when I read, I don't think about Jackson, Izzy, and Austin. I get to disappear out of this nightmare and enter a whole new world where time is irrelevant, and my pain disappears. But this past week, you showed me this life doesn't have to be a nightmare - it still has the potential to be a dream. You helped me realize something important these past few days: I've spent the past year of my life just trying to get through each day, one day at a time. I was just surviving. And thanks to you, I now know I don't want to just 'survive' - I want to *live*. I want to *thrive*.

I want to laugh again and just feel *everything* again. Even the sadness and the grief and pain. I want to feel it all because I want to feel alive. I'm tired of numbing myself. I didn't realize how empty I was until you showed me how full I could be, how full my life could still be." Tears as salty as the waves crashing behind her wet Margaret's cheeks, as she pours her thoughts and her heart into Will's open hands.

"Margaret," Will begins, only to be cut off by the woman he stares longingly at before him.

"Wait, I just…I need to say thank you. Thank you for all of it, Will. For talking with me, walking with me. For making me turn this trip into an adventure. For breathing life back into me. Last night, that kiss…it was a wonderful kiss. And I wanted it, I don't want you to think I didn't. I don't want you to think you did something wrong. Because you didn't do anything wrong. It was wonderful. But that was the problem. It threw me off. And I felt guilty for feeling wonderful, like I was cheating on Austin. But it's good because this has all helped me to realize I'm ready to start living again, but…" her voice trails off, losing its way and getting stuck somewhere in her throat.

"…But you're not ready to start loving again," Will finishes for her. She turns her eyes toward his as she wipes the tears from her face. Their eyes lock, and Will reaches out to gently tuck Margaret's whipping hair behind her ear, the tips of his fingers electrifying her body as they softly brush against her skin.

"I'm sorry."

"Don't be. Margaret, you're an amazing person. And it makes me so happy to hear you say these things. Because you have the most radiant smile of any woman I have ever met, and that smile should not be hidden behind a book all the time." Will smirks playfully at her. Margaret's melodic laugh carries across the rolling waves, her smile easy and free.

"Thank you, Will. For everything." Will brings her hand to his soft lips, planting a gentle kiss. Margaret takes a sip of her coffee, savoring the chocolate notes as she gives Will an assessing look behind the steam rising for her cup. "What do you say? One last walk along the beach before I have to hop on the shuttle?"

"I can't think of anything I'd want to do more." Margaret realizes she will miss seeing Will's smile after today. She's never met anyone with a smile that takes up their whole face the way Will's does.

The two rise from the table, and Will interlocks his fingers with Margaret's. She soaks up every last drop of the comfortable, easy feeling of being next to Will. The two talk easily about the ending of their trip, and what they'll do when they get back home. Will says he's going to book some hiking trips. Margaret talks about how she's going to read less. Not stop reading all together, of course. But just less. Maybe start a new hobby, she says.

But as Margaret has learned this past year, time stops for no one, and soon the minutes have been swept up by the sea, and it's time for her to head to the airport. Will walks her to the shuttle office, where her luggage and her books wait for her to take them back home. Margaret stares at her belongings, the wheels in her mind turning.

"Hold on," she proclaims. "Can you help me collect all my books?" Together the pair comb through her bags, collecting every book she brought with her. She observes the stacks before her for a moment, before taking a single book and placing it back in her carry-on bag. "Okay, can you help me bring these to the concierge desk?"

"Of course." Will grabs most of the books, and Margaret picks of the last of the stragglers. The pair brings them to the concierge, where Margaret asks for a pen. Inside each cover, she writes a simple note: *I hope this book helps you as much as it helped me.* After all the books have been signed, Margaret returns the pen to the woman at the desk.

"Can I donate these to the resort? For guests to check-out and read if they'd like?" she asks.

"Yes, of course! We have a small library in our lounge where guests can access books for reading pleasure at the beach or anywhere on the resort. I can take these for you and add them to the collection."

"Perfect. Thank you so much." Margaret's smile is beaming, and she feels as if a giant weight has been lifted from her shoulders as she and Will walk hand-in-hand back to the shuttle. Will beams proudly at her, as they descend on the shuttle sitting in the station.

"Well, I guess this is it," Will begins, rolling on his heels.

"Yeah. I guess so," Margaret avoids looking at him, too afraid of what she'll find there when she does.

"Margaret, keep in touch, okay? I mean it. I'd love to stay connected. I'd love to be a part of this next chapter of your life you're about to start living. Even if it is as 'just a friend.'" Will adds air quotes for emphasis, as he smirks playfully in Margaret's direction.

"Of course. We'll keep in touch. I'd say you've changed my life, Will, but I don't think that's fitting. You gave it a jump start when it was dead. You breathed life back into it. And for that, I'll forever be grateful." The two lock eyes, a bond formed between them that only a precious few in this world ever get to experience. Will leans forward and wraps Margaret in a strong embrace. She melts into him, letting his warmth mingle with her soul. As they peel away, he cups her warm cheek in his hand plants a soft kiss on her forehead.

She climbs onto the bus, picking a seat where she can still see her friend, and they share a smile and a wave as the bus pulls away from the resort. On the trek to the airport Margaret once again finds herself wiping away tears. But these are new tears. Tears of hope, strength, love, and gratitude for the future before her. A future that, for the first time since the accident, looks positive.

Once through airport security and settled into her chair at the terminal, Margaret leaves the one book she brought home in her bag and instead opens her phone and begins browsing animal shelters. "I need something that needs me. Time to find a friend." As she waits for her plane to be ready for boarding, she spends her time scrolling past countless faces of puppies and dogs looking for a new home. An animal whose heart has been broken like her own. An animal that will heal Margaret as much as she will heal them. Because Margaret knows, as she fondly recalls her loyal Watson, if there's anyone out there that can heal a broken heart, it's a dog.

Chapter Fourteen

Friday, June 16, 2017

T he shrill pierce of the doorbell through the air startles Margaret awake. She bolts out of her chair, wondering who the heck is ringing her doorbell so early. A quick glance at the clock tells her it's actually almost eleven, and she feels a little sheepish. She swings the door open to find a delivery man with an elaborate bouquet of flowers in his arms.

"Delivery for Margaret Heller," the man announces.

"Oh, yes, that's me." He hands the flowers over and pulls a small clipboard out of the pocket of his uniform.

"I need you to sign this," he explains, shoving the clipboard under Margaret's nose.

"Yeah, okay, just a sec," Margaret struggles to set the exceptionally large bouquet at her feet, then signs the clipboard. The man takes it, wishes Margaret a nice day, and is back on his way in a purple flower delivery truck.

She closes the door and carries the ornate vase into the kitchen, carefully setting it on the counter. She digs through the mass of petals and stems and finally finds a small, square card buried in the center of the arrangement.

Thinking of you today and wishing you peace during this difficult time. Love, your friends at Thomas C. Moore Elementary

Margaret feels a ping of guilt for having ignored all the texts and messages she has received this past week. Hopefully she'll get a chance to apologize to everyone at the funeral today.

Her stomach sinks. The funeral is today. A sudden wave of nausea threatens to overtake her, as she gingerly sits herself down in a chair at the table. The room is spinning around her. She's been dreading this day, and it's here. She closes her eyes, inhales several deep, slow breaths, steadying herself and the spinning room.

"One foot in front of the other. One step at a time," she encourages herself. She opens her eyes and rises from the table. "A shower. That's step one." She walks to her bathroom and begins the process of getting ready for what will be the second most difficult day of her life.

The sound of voices drifting up the stairs greets Margaret when she exits the bathroom after her shower. Grumbling to herself about invasion of privacy, she finishes slipping into her black dress, then walks downstairs while brushing the knots out of her wet hair.

"Margaret," AJ announces to the room, a soft, sad smile hanging on his face. He wraps his sister in a bear hug, and Margaret melts into his arms. "Glad to see you're up and showered already." Odette and Nancy are sitting at the kitchen table, pouring over papers together. Odette looks up and beams at Margaret.

"What's everyone doing here?"

"Well we thought we better come over here before we all make our way to the funeral home. You know, just make sure you're not lost in a book or asleep on the couch instead of getting ready." AJ smiles playfully at this sister, but Margaret doesn't return the gesture. She turns around and walks wordlessly back up to her bedroom, where she finishes primping herself.

When she comes back down to the kitchen, the trio of invaders have made themselves at home, and are eating sandwiches and drinking sodas. "Want one?" AJ asks, offering Margaret a sandwich in his outstretched hand. Margaret takes it and sits down in the last remaining empty chair at the table.

"So Margaret," her mother begins in the usual business tone Margaret is growing tired of. "How did those eulogies turn out?"

"Fine," Margaret lies. Her stomach drops realizing she still hasn't written them. *Guess I'll be winging it*, she thinks to herself.

"Good. Now, I printed off some programs for the service, Odette and I were just going over them. Take a look." Nancy slides a small booklet across the table to Margaret. On the cover of the booklet is one of her favorite pictures of Austin with the kids. It was taken during one of their camping trips near the boundary waters in northern Minnesota. They had gone hiking through the state park, and they found this enormous cave carved out from melting glaciers. Austin is in the center of the mouth of the cave, and Jackson's head is peeking over his shoulder as he climbs on his dad's back, a huge grin painted on his excited face. Izzy is nestled into her daddy's strong arm, giving him a big hug and flashing a cheesy grin at the camera. Austin is front and center, his smile so carefree and easy, his eyes shining with the joy of being with his kids. Margaret smiles warmly at the memory.

She opens the pamphlet and skims over the program, noting that she's the last one to speak, after the "open mic" portion of the service. "Looks perfect," she confirms, passing the pamphlet back to her mother.

"You keep that one somewhere safe here. You'll want to keep one for yourself." Nancy passes it back to her daughter. Margaret can't possibly think why she'd ever want to reflect on this day, but she obliges without protest.

The four family members sit together for a couple hours, talking and reminiscing on memories of the ones no longer with them. And for a little while, the vice around Margaret's chest eases its grip and her heart finds a smooth, calming rhythm deep within her.

Margaret walks through the doors of the funeral home with fear and trepidation clawing at her chest. She focuses on controlling her breathing, trying to placate her frantic heart. A man in an expensive-looking suit greets Margaret and her family warmly.

"Welcome. Nancy, it's nice to see you again," the man smiles, as he takes Nancy's hand in a firm handshake. "And for those of you I haven't met, I am Sean. I am the director here, and I'll be facilitating the service today. I am here for whatever you need. Come, follow me." Sean directs the small group into a large, open room to their left. The room is filled with several large, plush chairs, and a few floral couches that look like they came from her grandmother's house. "My team has been hard at work setting up the things you dropped off this morning, Nancy. How does it look?"

Near the entrance of the room is a podium, where a guest book sits splayed open, waiting for its pages to be filled. AJ, Odette, and Margaret had created six different poster boards of photographs - one for Jackson, one for Izzy, one for Austin, and three for family photos - and they were now spread throughout the room. Large, elaborate bouquets of various flower arrangements have been placed throughout the room as well, adding color and fragrance to an otherwise dark and dreary day. Centered along the back wall of the room is a table where the three marbled urns sit staring at Margaret. Her heart catches in her throat when she sees them, and she slowly makes her way toward the table. The most elaborate flower arrangements were saved for this table, giving beauty to an otherwise ugly sight to Margaret. Her eyes burn with the stinging assault of her tears as she runs her fingers lightly over the urns, tracing the names of the people she loves most. The table also contains some of the most loved artifacts from her family: Jackson's baseball mitt is mounted on a stand with his baseball picture framed, his participation medal hanging from the frame. A pair of Izzy's ballet slippers sit perched beside her urn, her tiara resting against the slippers. Austin's wedding ring hangs from the corner of Margaret's favorite photo from their wedding day, and the mug he *always* drank his Sunday morning coffee from stands proud beside the frame. The mug reads *Best Dad Ever* and had Izzy and Jackson's hand-prints. Margaret picks up the mug and pulls it close to her chest, closes her eyes, and lets the stinging tears make their escape.

She feels someone arrive next to her side, but decides to keep her eyes closed, praying that any moment she will wake up from this never-ending nightmare. "I hope you don't mind," Nancy begins. "I went to your house while you were at AJ's and took some things to bring here. I thought they should have something more to showcase who they were." Without opening her eyes, Margaret leans her head on her mother's shoulder.

"It's perfect," she whispers. "Thank you for taking care of this all, Mom. Thank you." Nancy's shoulder begins to tremble ever so slightly beneath Margaret's head.

"I didn't want you to have to do this, Margaret. Nobody should have to go through what you're going through. And to watch my only daughter..." a small sniffle cuts through the air. "...I can't take the pain away. But I could at least make some of this easier for you."

The mother and daughter stand together in silence, letting their broken hearts beat together for a brief moment.

"You must be Margaret," a deep voice rolls behind her. Margaret opens her eyes and turns to face Sean. "I'm so deeply sorry for your loss. A terribly tragic event." A 'thank you' cracks out of Margaret's dry throat. "The first hour will be in here, as friends and family gather to pay their respects." Sean is moving about the room as he talks, smiling at AJ and Odette as he passes. "After the hour is up, we'll usher guests who would like to stay for the service into the chapel. As Nancy's program outlined, I'll be facilitating the service very sparingly, leaving the memory sharing and storytelling to the guests. Margaret," his eyes bore into her heart. "You'll give the last remarks before everyone is ushered about once more, this time into the cafeteria for some light refreshments." Margaret nods, her stomach in knots as she thinks about the task before her. "If there is anything at all the four of you need while here, do not hesitate to let me or one of the staffers know. There are bottles of water and muffins in the kitchen for the four of you if you need anything to eat or drink before the refreshments are officially served. And with all that said, I will give you all some peace. Once guests begin to arrive, I will be floating around if needed." Sean tips his head Margaret's way, then exits through the doorway they entered.

Margaret falls into the nearest chair, bracing herself for what she knows will be an unbearable next few hours. The small group waits without filling the room with words, each of them dreading the impending barrage of condolences.

The first guests come through the door. Margaret rises from her chair, paints on a grim smile, and starts going through the motions expected of her.

Hugs. Countless arms embrace Margaret. It's the smells, not the faces, that stand out. Flowery perfumes, crisp colognes.

Hands. So many hands reaching out to touch her. They grasp her shoulders, squeeze her arms and hands.

Voices. The voices blend with the faces in a mingled, jumbled mess.

Margaret moves through the waves, never fully aware of who she is speaking to.

Smile, nod, 'thank you.'

The commotion is suffocating. The room is spinning. Everything is a blur from the tears welling in her eyes. A firm hand wraps around her arm and steers her away from the crowd. She looks up to see her brother, jaw clenched, his pink-rimmed eyes focused ahead of him. They exit the building, and he releases her arm. "You looked like you were about to pass out. Thought you could use some fresh air." Margaret notices his heaving chest and thinks he must have needed some fresh air as much as she did. The siblings let the birds hopping among the trees do the talking for them. Margaret turns her eyes to the sky and watches a robin cut through the air above her.

"It's so unfair. How can the sky be so blue today? How can it be so beautiful out here while it's so awful in there?" Margaret whines to her brother. AJ doesn't respond, just looks up at the cloudless sky with her, his shoulders slightly trembling as silent tears begin to roll down his face. Margaret opens her heart to the feelings ravishing within her, wraps her arms around her brother, and cries with him. Their sobs float to the clouds above them, carrying their dreams of the future with them. Eventually, the brother and sister make their way back into the building.

Margaret notices Austin's parents perusing Izzy's photo board. Carolyn is dabbing at her eyes with a flowered handkerchief. Seeing them standing in front of her daughter's memories, the granddaughter they never took the time to know, sends hot, angry waves through Margaret's veins, so she decides she'll try talking to them later, maybe at the refreshments after the ceremony, and turns on the spot to go the opposite direction. She is met by Carrie.

"Margaret." Carrie scoops her into a tentative, yet strong hug, and Margaret feels guilt welling inside her from when she last saw Carrie. When she pulls herself away from the embrace, she takes in Carrie's damp, pink eyes. The two friends take a moment to reminisce on memories their families had made together. Margaret fights the jealousy of knowing Carrie gets to continue to make more memories with her family, and she excuses herself from her friend before the jealousy bubbles over her. Back to mingling and going through the motions.

It's all a blur to Margaret. The greetings, hand shaking, hugging, tears, condolences. One minute she's standing in the memorial room, and the next someone has ushered her into the chapel, where she sits with her mother on one side and AJ on the other. Austin's parents sit beside Nancy. Margaret tries to listen as friends and families step up to the microphone to share stories, but her brain is fuzzy and her eyes are heavy, and at the end of the day she won't remember any of it.

Suddenly, AJ is nudging her. "You, Margaret," he whispers. "It's your turn. Go up and give your eulogy."

Margaret's stomach jolts violently. She rises on shaky legs and drags her feet with heavy trepidation to the podium. Using the podium to help her stand, she looks out to the crowd before her. *Where did all these people come from?* She doesn't recall interacting with so many people during the memorial hour. But the room is full. More than full - it is overflowing. There aren't enough seats in the chapel. Visitors are standing along the side walls and in the back of the room. Margaret's heart swells at the sight of so many people who have loved her family over the years. A lump forms in her throat as the tears begin to cascade freely down her face. She inhales deeply, attempting to calm her anxious heart, and looks out into the crowd before her.

"I'd say what a beautiful sight it is to see so many people who loved my family, but, really, it's an ugly sight I'd rather not see." Margaret notices her mother shift uncomfortably in her seat. "I still can't wrap my head around the fact that this is real life. That this is not just some nightmare that I can't wake up from." AJ clears his throat loudly. Margaret sighs, closes her eyes, and tries to organize her scattered brain into something coherent about the family she'll never see again. When she opens her eyes again, they lock with Odette's. She feels love radiating from her sister-in-law's tear-filled eyes.

"I'm not going to stand up here and say something cliche about telling the ones we love how much we love them when we have the chance, while they're still here. Because you know that. We all know that. Everyone always says it. 'Life is short, so always tell the people you love that you love them.' We know that already. So instead I'm going to tell you that life is unfair. Because it is. Life doesn't care if you are sweet or nasty, big or small, old or young. It will do with you whatever it wants. Life doesn't care about your plans or dreams. Life has its own agenda, and you can't do anything to change it." Margaret pauses to grab a tissue from her pocket and dries her face. She sees her mother's uncomfortable, flabbergasted face staring in horror her way. She closes her eyes, takes a deep breath, and continues.

"Izzy was the spunkiest, most determined little girl I have ever met. She was brave and fearless, and if there was something she wanted, she worked to get it. She was going to be a CEO someday, of that I had no doubt. Jackson was my rule-follower and my snuggler. He was calculated and intentional in everything he did, always acutely aware of the emotions of those around him. I dreamed of him doing something for people when he grew up, maybe a nurse, doctor, or teacher. And Austin," Margaret's voice cracks. She takes a steadying breath. "Austin was the proudest daddy, and my very best friend. We were going to grow old together watching our kids grow alongside us, building their own lives." She fiddles with the corners of the tissue in her hands. "I guess, if something like this had to happen, I'm glad they all went together. It helps knowing that they have each other, wherever they are."

Margaret begins to spin her sapphire wedding ring as she tries to continue to organize her thoughts. The sound of intermittent sniffles cut through the air. "When I think back on the ridiculously short time I had with my family, it's the everyday moments that shine the brightest. Like when Jackson lost his first tooth while biting into an apple, and the tooth got stuck in the apple. I'll never forget how big his eyes grew in surprise, and the sound of his contagious giggle at the sight of his tooth sticking out of that green apple. Or when Izzy would crawl into my bed in the morning and put both of her tiny hands on either side of my face and give me the wettest kisses. Yes, it's the little, everyday memories that I'll miss the most. It's sitting cross-legged on the floor playing the matching game. Holding their tiny hands while we walk to the park. It's kissing Austin goodnight at the end of every day and good morning at the start of each morning. The way he *always* drove with one hand on the wheel and the other hand wrapped in mine. It's the squeals of excitement when the kids caught their first fish. The cheesy grins and musical giggles as we chased each other around the house. It's those everyday moments that I'm going to miss more than anything in this world. Because it's the everyday moments, the mundane, the things we take for granted - those are the things that make life, *life*." Margaret's tears are flowing freely, and she stops to clean her face.

"So bask in the blissfully ordinary while you still have it. Soak up the little things. Because the little things are the building blocks for the big things. And because one day, the little things will be the most important things. They'll be the things you come to love the most. They'll be the brightest thing in this life you build."

Margaret grabs another tissue from the podium as she makes her way back to her chair. AJ takes her hand in his, as she sobs into her tissue, reliving the everyday moments that made her life beautiful.

Somehow Margaret survives the day and finds herself standing alone in her kitchen. Odette and AJ had offered their guest room again, but Margaret is so exhausted and drained, she just wants to be alone. "I have to learn to be alone at some point," she lectures herself. The three marbled urns stare at her from their place on the counter, as the ticking of the clock echoes throughout the empty house, reminding her of the cruelty that time refuses to stop, even for those that beg.

"I'm alone," she whispers, letting the words fill the room around her. Panic claws at her heart. She gasps in ragged breaths, clutching her chest, trying to steady her breathing. Reality begins to invade from all sides, the stillness of the house closing in, threatening to suffocate her under the weight of its aloneness.

Margaret runs outside and collapses on the front porch, gulping in deep breaths of the cool, refreshing evening air. Once her heart rate has slowed, she turns back into the house only to grab her car keys and purse. The tires on the van squeal as she backs out of the driveway. An hour later, the front door to her house opens again, and she enters carrying five bags full of new books. "Exercise is still overrated," she mutters, as she struggles with the weight of the bags while trying to kick off her shoes.

She trudges into the living room and drops her haul on the floor. With great care, she pulls each book out of the bag and sets it on the coffee table in the center of the room. She stares at the twenty-seven books now stacked neatly on the table before her, trying to decide which one to read first.

Tick.

Tock.

Tick.

Tock.

Margaret glares up at the clock perched above her fireplace.

Tick.

Tock.

Tick.

Tock.

The clicking of the machine rattles around Margaret's empty chest, bruising her wounded heart further with the gruesome reality of time. She pushes herself off the floor, drags a chair into the room from the kitchen table, climbs up and pulls the clock from the wall. Her stomps bounce off the lonely walls in the house as she makes her way outside and throws the device into the garbage bin. She pauses when she re-enters the house, assessing to see if there are any other aggressive devices that need to be removed.

"I'm alone." She says it louder this time, letting the words sink their fangs into her heart. She gazes up at the stairs before her. The stairs that lead to her bedroom, where she used to lay with her husband. The stairs that would take her to her children's rooms, where she used to read them bedtime stories and cuddle beneath their blankets with them, their breath warm on her face. She can't bear walking up those stairs, so she turns her attention back to her books. Margaret reaches for the book closest to her, lies down on the couch, and leaves the pain and anguish of reality behind her.

Chapter Fifteen

Epilogue

AJ and Odette stand with large smiles and open arms as Margaret arrives to baggage claim. She allows herself to be buried in the warmth of AJ's burly arms as he gives her a strong hug. "Welcome home, sis." But Margaret only embraces her brother for a moment before she's pushing him away and reaching out to take her niece from Odette's arms.

"Hi baby girl. Did you miss Auntie?"

"We all missed you, hon. How was your trip?" Odette asks, as she pecks Margaret's cheek.

Margaret spends the rest of their time together reliving the past week, giving the couple all the details. "Sounds like the perfect getaway," Odette concludes as Margaret finishes detailing the night of the wedding, leaving out Will's attempted kiss.

"It was." Margaret stares dreamily out the car window, already missing the island and her new friend. "Oh, and I think I'm going to get a dog."

"A dog?" AJ keeps his focus on the road, but Margaret sees the curve of a smile from the side of his check. "Huh. A dog. Remember Watson? He was a good mutt." AJ gives a nod, seemingly more to himself than to Margaret. "Yeah, a dog. I think that's a good idea."

"Me too." Margaret smiles to herself. She'd been thinking about dogs almost her entire flight home, and the more she chewed on the idea, the more sure she became it was a great choice. She had even started browsing the websites of local shelters as she had waited between her connecting flights. A faithful dog had healed her heart before, and she was sure a dog could help heal her heart again.

When they pull into Margaret's driveway, the sun has long said its goodbyes, and the sliver of the moon is peeking between hazy clouds. Margaret peeks over to her niece in the seat beside her. Mary Kate is breathing slow and steady, her eyelids fluttering ever so lightly as she dreams of whatever innocent babes dream of. Margaret runs a soft finger across the sleeping child's cheek and places a warm kiss upon her forehead, feeling nothing but gratitude to have this beautiful child in her life. She whispers a goodbye to Odette and shimmies out of the car. She walks to the back of the car where AJ is lifting her luggage from the trunk.

"This feels a lot lighter. I remember your suitcase being insanely heavy. How come it's so different?"

"I left some baggage in Hawaii," she smiles to herself.

"Well alright then! I gotta get the girls home, but call if you need anything. Come over tomorrow for burgers - Mary Kate would love some play time with her auntie." He parts with a quick hug and a peck on the top of her head.

"Thanks, AJ."

The door closes behind her brother, and Margaret is left alone in the house. As she stands in the entrance, she closes her eyes, and inhales deeply, Austin's face swimming before her. She recalls all the momentous times before that she has walked through the doors of this house. The very first time they walked through after closing on the house, Austin ran screaming playfully from room to room, shouting with joy that it was all their own, as Margaret stood laughing with him, one hand on her very swollen belly. Soon after that they entered carrying a tiny, sleeping Jackson through the doors for the first time. And it wasn't long until they brought Izzy through the door, her loud wails already telling the world she'd be a force to be reckoned with.

Silent tears escape her eyes even though they're tightly squeezed shut, as she thinks of her family and all the memories they packed into this house. A soft, grateful smile grows on her face as her mind wanders to Will. Thanks to him, she's just made another momentous entrance through those doors.

She opens her eyes, with a new resolve. Today is the first day of the rest of her life. No more hiding in a book. No more avoiding thinking about her family.

She thinks of Keith and his story he shared with her the night of the wedding. Her soft smile stretches to her eyes. *It's time to turn this house back into a home.*

Acknowledgments

Margaret's story started coming to my life during my daily commutes to and from work years ago. After well over a year of her story growing more and more vivid with each passing drive, I eventually decided to sit down and try to write it out. I had been a reader and writer my whole life, but my writing was typically poems and short stories. While I had always dreamed of becoming a published writer someday, I never thought I actually had the discipline to sit down and write an entire novel. Well, I underestimated myself. With the helpful nudge of NaNoWriMo, I eventually put Margaret's story on paper. And shortly after her story was officially born, two more stories took shape in my mind (and my notebooks).

Running Home would not have come to life without the helpful hands of many people in my life.

First and foremost, I need to thank my beta book club group. Our virtual book club was the best part of my writing experience. You all had such wonderful insight and opinions. You are all a part of breathing life into Margaret and her story. From the very bottom of my heart, thank you. I appreciate you all so much.

Thank you to my editor, Savannah. Your insight was so valuable and I truly appreciate the work you put into helping me polish Margaret's story. I am looking forward to our continued relationship in more stories to come.

Thank you to Esther, my cover designer at Meraki Cover Designs. You did beautiful work and truly brought my story to life through imagery.

Thank you to YOU, my reader. Maybe you bought my book because you are my aunt or cousin or friend and want to support me. Or maybe you are a stranger and were sincerely intrigued by the cover design, or the blurb, or genre. Wherever you fall on the reader spectrum, thank you for choosing to read Margaret's story.

Lastly, but certainly not least, thank you to my husband. For helping me make time for my dreams. For supporting me in putting myself first at times. And for seeing a diamond in my potential when all I could see was a lump of coal. You are my everything.

About the Author

Katie Macmillan lives in Minnesota with her husband, two sons, and their sweeter-than-sugar pit bull. When she's not working, mothering, or writing, Katie likes to spend her time playing in the kitchen. She likes thunderstorms, baby snuggles, and a good, creamy, spicy chai tea. If you sit in the passenger seat of her car, you'll have to listen to country music with the windows rolled all the way down. Katie thinks any day with sunshine and blue skies is a good day to be alive.

www.ingramcontent.com/pod-product-compliance
Lightning Source LLC
Chambersburg PA
CBHW031020160726
47991CB00005B/1807